2019

THESE WITCHES DON'T BURN

ISABEL STERLING

RAZORBILL

RAZORBILL

An imprint of Penguin Random House LLC, New York

First published in the United States of America by Razorbill,
an imprint of Penguin Random House LLC, 2019

RAZORBILL & colophon is a registered trademark
of Penguin Random House LLC.

Visit us online at penguinrandomhouse.com

LIBRARY OF CONGRESS CATALOGING-IN-PUBLICATION DATA IS AVAILABLE
ISBN 9780451480323

Printed in the United States of America

1 3 5 7 9 10 8 6 4 2

Interior design by Corina Lupp

For my wife, Megan.
Meeting you changed everything, including this story.

1

THEY SAY THERE'S A fine line between love and hate.

I used to think They were idiots. Most people are. What could some faceless They know about love? Or hate for that matter. But then I dated Veronica Matthews.

Veronica. Matthews.

The girl who pulled me out of the closet so fast and so completely my head was still spinning weeks later. Our first kiss was life-changing. Identity-altering. Even after a year of dating, I still don't have the right words to describe it.

My parents were surprised, though they recovered quickly, when I walked into the kitchen the day of the kiss to announce, "Mom. Dad. Turns out, I'm gay."

Dad dropped his sauce spoon on the floor. He blinked a few times, then shrugged. "Oh, well, okay then."

Mom picked up the sauce spoon and rinsed it in the sink. "Want to talk about it?"

I remember shrugging. Dad and I do that a lot. "Nope. Just thought you should know."

And that was that.

Veronica Matthews taught me about love, and I guess They were right. There really was a fine line to cross to hate. The same girl who dragged my ass out of the closet later tore my heart from my chest with her meticulously manicured nails.

I hate her. The stupid, self-centered—

Someone clears their throat in front of me. I tear my gaze away from Veronica, who's in the back of the shop by the prepackaged potions, flirting with a girl whose name I can't remember. She looks familiar, with her warm brown skin and a tumble of tight black curls. I think she was on the cheerleading squad with Veronica.

Evan Woelk, a tall, skinny white boy with guyliner thick around his dark brown eyes, stands on the other side of the counter. He smiles when I finally turn my attention his way. "Hey, Hannah." He drops a pile of merchandise next to the register and shoves his hands deep in his front pockets.

"Find everything okay?" I ask, stifling a cringe as Veronica giggles. Even the lavender incense burning on the counter behind me can't calm my nerves when she's around.

Evan nods and watches the total go up and up as I scan his items. Black candles. Twine for binding rituals. A book on hexes. Incense. An all-black athame, both edges of the knife sharp even though the blade is only used for directing energy. I fight the urge to roll my eyes. Yet another Reg playing at being a witch.

I ring up the last item and glance at Evan. He has the whole goth thing going on—black jeans, a tight black shirt, and rings on every finger—which makes this all the more ridiculous. "Eighty-four ninety-five." I bite my lip as he swipes his card. Part of me wants to warn him. Even if Wiccan magic is child's play compared to what I can do, it's still dangerous to mess with forces you don't understand.

Not that I'll actually say anything. To expose my secret is to risk banishment.

Or worse.

Evan accepts his bag with a tight smile. He shifts on his feet, not leaving. I plaster on my work smile, but I'm itching for him to go. Veronica's still giggling over something What's-Her-Face has said. I don't want to deal with her, but I can't leave the counter with a customer in the shop. I never considered myself the jealous type, but if those two don't get out of here soon, I'll—

"Is that Veronica?" he asks, pointing at the pad of paper in front of me. The one with my half-finished Veronica-turned-evil-demon sketch. "I heard you two broke up."

Heat burns at my cheeks. I crumple the page and toss it in the trash. "I really don't want to talk about it." Of course he's heard. The whole school gossiped about our public breakup for weeks.

"Forget I asked." Evan brushes his dark hair out of his eyes. It's a wasted effort, as it flops right back into place. "Are you going to the bonfire tonight?"

I offer a half smile, my thanks for the subject change. "I think Gemma wants to go." And if my best friend wants to go to the annual end-of-school-year bonfire in the woods, there's no way she'll let me skip it. "I take it you're going?"

"Wouldn't miss it." He raises his bag of magic supplies, the athame poking out through a small tear in the plastic. "See you tonight."

"Later," I say, but I roll my eyes once Evan is gone. I get enough of the wannabes from the tourists who visit Salem. It's even more annoying when the locals do it, too. They act like it's all about the wardrobe and accessories. Here, buy a necklace and a few candles. That *totally* makes you a witch. If they had any clue what *real* witches were like, what we're capable of . . .

They probably wouldn't sleep very well at night.

Veronica's laugh trickles through to the front of the store. Familiar pangs of desire work down my spine, but the ice in my veins squashes the feeling. I want her out of this shop. I want her out of my *life* long enough for me to get over her.

But no. If only I were so lucky. The selfish, *gorgeous* bane of my existence belongs to the same coven as my family. Which was great while we were dating, but now . . .

"Oh, Hannah. I forgot you work here." Veronica sidles up to the counter with a small basket of candles and incense, the lie falling effortlessly from her glossy lips. "How are you?"

I reach for the candles she deposited on the counter and ring them up. "What are you doing here?"

"Shopping." She smirks and shares a look with What's-Her-Face, who snaps her gum.

"This tourist trap overcharges, and you know it." I shove the candles into a paper bag, letting my shoulder-length brown hair fall past my face. It creates enough of a barrier to keep from looking at her.

"Maybe I wanted to see you." Veronica's voice is sweet like honey, but I can hear the poison beneath her words. "You're not returning my texts."

"Yeah, well, take a hint." I place the last of the incense in the bag. "That'll be forty-four ninety-three."

She hands over cash, her fingers lingering on mine. A shiver crawls along my skin, but I won't let her see that. I *can't* let her know she still affects me that way. "It doesn't have to be like this, Hannah." She almost seems sincere.

And the way my name sounds rolling off her tongue? I have to swallow around the lump in my throat before I can speak. "Thank you for visiting the Fly by Night Cauldron. Have a nice day."

"Come on, Ronnie, let's go." What's-Her-Face, who Veronica never bothered to introduce, pivots and hurries toward the exit, her heels clicking against the floor.

But Veronica pauses. Lingers. As if there's more she came to say. My heart pounds in my chest, and I'm sure she must hear it.

I tug at my uniform again. "Since when do you let people call you Ronnie? You hate that."

My ex watches her friend leave, and when she's sure we're alone, she leans against the counter, staring up at me through her lashes. "Be careful, Hannah. I might think you're jealous." A deliberate breeze brushes my neck, laced with a current of Veronica's power. The smoke from the incense swirls its way between us, caressing my cheek and slipping along Veronica's collarbone, drawing my eye to the bit of exposed skin.

"What the hell are you doing?" Even though I don't see anyone else in the shop, I keep my voice low so no one overhears. "If Lady Ariana caught you using magic in public—"

"Relax, Hannah. It's not like she'd ever step foot in a place like this. No one's going to know." She fixes me with her emerald stare, but I back out of reach. Using magic in public is a surefire way to lose coven privileges. And I, for one, don't want my training delayed because my obnoxious ex is careless.

Veronica sighs and pushes away from the counter, releasing her hold on the air. The wind dies and resumes a more natural path. "Happy?"

I don't dignify her with an answer. She knows what would happen if a Reg caught us. If our high priestess found out.

"Listen, Hannah." Veronica fusses with her bag of candles. "I wanted to know . . . Are you coming to graduation tomorrow? I think I finally perfected my speech."

"Really?" I cringe at the encouragement in my voice. Instincts from a lifetime of friendship are hard to quell, no matter how much she hurt me. I cross my arms and glance around the shop to make sure we're still alone. "No, I'm not. I'd rather let the Council strip my magic than sit through that."

The words hang in the air between us, charged with more power than Veronica's manipulated wind. Her lips part, but nothing comes out. I wonder if she's thinking about the day we went shopping for her graduation dress. If she remembers what we did the night she was officially named valedictorian, after her parents went to bed. Guilt clutches at my chest, but I push it away.

It's her fault we're not together anymore. She's the one who hurt *me*.

Veronica shifts the bag to her other hand, and a mask settles over her features. Gone is the hurt. Gone is the girl I loved, replaced by the one who broke my heart.

What's-Her-Face leans back into the shop. "Everything all right in here?"

"Of course." Veronica smiles her perfect smile, brandishing it like a weapon. "Just thought I forgot my receipt. Let's go." She turns away, loops her arm through her friend's, and disappears out the door.

As the bell jingles their departure, my heart threatens to burst. The tears sting, but I won't let them fall. I won't give Veronica the satisfaction.

If she thinks she can show up at my work all summer, she's sorely mistaken. Because when it comes to holding a grudge, I'm an Olympic champion.

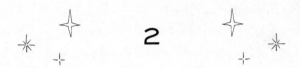

2

AFTER I CLOCK OUT for the day, I swing by the dance studio to pick up Gemma from her ballet class. She's easy to spot, standing nearly a head taller than her classmates. When Gemma hit five ten in ninth grade, everyone tried to get her to join the basketball team, but her body is built for dance. Even walking is a performance; she practically floats into my car.

"You ready to rock the hell out of this bonfire?" Gemma slides on her seat belt and pulls her blonde hair loose from its bun.

I shrug and pull into traffic.

Gemma scowls. "I know that face, Han. What'd Veronica do?"

There isn't a single subject change that'll distract Gemma when she's wearing that expression, so I fill her in on the Veronica Incident. Minus the whole Veronica-doing-magic-in-public thing. The only secret I've ever kept from Gem is my status as an Elemental Witch, and that's a secret I'll take to my grave.

When I finish my story, there's a murderous gleam to Gemma's eyes. "You should ask your boss to ban her from the store."

"That seems a little extreme," I say as I make the final turn down my street.

"Everything about Veronica is 'a little extreme.' You need space." Gemma reaches for my hand when I throw the car in park.

"At the very least, promise you'll enjoy the bonfire tonight? Party until you forget all about her?"

"Promise."

A few short hours later, as the sun dips and the sky blushes, Gemma has succeeded in step one of our mission. We're ready to party.

The crackle of the bonfire greets us moments before we step through a thicket of trees into the hidden clearing that has hosted generations of Salem High students. Beside me, Gemma scans the party. "Is it me, or does everyone look hotter out here than in class?"

I survey the dancing teens. I'll say one thing for sure: there's a lot more skin showing here than in school. "How do you have beer goggles already? I'm pretty sure you have to drink first."

"I'm serious. Maybe it's the firelight." Gemma heads for the keg, where she fills a cup, takes a swig, and grimaces.

"That good, huh?"

"The first drink is the worst. You're too sober to forget how shitty it tastes." She raises the cup but pauses before taking another sip. "Are you okay?"

"I'm fine." I force myself to focus on Gemma instead of the growing crowd around us. I refuse to spend the entire night searching for Veronica and What's-Her-Face. Gem levels me with a look, and I sigh. "I will be. Promise."

Behind us, someone adds more wood to the bonfire. The flames snap and crackle along the logs, and I turn to look. My skin tingles with untapped magic as I near the fire, drawn forward like a bug to a zapper. I can't let myself give in to its song. Not here, surrounded by Regs. Gemma follows, and we stand together beside the bonfire, swaying to the music pouring from someone's truck.

I step closer to the flames, until I feel the lick of heat against my face. The energy cascades over me, through me, driving out the lingering hurt from seeing Veronica. Numbing bad memories like a magical novocaine.

Gemma touches my elbow. I turn, half-dazed, and she nods in the direction of Nolan Abbott. Nolan will be a senior next year, like us, and the new soccer captain has his eye on my best friend.

"Looks like someone has an admirer tonight." I nudge Gem in the shoulder. "Are you interested?" I waggle my eyebrows.

She returns Nolan's appraising look. "Not my usual type," she says at last, "but what the hell. A summer fling never hurt anyone." But then she pauses, biting her lip. She glances back at me. "I can't abandon you."

"It's fine. I'll hang by the fire."

"Are you sure?" Gemma flashes me a look, and I nod. "When I come back, I want to see you in full party mode. No moping about you-know-who."

I raise my middle three fingers to the star-speckled sky. "Scout's honor. Now go."

Gemma grins and glides across the clearing to Nolan, who's trying to look like he's *not* waiting for her. He grins wide when Gemma arrives, and I turn back to the fire.

"Hannah?"

I hear my name but don't look. Instead, I lose myself in the flicker of flames and the pulse of music.

"Earth to Hannah. Come in, Hannah." The voice is closer now, a teasing edge to the deep timbre.

I grin when I realize who's disturbed my fire gazing and turn to greet him. "Hey, Benton. Excited for graduation tomorrow?"

"Excited. Relieved. Contemplating my place in the universe."

He laughs, showcasing the dimples that sent Gemma into full-on crush mode back when we were freshmen and Benton was the new sophomore in Salem. "It still feels so surreal, you know? I can't believe I'm *done*."

I nod, even though I still have another year left. "Art class won't be the same without you."

"I'm sure you'll manage." Benton's eye twitches like he meant to wink but thought better of it halfway through. He stares at the fire instead of looking at me.

"So . . ." I say, wishing I had a bottle or something to occupy my hands. "Any fun plans before college? Are you going to throw another pool party this year?"

"I don't think so. My parents were not pleased with the amount of beer cans they caught me fishing out of the water."

That earns a laugh. There were a *ton* of people at his place last year. "What if it's just us? I promise to be a courteous guest." I nudge him with my elbow. "Come on, there have to be some perks to being your art buddy all year."

Benton's cheeks flush pink. "I could probably swing that." He runs a hand through his hair, and I catch the flash of a tattoo.

"Nice ink. Is that new?" I gesture to the black triangle on his wrist. "I don't remember seeing it in class."

"What? Oh, yeah. It's an early graduation gift to myself."

"What does it mean?"

Someone adds more wood to the fire, and sparks flare into the sky. Benton steps back, shielding his eyes. Reluctantly, I back away, too. Nothing compares to the gentle lick of flames across my skin, to the rush of power that comes from contact, but this isn't the place. As an Elemental, fire won't burn my skin, but I don't want to attract any questions if my clothes burn and I do not.

Benton runs a finger along the triangle on his wrist. "It's delta. The symbol for change. It's the only thing in life you can really count on."

I nod and fall silent. Benton doesn't continue, and I don't push. Instead, I lose myself to the fire's dance. Another shot of sparks dots the sky. Chills tingle down my back. If only I were alone, the things I could do with a fire this size . . .

Benton sidles closer to me, and something in his posture draws my attention away from the flames. I have to crane my neck to meet his stare. "How are you, really?" he asks. "I know things have been rough since you and Veronica split." He shoves his hands in the pockets of his ripped jeans, but he's standing well inside my personal bubble.

"Rough's one word for it." The mention of Veronica is a shot of poison right to the heart. I want to be home, in bed, where I can hide the tears pressing behind my eyes. Benton should know better. He was there. He saw the shouting match outside our bus back to Salem. He and Gemma comforted me on the horribly awkward ride home.

"I'm sorry." Benton tugs at his hair, which makes it stand on end for a moment before it falls. "Um, so I was thinking. I know the timing sucks, but . . . do you want to get coffee sometime?"

I stare at my friend. Unblinking. Confused. Slightly horrified.

"I totally get if it's too soon. I do. And normally I wouldn't ask someone out this soon after a breakup, but I'm leaving for Boston in August, and I didn't want to leave without trying, and—"

"Are you seriously asking me out right now?"

Benton falters. This clearly isn't going the way he rehearsed it in his head. "Um . . . yes?"

"Why?"

"Because you're funny. And kind. And smart. And—"

"And a huge lesbian," I add before this can get any more awkward. "I thought you knew that."

Benton stares at his shoes. "I did. I do."

"So, what?" I ask, fury and betrayal rising from deep in my gut. "Did you think you could turn me straight?"

"No! No, of course not." He blows out a breath and laces his hands on top of his head. "I feel like such an asshole right now."

The tension in my chest loosens. A little. "Let's pretend this never happened." I hold out a hand. "Friends?"

"Friends." Benton shakes my hand, but his forehead crinkles. "I don't get why Savannah told me to ask you out. She said you were bisexual. She even said you had a crush on me."

I don't hear whatever he says next. Savannah. *That's* her name. What's-Her-Face from the store this afternoon. I grab Benton's arm. "Savannah told you? When?"

Benton glances at the place where my fingers circle his bare skin. I let go. "Like ten minutes ago." He kicks at a pebble on the ground, sending it skittering into the fire. "This is so messed up."

"No kidding." I'm already scanning the crowd for her expanse of dark curls. "Where was she when she told you?"

"Over there." He gestures toward the other side of the clearing, across a throng of writhing bodies.

"Great, thanks." I take off toward the swell of dancers moving their hips to yet another wordless song with pounding bass. The crackle of fire is loud in my ears, but familiar laughter breaks through. My hands ball into fists.

"Where are you going?" Benton's words chase after me.

"To find Veronica." *And end this.*

$$\dashv\vdash \quad \text{\Large *} \quad \dashv\vdash$$

The field around the bonfire is packed tight with seniors who are going to be painfully hungover for their graduation tomorrow. I weave through their gyrating bodies, careful to dodge the cups of beer. I'm going to kill Veronica when I find her. She's lucky it's against Council law to attack another witch.

I'm almost to the back of the crowd when I hear her voice, low and sharp as she speaks to Savannah. I squeeze past the edge of the crowd and spot them.

Savannah leans against a tree and reaches for Veronica's hand. "Come on, Ronnie," she soothes. "After what she did to you? She deserved worse."

Veronica hisses something in response, but I can't make out her words.

My throat closes, and I see red. I am fire—pure passion and perfect aggression. All the frustrations from the shop today crackle inside, ready for a fight. Savannah sees me first. A smug look pulls at her purple lips, the color bold and sophisticated against her skin tone. Veronica turns, eyes flashing in the moonlight. She wipes her face free of expression, settles on her perfect mask.

Just seeing her, watching her as she watches me, makes my skin flush hot. I wish, not for the first time since we broke up, that I could forget how good it feels when her body is pressed against mine.

"What the hell is your problem, Veronica?"

Veronica drains her cup and passes it to Savannah. "Could you grab me another drink? I think Hannah needs a word." She stares at me the whole time she speaks, like she's watching to see how mad I am, to see how far she can push until I lose all sense of myself.

Times like this I can't believe we ever dated.

Savannah glances between us, the victory vanishing from her eyes. She takes Veronica's cup and stalks off toward the kegs.

Veronica raises a brow in mock concern when her friend is out of earshot. "Is something wrong? You look a little pale."

"You know exactly what you did."

She tilts her head. "I haven't done anything."

"Okay, fine, you had your little Reg friend do it." I snort when she still looks confused. She's actually going to make me say it. "She told Benton to ask me out. Lied and said I'm bisexual to convince him to do it."

Veronica examines her manicure. "There's nothing wrong with being bi, Hannah."

"I never said there was. But I'm *not* bi. You had no right to lie about that." My whole body shakes as I stifle the screams bubbling up inside. But Veronica just stands there, smug. "Why are you doing this? What could you possibly gain from making my life miserable?"

She glances up, and I swear she looks sorry. Almost. "I don't want you to be miserable." Veronica peers out over the crowd of dancing teens. "But you're a cute girl. You have to learn to deal with guys coming on to you."

"Excuse me?"

Veronica steps closer until she's towering over me. "Isn't being single the worst?"

And there it is. Dangling in the air between us.

A humorless laugh pushes through my chest. "Is that it then? You'll make single life so miserable that I'll run back to you?"

"You and I were good together, Hannah." She brushes a lock of hair behind my ear and trails her fingers down my neck, my arm, raising goose bumps all the way to my wrist. Which is not helping. "It doesn't have to be over between us." She wraps her arm around my waist, pulling me forward until our bodies are flush.

My skin burns, and I'm tingling all over.

Until I recognize her touch, her possessiveness, as the same controlling bullshit that ended us in the first place.

I push Veronica away, stepping back until the cool air swirls around me. "Don't. Just don't. This is your fault, and you know it." I reach into my pocket and grip the keys resting there. I need to find Gemma and get the hell out of here.

Veronica glares at me. "Rewrite our history all you want, but you broke up with *me*."

"Like you gave me a choice! What did you expect me to do? Go on like everything was normal? Pretend New York never happened?"

"Yes! It was one bad weekend, Hannah. You didn't even give me a chance to explain." She's close now, shouting inches from my face. Heads turn in our direction. Judging glances. Curious stares.

"I don't want to fight about this every time I see you." My voice is hardly more than a whisper, but I know she can hear me. The air between us tells me she's barely breathing. "I want to move on with my life."

"Fine." The word lands like a slap to the face. "Take responsibility for the breakup and this stops."

"Like hell."

Veronica glowers at me. She starts to say more, but a piercing scream splits the night.

The music stops. Someone giggles until they're told to hush. I spare a glance for Veronica and then race toward the source of the scream. Our classmates may need another shout to pinpoint the location, but the wind carries the panic, and the sounds of stifled sobs, right to me.

Please don't let it be Gemma.

Someone falls in step behind me. I glance back, and Veronica is on my heels. We're alone in our chase. For now.

The energy in the air grows oppressive. We're close. Really close. There's a whimper just ahead, and I rush forward through a cluster of trees and—

"Son of a . . ." I trail off as Veronica stumbles to a stop beside me. The scene before us is like something out of a bad horror film. Fire flickers a few yards away, but what captures my attention is the girl on the ground.

Covered in blood.

3

IT TAKES ME A second longer than Veronica to recognize the blood-soaked girl.

"Savannah." Veronica rushes forward and drops to her knees beside her wide-eyed friend. "What happened?"

"I don't know." Savannah's voice breaks, and she wipes at the tears on her face with one hand, holding the other gingerly across her chest. "I saw another fire, so I came to see who was partying over here. But then I slipped . . ."

We glance behind us at said fire. It's not a bonfire, not like the one I left Benton standing beside. This looks more like someone carved a circle into the earth, maybe six or seven feet across, and set it ablaze.

"It's okay. Everything's going to be okay," Veronica says, but she looks at me like she thinks the opposite. The air is thick with malice. The fire burning behind us is vicious and hungry. Even the earth—usually a calm and steady element—feels shaken.

Something wicked happened here.

Veronica turns back to Savannah. "Where's the blood coming from? Where are you hurt?"

"It's not . . ." Savannah loses her voice to tears. I wait, worry clawing at my skin. "It's not mine." She looks up, and my gaze follows.

The mangled remains of a raccoon swing from a noose above us. A red slash forms a gruesome smile across its stomach, spilling flesh and blood to the ground. Meatier bits stick to its broken ribs and dangle suspended in the air. A piece slips free and lands beside Savannah. My stomach clenches. Bile burns my throat, and I swallow to keep from getting sick.

A hand touches my back, and I flinch away.

Veronica scowls. "It's me. Relax."

"Relax? She is *covered* in blood. And god knows what else." I retch and walk farther away from Savannah, toward the flickering fire. My heart aches for the poor creature. "I've got a bad feeling about this."

"No kidding," Veronica snaps, but then she stops short and reaches for me. "Look."

I follow her pointed finger to the flames. "I know. I saw the fire. I'm not completely oblivious."

"Then shut up and really *look*."

Gasoline and wood smoke—and not a small amount of panic—choke the air from my lungs when I finally do as she says.

That's not a circle carved into the earth and set aflame.

It's a pentacle.

My hands shake, and I stumble away from the fire. A pentacle near a blood sacrifice means one of two things, and neither is particularly great. Either a Reg is dabbling in dangerous magic . . .

Or there's a Blood Witch in Salem.

"Do you think she followed us?" I ask, keeping my voice low so Savannah won't hear, but I can't bury the fear. The panic. If this isn't a Reg prank—please, *please* let it be a Reg prank—then it has to be a Blood Witch.

Of the three Witch Clans, Blood Witches are the only ones

who use animal sacrifices in their magic. And they don't have a good reputation for respecting human life—Reg *or* Clan.

On reflex, my fingers rub against my jaw. I can almost feel the long-healed bruise there. The cut on my skin. The—

"Hey, it's okay." Veronica pulls my hand from my face. "She has no idea where we live. This isn't her. Come on, let's get this cleaned up." She releases me and rushes back to Savannah's side. "Can you stand, sweetie? We need to get out of here."

Sweetie? Are Veronica and Savannah— I push the thought away. I have more pressing concerns right now than whether or not my ex is hooking up with one of the hottest girls in Massachusetts.

"I think so." Savannah reaches for Veronica's outstretched hand. "But my wrist . . . I think it's broken."

Branches snap in the distance. Someone calls my name. A second later, Gemma and Nolan spill into the small clearing, followed by a few of Nolan's teammates.

"Oh, thank god, there you are." Gemma rushes over and flings her arms around me. "When I couldn't find you by the bonfire, I thought for sure—" Her voice dies when she sees Veronica supporting Savannah's weight. "What's going on here?" She looks up and gasps. "And what the hell is *that?*"

Nolan steps forward and slips in the puddle of blood. A string of muttered curses fills the tense air as he wipes his previously pristine Adidas on the grass. Behind us, the crowd grows as classmates follow the soccer team into the clearing.

"Ha-ha, very funny." Nolan sounds anything but amused as he scans the tipsy group behind him. "You got us. Joke's over."

A murmur works through the crowd, but no one responds.

Something violent flashes through Nolan's eyes. "I'm not kidding, assholes. Clean this up. Prank's over." When no one answers, he tries another angle. He plasters on his most charming smile and approaches Savannah. "What happened? Who did this to you?"

Savannah eats it right up.

"I saw the fire and thought someone set up a quieter party. I didn't see the blood until it was too late." She cradles her injured arm carefully against her chest.

"Did you see anything else?"

To my surprise, Savannah nods. "I saw someone running away."

Relief washes over me. "Was it someone from school?" If a Blood Witch did this—if *she* were here—there's no way they'd stick around long enough for a Reg to spot them. This has to be a prank. A cruel—and super gross—prank.

But Savannah shakes her head, puncturing my sense of surety. "I didn't see their face. They were wearing a hoodie."

At that, Nolan circles the crowd, moving along the edge of the burning pentacle. "All right, which of you assholes tried to ruin my bonfire?" He stops in front of Evan, who's wearing a black hoodie and even thicker eyeliner than he had on in the store. "Looks like we've found our witch. Shall we break out the gallows?"

Nolan's teammates laugh, but I flinch at his words. At their meaning. Though no Elementals died in Salem's witch trails, a few Caster Witches perished alongside the accused Regs. Nolan's cruel smile makes me want to hit something. Preferably him.

Gemma sidles closer to me and makes a face. "I can't believe I made out with that asshat, like, five minutes ago."

"So much for your summer fling," I say, casting her an apologetic look.

Nolan steps closer to Evan, sizing him up. "What's the matter? No spells to make you disappear?"

"Back off, Abbott. I didn't do anything." Evan shoves Nolan and separates himself from the crowd of soccer players gathering around him.

Nolan looks to his teammates and grins. "Not until you clean up your mess."

"Screw you." The fire in front of Evan casts a strange glow on his face. He curls his hands into fists like he's ready for a fight. Like he's been hoping for one all along.

There is no version of this story that ends well. I need to get out of here. Now. I turn to Gemma, but she's not there. *Dammit, Gem. Where are you?* I push through the crowd and find her ending a call on her phone.

"We gotta go." I reach for her arm, but her hand flies to her mouth. There's a deep *thwack*, the unmistakable sound of a fist connecting with someone's face.

I turn as Nolan stumbles back against a tree, touching his lips. His fingers come away with blood. He lunges forward, catching Evan around the waist.

The boys hit the ground and roll, first Nolan on top, then Evan. Fists fly. Half the soccer team joins the fray, some pulling the guys apart, others adding their fists to the fight. They roll down the small incline toward us, heading right for the—

"Keep them away from the fire!" I rush to the pentacle, pushing frozen onlookers out of the way, and kick dirt over the blaze.

Veronica falls to her knees beside me, using a sweater to pat at the flames, but the fire is dying faster than it should. I glare at her. Even if she doesn't care about getting in trouble with our high priestess, even if she thinks no one in our coven will ever find out, this place is crawling with Regs. If anyone saw her using magic to put out the flames, it could spark a repeat of our town's most infamous history. Witch Hunters may be a thing of the past, but it's not a past I'm eager to repeat.

Gemma rushes forward to help, but the fire's stubborn. It's only a matter of time before Evan and Nolan roll this way. And if their clothes catch on fire, this night will get a million times worse.

Someone knocks into me, throwing me off balance. I fall forward, and my magic reacts on instinct, ready to protect me from the flames. Ready to expose a centuries-old secret.

Hands grip my arm, then circle around my waist. I'm hauled upright and my magic recedes. When I'm standing on my own, I turn and fling my arms around the person standing there. They just saved me—and my entire coven—from exposure.

I pull away to see who it is. "Benton." The blush on his cheeks makes me step back. It probably wasn't the best idea to hug him so soon after turning him down. "Thank you."

Benton grips the back of his neck, his face still blooming with color. "Yeah, no problem. It's the least I could do after the whole . . . well, you know."

"No, seriously. Thank you. That would have . . ." That would have been the end of life as I know it. "Thanks." I turn back to check on the fire, but my help isn't needed. A few of the guys have dragged over the keg and are spraying down the flames.

"Like I said. No problem." Benton spares a fleeting glance for the dead animal hanging from the tree and grimaces. "I'll catch you later."

I grin, but I don't think the pun was intentional. "I'm going to hold you to that pool day."

"Only if you bring those triple chocolate brownies you made

last year," he says, and I'm surprised he remembers. I agree, and Benton waves, heading back toward the main bonfire.

Once he's out of the way, Gemma rushes in and wraps me in a hug. "Thank god Benton was there."

"I know." I squeeze back and release her.

Gemma's gaze trails after Benton as he leaves, and she lets out a dreamy sigh. "I should have spent the night with him instead of Nolan. He's much more my type."

"I thought you were over him?" I promised Benton I'd forget about our awkward encounter, but I don't want Gem to set herself up for heartbreak either. She shrugs, and I nod in the direction he disappeared. "Come on, we should get out of here."

"But we have to wait."

"For what? The guys will get the fight under control."

Gemma shakes her head. "That's not what I meant. Savannah needs a doctor, and I—"

"Oh, Gem. Please tell me you didn't." Her stubborn look says she most certainly did. She already called for an ambulance. I sigh. "The paramedics don't need us here to do their job. Let's go. Unless you *want* our parents to find out you were drinking." At that, Gem loses her smile and nods.

But before we can take more than a step, sirens wail and police lights pierce the trees.

—|—   —⁎—   —|—

Paramedics wrap Savannah in blankets and load her in the back of an ambulance; its flashing lights create a patchwork of dancing shadows in the woods. Gemma and I stand huddled together as police swarm around us. They question classmates and send them home, confiscating keys from anyone who seems even a little bit tipsy, forcing more than a few teens to call home for a ride.

Veronica approaches, all her earlier bravado gone, the smirk wiped clean from her face. "Can we talk?"

Gemma casts me a glance. I nod, and she steps a few paces away. In her absence, Veronica leans against the tree beside me. "That was pretty intense, huh?"

A police officer comes near, so I make a noncommittal noise. Once the officer passes, the fear bubbles up again, and I can't hold it back. "Do you think she found us?" My voice shakes, but Veronica knows who *she* is. The Blood Witch in New York who took control of my body, who forced me to my knees, with only a single drop of my blood. "We have to tell our parents."

"No, we don't." Veronica grips my shaking hands in hers, and I almost feel safe. "There are no Blood Witches in Salem, Han. This was a prank. We're fine."

"But—"

"Hannah, no." Her words grow harsh, and she drops my hands. "We swore we would never tell anyone about what happened on that trip."

"But if she's here—"

"But *nothing*. She's not here, and what we did in New York could send us straight to the Council. We could lose our magic." Veronica goes silent as another officer walks past. "Use your head."

"We have to say *something*," I whisper, scanning the crowd for any members of Salem PD I recognize. "My dad will hear about the raccoon and pentacle at work."

"So? Your dad is smart enough to know this is either a Reg prank or some kind of pagan ritual. Either way, it doesn't involve us or our coven." Veronica sighs. "I've worked too hard to miss graduation. I'm not going to skip my speech because you're afraid of a Blood Witch who doesn't even know what state we live in."

When she puts it like that, I can't deny the logic in her words. But I hate admitting that she's right. "Fine," I say, clipping the word short. "I won't say anything about tonight until after graduation."

Veronica looks like she wants to argue, but she shakes her head. "I'm going with Savannah to the hospital. You good?"

"Yeah. Yeah, I'm fine." I bounce forward on the balls of my feet and ignore the stinging in my eyes. "Go ahead. You don't want to miss your ride."

Veronica worries at her lower lip. I think for a second she might say more, but she shakes her head and disappears into the back of the ambulance.

My chest aches to see her like this. Vulnerable. Afraid. *Not* trying to make my life miserable. It's so much easier to deal with all the emotions swirling inside—the betrayal, the hurt, the lingering attraction—when we're fighting.

"Hannah?" Gemma steps close and wraps her arms around me. "You okay?"

"I will be." I soak in her warmth and watch the ambulance drive off. Someone took down the mangled raccoon, bagged it up, and carted it away. I'm not sure what happened to Nolan or Evan after the fight. I didn't see either of them in handcuffs, so that's probably a good sign.

Gemma and I tried to leave earlier with the rest of our classmates, but someone told the cops I was the one who found Savannah. Never mind that Veronica and I found her together. Veronica gets to ride off in an ambulance while I'm stuck out here with the raccoon blood.

Lucky me.

I'm about to ask one of the officers if we can leave when a man with short brown hair and a tall, lean frame heads our way. Unlike the rest of the cops, he's not in uniform. He's wearing a dark gray suit with black dress shoes. Not exactly bonfire-in-the-woods attire.

"Good evening, ladies. I'm Detective Archer. Which of you is Miss Walsh?" He taps a pen to his small notebook.

It must be a slow night if they sent a detective out for this. "I'm Hannah Walsh," I say, and release Gemma's hand, reminding myself to breathe. I let Veronica's earlier conviction steady my nerves. Nothing that happened tonight has anything to do with the Clans. This wasn't a Blood Witch. We're safe.

"You found Miss Clarke this evening?"

I assume he means Savannah. I don't actually know her last name. "Yeah. Veronica and I heard her scream over the music. I happened to get here first. But, like, by a second. Tops."

The detective stares at me like he's waiting for me to say more. His attention is unnerving; it prickles along my skin, making me shiver.

"I'm not sure what else I can tell you. We barely beat the others here," I add when he *still* doesn't speak.

Detective Archer scribbles something in his little notebook. "And did you recognize the symbol burned into the ground?"

"Umm . . ." How much is dangerous to admit? I'm a terrible liar, always have been. Some say it's an admirable quality, but those people must not have any real secrets to keep. "Yeah, sure. Of course," I answer after the silence has stretched on far too long. "I've lived in Salem my whole life. I know a pentacle when I see one."

"And you're aware the pentacle is a symbol of witchcraft?" The detective stares at me, unblinking.

I catch myself rolling my eyes, but not fast enough to prevent it. Gemma shoves an elbow in my ribs, and the detective cocks a brow. "Sorry, it's just . . . Salem. Witch trials. It all kind of comes with the territory."

Detective Archer stops with the note-taking for a second and really looks at me. "Well then, it's a good thing I met an expert on my first assignment."

"I'm not an expert." The words fly out of my mouth before I realize they're in my brain. I've barely said anything. How could he— Then the sarcasm registers, followed by the rest of his sentence, and embarrassment burns my cheeks. "You're new here?"

The detective gives a quick nod and returns to his notes, flipping back a couple pages. "Can you explain why you and your friends tried to hide evidence?"

"We didn't—"

"You didn't destroy the burning pentacle?"

I glance at Gemma, but she's still tipsy and hasn't spoken. I try to act like this whole conversation isn't hitting too close to home. "We didn't want the guys to roll through the flames and catch themselves on fire. I didn't think it was evidence."

"Right. The fight between Nolan Abbott and Evan Woelk. Any idea whether either of them might be involved with the sacrifice?" Detective Archer holds his pen poised and ready.

"I don't know. We don't really run in the same circles." I glance back toward the pentacle and it hits me. Evan came into the store today. He could have used the athame to kill the animal . . .

Beside me, Gemma shivers. "Um, sir? Could we go home now?"

The detective looks to Gemma. "Perhaps. Do you have anything to add, Miss . . ."

"Goodwin," she says. "Gemma Goodwin. And no. I got here after Hannah. I'm the one who called for the ambulance." She tucks her hair behind her ear and flutters her lashes. I love the girl, but damn is she a suck-up sometimes.

Detective Archer flips the page on his little notebook and scribbles something down. Each second that passes feels like an hour, and I reach for the phone in my pocket. It's late. *Really* late.

"Umm . . . Detective? We're going to miss curfew if we don't leave soon." I haven't had a curfew in ages, but it seems like a normal enough excuse for the detective.

"Right, of course." He asks a few more questions, makes sure Gem isn't driving, and sends us on our way.

Gemma and I walk in silence back toward my car. It isn't until we're safely on the road that Gemma speaks. "What do you think happened back there?" Her voice is a whisper, barely audible above the soft music coming from the speakers.

"I don't know." I grip the steering wheel. There are too many possibilities taking up space in my head. Was it Evan? If so, what purpose could he have for a ritual like that? And if Veronica's wrong, if this wasn't a Reg, we have bigger problems than a ruined bonfire.

Gemma rests her head on the window, her eyelids drifting shut. "That poor raccoon. Here's hoping it was a one-time thing."

"Fingers crossed." I turn off my high beams as another car comes into view, and by the time I flick my brights back on, Gem is asleep.

In the dark, with only the moon and my headlights to guide us, an icy fear grips my spine. I try very hard to fully convince myself that this was a Reg. That it was Evan, taking his goth look way too far and dabbling in the more destructive parts of pagan magic.

Because if there's a Blood Witch in town . . .

No one is safe.

4

BANGING PANS AND THE smell of sizzling bacon pull me out of restless sleep. Fragments of nightmares cling to the edges of my consciousness, but they dissolve into smoke when I try to force them into focus.

All things considered, that's probably for the best.

Gemma stirs on the air mattress below me. There was a time when we'd take turns hosting sleepovers, but ever since I came out last year, her parents have been more than a little awkward around me. Suddenly, their house had all these new rules—keep the bedroom door open, no hangouts without adult supervision, sleepovers have to be in separate rooms—like they were afraid my queerness was contagious.

"Good morning," I singsong when she finally rubs at her eyes and sits up.

"Morning," Gem grumbles back. She stretches her arms over head and yawns loudly. "So, last night was a hot mess."

"And gross," I add, a chill creeping up my spine. I pull the blankets tight around my shoulders as I sit up, a fluffy shield against the memories of mangled animal parts and dripping blood.

"I can't believe you talked to She-Who-Must-Not-Be-Named without someone getting killed." Gem grabs the toothbrush from her overnight bag and heads for the door. "It's a summer miracle."

"Hilarious, Gem. Really."

"You know you love me," she says, and glides out the door. The smell of bacon intensifies with her departure.

While Gem uses the guest bathroom in the hall, I throw my hair into a ponytail and reach for my phone, desperate for news. Maybe the police already caught the misguided Reg dabbling in sacrificial magic.

I punch in my passcode, and I'm shocked Mom let me sleep in so late. Normally, anything past nine results in a lecture. Out of habit, I check my notifications before searching for news. I'm tagged in a few blurry photos from the bonfire, my pre-party pic with Gem has a decent number of new likes, and there's an unread direct message waiting for me. Without thinking, I open the message and freeze.

It's from Veronica.

Seeing her name pop up sends tears prickling in my eyes. I should delete it unread. Block her account so she can't send any more. But I can't. I have to know. Maybe she's writing to apologize. Maybe last night made her regret what happened between us. Maybe . . .

> Hannah,
>
> I'm graduating today. Top of my class, just like I promised when we were kids. I did it, Han. I really did it.
>
> You should be there, sitting in the front row. I wrote so much of my speech for you. It won't be right without you there. Everyone is coming, all the families. Doesn't that mean anything to you? We've been friends our entire lives. What happened in NYC shouldn't change that.
>
> I would go if it were you.
>
> —V

I read her message again—coded to avoid mentioning the coven—torturing myself with her words. Should I go? *Would* she really go if our places were reversed?

A door opens and clicks shut in the hallway. I wipe the tears from my face and delete our message history. My chest constricts as years' worth of exchanges disappear in an instant. I want to undo it the second they're gone, but like our relationship, what's done is done.

My door opens and Gemma steps inside, her hair wrapped tight in a towel, her shirt sticking to her not-quite-dry skin. "What're you doing?"

"Nothing." My voice sounds guilty, even to me.

Gemma cocks her head to one side, which looks ridiculous with the huge towel engulfing her hair. "Then why do you look like someone punched you in the gut?"

"I don't—"

"It's Veronica, isn't it?" Gemma crawls into bed beside me and reaches for my hand. "What'd she do this time?"

I stare at the ceiling, as if that will stop the flood of emotions drowning my eyes. "She wanted me to go to graduation." *Which started twenty minutes ago.* She might be giving her speech right now, staring into a sea of faces, hoping to find mine.

"Are you upset you missed it?"

Yes. No. Maybe. I shake my head. "No." I pick at my comforter. "Does that make me a terrible person? We've been friends since we were in diapers, long before she was my girlfriend."

"Is that her excuse?" Gemma wraps her arm around my shoulders. "She hurt you, Hannah. Don't let her guilt trip you for trying to heal. You don't owe her anything."

"I know." If only things were that simple. If only I could delete her from my life completely. "But—"

"No *but*s. You made your choice, and so did she. It's too late to go now anyway." Gemma pulls away and removes the towel from her head. "Do we need to have a ceremonial burning of Veronica's things?" She gestures toward my closet, where she hid all my relationship keepsakes in a shoe box. "I know I said to hang on to them, but maybe you need a good purge."

"Girls!" Mom calls to us from the bottom of the stairs before I can reply. "Breakfast is ready."

Gem lights up at the mention of food. She runs a comb swiftly through her hair and bounds for the door. I trudge after her, a clumsy ogre in the wake of her ballerina's grace.

"Good morning, Mrs. Walsh," Gemma says with a smile. "Need help setting the table?"

"Already done, but thank you." Mom points down the hall to the dining room. "Go on ahead, I just need to grab the toast."

Gemma doesn't need to be told twice. She practically sprints down the hall and disappears into the dining room. But I don't follow. I head for the kitchen, trailing after Mom.

"Hannah?" Mom pauses with a plate full of toast in her hands. "What's wrong?"

"Something weird happened last night. At the bonfire, Veronica and I—"

"Marie! You coming?" Dad's voice carries through the house, deep and rumbling. "The eggs are getting cold."

Mom shifts the plate into one hand and places the other on my shoulder. "I'm sorry you had a bad night, Han. I know you and Veronica aren't on good terms right now, but you'll have to learn to be around each other sooner or later. We can talk after brunch."

"No, Mom—"

But she's already gone. I follow her into the dining room where fried eggs, fruit, and a small mountain of bacon load up each plate. Mom sets the toast in the middle of the table, and we take our seats.

Dad smiles at me over his coffee. "Good morning."

I mumble a response around the piece of bacon I shoved in my mouth.

"How was the bonfire?" Dad asks when I chomp on my toast instead of saying hello.

Gemma drops her fork back onto her plate. "You won't *believe* what happened." She leans forward, and my mouth is too full to tell her to hush. "Someone killed a raccoon and burned a pentacle into the ground. There was blood *everywhere*. And then there was this fight, and a girl broke her arm. Not from the fight, she got hurt before. Wait, let me back up. I'm not telling this right."

"Geez, Gem. Take a breath in there somewhere," I say in a futile attempt to lighten the mood. My parents turn to stare at me. A crease deepens in Mom's brow.

"Sorry, I didn't mean to forget the most unusual part." Gemma cups her hand to the side of her mouth and mock-whispers to my parents, "Hannah and Veronica talked without killing each other."

Dad chuckles politely. "Now, that *is* something."

As Gemma launches back into her story, describing the bloody scene with more detail than most people find appropriate for breakfast conversation, last night's worries slither through my brain. I know Veronica said this was a Reg, but what if it wasn't?

"Mom? Do we have any jelly?" I ask, standing up from the table. "Could you help me find it?" I shoot her a look and hope she reads the meaning there.

She meets my gaze and nods. "Sure. There should be some in the fridge."

"Do you have strawberry?" Gem asks as she spears a piece of cantaloupe with her fork, oblivious to how much I'm panicking.

"Probably. I'll look," I say, and lead Mom into the kitchen. I don't know how to explain this with Gemma in the next room, chatting to my father about last night's fight.

"What's going on, Hannah?" Mom asks, opening the fridge and pulling out a jar of jelly. "What's this about an animal sacrifice?"

I glance back to the dining room, but we're far enough away that I can't make out Gemma's words. Even so, I keep my voice low as I tell Mom everything that happened last night. Savannah's scream. The sacrificial raccoon. The pentacle. I leave out the part where Veronica used her magic in public. I may hate my ex, but I don't hate her that much.

When I'm finished, Mom lets out a long sigh. "Regs in this town . . . Their foolishness never ceases to amaze me."

"What if it wasn't a Reg?"

Mom cuts me a look, her eyes flashing. "You think this was a Blood Witch?"

I nod, fingers trembling.

"Hannah." Mom rests a hand on my shoulder. "There haven't been any Blood Witches in Salem since the trials. What makes you think they'd come back now?"

Oh, I don't know. Maybe because Veronica and I stumbled into a turf war between a Blood Witch and a group of Casters when we went on our school trip to Manhattan last month? Maybe because said Blood Witch threatened to kill me if she ever saw me again? But I can't say that. Any of it. "I could feel it, Mom. There was an energy to that ritual. Something more than a Reg playing a prank on us."

Mom considers me, her gaze sweeping across my face. I worry she'll see all the things I'm hiding from her, but she doesn't say anything. Instead, she rolls her shoulders and cups her hands together. Air swirls in the space between them, spinning faster and faster until it starts to glow. "I'll let Lady Ariana know."

I swallow. Hard. If anyone can determine whether there's a Blood Witch in town, it's our high priestess. Unfortunately, she's also the person most likely to sense I'm hiding something, and she's not exactly someone whose shit list you want to be on. Ever.

Mom whispers something into the spinning orb and sets it free. Though I can't see or sense it—that particular skill is one I won't learn until I'm eighteen—I know it's traveling across town to take a message to Lady Ariana. A few seconds pass, and Mom tilts her head like she's listening to a response. "We'll finish brunch, then you and Veronica will show Lady Ariana what happened last night."

Before I can protest about the inclusion of my ex, Mom turns and carries the jelly back to the dining room; I follow, my feet dragging against the carpet. The wall zaps me with static as I brush past.

"The closest we had in the fridge was raspberry. Is that okay?" Mom asks, her voice free from the worry that closes my throat.

"Raspberry works." Gemma reaches across the table and takes the jar from my mom.

I slip into the chair next to my best friend. Her presence doesn't do anything to dissolve the pit of worry in my stomach. I pick at the eggs on my plate. They've gone cold.

+-　*　-+

After brunch, I stall as much as I can before we have to meet Lady Ariana in the woods. When I've changed my outfit for the fifth time, Mom finally drags me out of the house. We drop Gemma at her place, then head for the site of last night's bonfire. With the detour, we're the last to arrive at the woods. Veronica and her parents—Mr. and Mrs. Matthews—are waiting outside their car, but Lady Ariana is still in her ancient Impala. It's old enough to be rusted and rotted through, but the metal is in pristine condition. One of the many perks of being an Elemental High Priestess.

As Dad shifts our car into park, Lady Ariana swings open her door and steps out. Her silver hair is pulled into a tight bun, the lines around her eyes and mouth set deep. She glides across the earth with the kind of grace only age and power can bestow. I hastily scramble out of our car and stand beside Veronica's family.

Lady Ariana stops before us; her eyes narrow, almost imperceptibly. "Show me."

I nod and stumble forward, Veronica close behind. Our parents wait for Lady Ariana to pass before bringing up the rear of our multigenerational investigation team. The ground before us is trampled, the grass squashed beneath the comings and goings of nearly one hundred Salem High students. With the amount of police presence last night, I'm surprised there isn't any crime scene tape blocking off the area.

When we reach the spot where Veronica and I fought last

night, Veronica stops. "We were here when we heard the first scream." Her voice is subdued, but I don't trust it. She's still wearing her graduation dress, the deep maroon beautiful against her white skin, the hem skimming the top of her knees. The clothing choice feels deliberate, like she's trying to remind me of what I missed.

"We followed the screams this way." I shove past Veronica, feeling oddly underdressed in my denim shorts and the orange Salem State T-shirt Mom got me when the university bookstore was having a sale. "This is it. The raccoon was hanging there." I point to the branch that held the sacrificial animal last night. The ground beneath is still red with blood.

"You two," Lady Ariana says, pointing at me and Veronica, "stay here." Our high priestess crosses the small clearing, kneels, and places her hands just outside the pool of blood. She closes her eyes, takes a deep breath, and that's when the show really begins.

Wind kicks up and swirls around us, pulling loose strands of hair out of my ponytail. Goose bumps prickle across my arms, and I shiver despite the late June heat. A slight tremor works through the earth, like the gentle ripple of a pond after a pebble's been tossed in. The amount of magic in the clearing is heady. Intoxicating.

After a moment, Lady Ariana stands, eyes still closed, and presses a hand against the trunk of the tree. I hold my breath, waiting as she reads the energy flowing through each ring of the tall oak.

Mom fidgets beside me. "Was this the work of a Blood Witch?" Her voice trembles, and I wonder if she's thinking of all those bedtime stories she told me—the ones with Blood Witches so powerful they could control your mind or stop your heart with a single thought. I wonder if she's ever faced a Blood Witch before. If she knows how terrifying their strength and speed is. How quickly their wounds heal.

Lady Ariana shakes her head and pats the side of the trunk like it's a beloved pet. "There's no indication of magic by the tree. None in the blood."

"So that's it? We're still the only Clan in Salem?" The relief that flows through me nearly brings me to tears. We're safe. She didn't follow us home.

Lady Ariana purses her lips. "Did I say I was finished?" With swift, sure steps, she crosses to the remnants of the fiery pentacle. As she kneels, Veronica reaches for me and digs her fingers into my bare skin.

I yank my arm from her grip. *What?* I mouth the word to avoid disturbing Lady Ariana.

Veronica nods toward the ashy pentacle. Her eyes grow wide as Lady Ariana puts a hand to the earth.

And then I remember.

Veronica used her magic to help put out the fire.

I see the moment Lady Ariana senses magic in the ashes. Her eyes cloud over; a brisk wind blasts into us, knocking me back a step.

And then the earth swallows us whole.

"I'm disappointed in you." Lady Ariana approaches with slow, deliberate steps. She stares down at us, where we're buried to our necks in the ground. "Especially *you*, Veronica. How dare you use your gifts in the presence of non-witches."

Our parents go pale. My mom's jaw falls open.

Even with most of Lady Ariana's wrath focused on Veronica, panic claws at my chest. Every instinct shouts at me to dig my fingers into the ground and pull myself free, but that's exactly what she wants. So I remain still.

Power crackles around our high priestess, and it's like every element stretches toward her, eager for her energy. The soft breeze whips into a gale. The trampled grass around her feet stretches back to its full height, growing vibrant and green. I suck in a breath as the earth around my legs tightens, moving up and up until it pushes out my breath.

"I demand an explanation." Lady Ariana's voice is quiet, and yet it permeates the air, burrowing in my ears, making her disapproval inescapable. "I found no traces of Blood Magic. So I ask again, child. Why did you use your magic so carelessly?"

Veronica tenses beside me. A strangled cry passes her lips, and she struggles to inhale as the earth tightens around her chest. Her parents share a worried look, but they don't intervene. No one intervenes when a high priestess is disciplining her coven. "I wouldn't have done it if there had been another way," she says between gasps.

"Altruism is no excuse for breaking the Council's laws."

"But—"

"The Council leaves no room for exceptions. Our very existence demands absolute secrecy." Lady Ariana sighs like she's about to do something she finds distasteful.

"Wait!" I struggle against the earth, but it doesn't budge. "It's not her fault. She didn't have a choice. These guys, they were fighting, and they almost rolled into the flames. No one noticed her. I swear."

"Were these 'guys' Regs?"

The earth tightens around my chest. "Well, yeah."

A sad smile softens her wrinkled face, and I catch a glimpse of something no one else gets to see in her. The love—and disappointment—of my grandmother. "I expect more from you, Hannah. The last time witches grew careless with their magic, the Regs rose against us. Witch Hunters killed hundreds of witches before we formed the Council and put them down. They killed Casters in this very town. You know this."

"I know," I grumble. I'm not the one who needs a history lesson. "We don't use our magic in public. We don't risk ourselves for Regs. It's not our place to save them from themselves," I say, repeating her weekly reminder at coven meetings.

"You may know, Hannah, but you do not understand." My grandmother sighs and transforms again into Lady Ariana, high priestess of one of the largest Elemental covens in America. "You will learn. In time."

I don't like the sound of that.

"Veronica, our next private lesson will be delayed a month."

Beside me, Veronica blanches. "A month? But our next lesson isn't until August. If you add another month, I'll be away at college!"

"You should have thought of that before you chose to use your magic so carelessly. Be grateful I don't send you to school with a binding charm." Lady Ariana's threat hangs in the air, turning my stomach even though her words weren't aimed at me. The thought of wearing a binding ring again, of forcing my magic out of reach, is almost unbearable. "Hannah, you will share in Veronica's punishment. I'm moving your final initiation back thirty days."

"But I didn't do anything!" All the magic I've been dying to learn my entire life—air messages and scrying and creating fire from nothing—slips further out of reach.

"Isn't that a bit harsh, Mother?" Dad says, coming to my defense. "Hannah did tell us about the Reg ritual this morning."

Lady Ariana's expression remains impassive. "Did she mention Veronica's transgressions?" When Dad doesn't reply, she shakes her head. "I cannot show her favoritism, Tim, just as I couldn't do the same for you. She and Veronica will share an equal punishment. And for her outburst, she's banned from this week's usual lesson as well."

Anger and bitter disappointment flare inside, and it takes every ounce of self-control to keep my mouth shut. To hold back the tears stinging my eyes. I glare at Veronica, whose own *outburst* didn't lengthen her sentence, but I don't dare say anything. With my luck, I'd lose another week of lessons for breathing too loud.

"Come." Lady Ariana ushers our parents back toward the cars. "The girls need time to consider their actions." She glances at me over her shoulder, and I catch a brief hint of familial love. "Good luck."

5

WE'RE TRAPPED.

It takes every ounce of the control that's been hammered into me my entire life to keep the panic at bay. I reach for the earth, trying to convince it to let me go, but it's still saturated with my grandmother's power. Her magic is strong. Unyielding. Just like her.

We're not going anywhere.

"This is ridiculous," Veronica grumbles once she's sure we're alone. "I have three graduation parties tonight. This is going to ruin my manicure."

I close my eyes—partially to stop myself from rolling them at Veronica's out-of-whack priorities—and push against the earth's power, begging it to move, to soften, to loosen its hold. Nothing. Not the barest of budges. "Yeah, well, maybe you shouldn't have used your magic in public. You've gotten careless."

"Well, if *you* weren't so irrationally afraid of Blood Witches, Lady Ariana never would have found out." Veronica curses as she struggles against the immovable earth. "This is just as much your fault as mine."

"It's not irrational to be afraid of someone who tried to kill you," I snap back, and Veronica finally shuts up. I reach again for the earth's power, but I'm like an ant trying to move a mountain. It doesn't help that earth has always been my weakest element.

Veronica doesn't seem to be having better luck. She struggles and groans but stays firmly rooted in the ground.

While we strain our magic to dig ourselves out of these vertical graves, my mind drifts back to last night. What reason could a Reg have for doing this? What did they hope to accomplish? And then there's the bigger question: Who?

Evan still seems like the best suspect given his purchases at the Cauldron, but that doesn't mean it was him.

There's also Nolan. He certainly had a strong reaction to the sacrifice. Was he actually pissed or simply using his outrage to hide his involvement? He had plenty of time to perform the ritual before Gemma and I arrived in the woods.

Or maybe this wasn't even meant to be a spell. Maybe Savannah was trying to mess with me again. After she slipped in the blood and hurt her wrist, she could have faked seeing someone else run away from the scene of *her* crime.

"This is useless." Veronica sighs, her forehead damp with sweat. "There's no way we can overpower Lady Ariana's magic."

Veronica's right, but I don't say so. I don't say anything. Despite what she thinks, this whole thing is her fault.

The breeze picks up, fluttering the grass that's practically at eye level. Lady Ariana spelled the earth, but she didn't touch the *air*.

"Do you remember when Gabe was eight, and he slipped off his binding charm without permission at our Beltane celebration?" I ask, the memory of Veronica's younger brother bringing a smile to my lips despite everything.

Veronica laughs. "He got so dizzy from dancing around the maypole that he spun a cyclone that nearly uprooted all of

Lady Ariana's gardens." She glowers. "His first initiation was only pushed back two weeks for that."

"He was a child, V. Of course his sentence was lighter." I scowl at her. "And he was surrounded by the coven, not a bunch of Regs."

"What's your point?"

"My *point* is that I have an idea." I reach for the air, my magic humming under my skin, and grab hold of its will. It resists at first—air is a slippery element—but soon it bends to my call and starts to spin.

It takes all my focus to spiral the air into a thin cyclone and keep it from growing too large. The mini tornado pulls my hair loose and whips it around my face. As the wind reaches maximum velocity, I send the cyclone tunneling into the ground. Dirt flies into the air, and my makeshift shovel loosens the earth that binds me. I push until my muscles ache, until my power fades, and I only hope it's enough.

When the wind calms, and the dirt settles, Veronica and I are both covered in debris. I climb out of my loosened grave and fall onto my back, chest heaving from the effort.

"Clever," Veronica says, a smile on her face. If I didn't know better, I'd think she looked proud. The warmth in her gaze, the familiarity of that old us-against-the-world look in her eyes, punctures the armor around my heart.

I can't do this. Not anymore.

As Veronica takes a deep breath and copies my technique, I pull myself up and escape the clearing, struggling against the pull of the wind at my back.

"Hannah, wait." Branches snap behind me as Veronica

rushes to catch up. She pulls me to a stop one bend before the cars, where we're still hidden from view.

I flinch away from her touch. "What do you want?"

Veronica steps forward, but she doesn't snap back. She looks . . . confused. "Why'd you do it?"

"Do what?"

"You stood up for me. Against Lady Ariana, of all people. Why?"

I force a shrug, but the movement is constricted by her closeness. "If Benton hadn't caught me, I might have done the same thing."

"But you didn't." Veronica shakes her head and steps closer. She trails her fingers down my bare, dirt-streaked arm. "I think it's more than that." She tries to lace our fingers together. "Do you still love me?"

Her words rattle through my rib cage, and it's all I can do to shake my head. I pull my hand from hers and step out of reach. I can't let her see how much my skin sings under her touch. How true her words *used* to be.

"Come on, Hannah." Her voice is breaking, and I can't bear to look at her. "We were so good together."

But we weren't. "I can't do this right now." I try to turn away, but Veronica blocks my path. She steps closer, and her familiar scent—floral body wash and coconut shampoo, now with a hint of earth—washes over me. It floods my senses until I'm drowning.

Veronica leans forward, her forehead resting against mine. "You can't deny you miss me," she whispers, her breath warm on my face. "I miss you so much."

I want to tell her no. Tell her she's wrong, that I never loved her, but I can't. I did love her. First as a friend and then as the girl

I thought I'd marry. And now, with her so close, that's the only part I can remember.

In my silence, Veronica leans in and closes the final gap.

And then I'm flying.

Her lips are warm against mine, and all the feelings I tried to bury flare back to life. The love, the passion, the *heat* of everything we shared. Against my better judgment, I kiss her back. Nothing about this moment is tender. It's frantic. Hungry. Full of hurt.

I wrap my arms around her waist, my hands slipping along the thin fabric of her dress. The one we picked out together. I pull her tighter to me, until our bodies are flush, but it still isn't enough.

Veronica bites my lip, and the pain reminds me of all the reasons this has to end. I pull away, hating how much her sudden absence affects me. My body doesn't feel whole without her pressed against it.

"We can't do this. *I* can't do this." My breath comes out in a rush, and I'm powerless to stop the tears. "We're over."

"But why? We were perfect together. We can have that again." Tears pool in her eyes, making the green shine bright. "You want me just as much as I want you. That kiss proves it."

"It only proves I'm lonely."

"Oh, please. There was *passion* in that kiss." Veronica brushes away her tears, her movements harsh, like she hates to show weakness. But then she softens. "I love you."

"No, you don't." I shove past her and continue toward my parents' car. I'm bursting with all the reasons we can't be together. "You loved having a girlfriend who never said no. The *second* I stood up for what I needed, you abandoned me."

Veronica grabs my arm and spins me back to face her. "That's not true."

"It is!" My voice reverberates through the woods, startling birds into flight. "I told you I wasn't comfortable with those Caster Witches, but you didn't care! You were so busy trying to impress them that you didn't listen to me."

"Hannah—"

"No. You don't get to spin this. Not again." My breath comes in short, painful gasps. A phantom ache spreads through my limbs. "You didn't even help me when I was *attacked by a Blood Witch*, because you were too busy sucking up to people we were never going to see again."

The memories threaten to pull me down like an undertow. Pain blossoming across my face. My blood on the other witch's hands. Her smile as she took control of my body and forced me to my knees.

"Can I speak now? Or are you going to cut me off again?" When I cross my arms and say nothing, she continues. "I'll admit, the thing with the Blood Witch was not my best moment—"

"She nearly *killed* me. Do you have any idea what it feels like, to have your body possessed by Blood Magic?"

"—but you can't throw away our entire history because of one bad decision," she finishes, like she wasn't even listening to me. Which is half the problem right there.

"Fine, forget New York," I say, even as I remember the feel of the witch's hands closing around my throat. Veronica was so taken by the trio of Caster Witches we met in Manhattan that she refused to listen to me. She even abandoned me in Central Park when I begged her to stop talking to them. The

Blood Witch attacked moments later, mistaking me for one of the Casters.

I shake the memories away and focus my anger on Veronica. "Our entire relationship was me doing whatever *you* wanted. You decided when we'd hang out and what we'd do. You always picked the restaurant. You even tried to decide how and when our relationship would end!"

Veronica falls back a step, confusion creasing her brow. "What are you talking about?"

"I'm not oblivious, V. I caught every one of your 'long distance is *so* hard' and 'holding on to high school partners in college is almost impossible' hints. I know you were planning to break up with me when you left for school."

"I never said I wanted to break up with you." Tears shimmer in Veronica's eyes, but she doesn't let them fall. "I'm not wrong. Long distance *is* hard, but I think we can make it. I want us to make it."

"It doesn't matter. Not anymore." I step around her and head toward the cars. "It's too late to go back to the way we were."

"Why?" Veronica reaches for my wrist and holds firm. "Why can't we go back?"

She'll never understand. The realization washes all the fight out of me, leaving behind only heartache. I gently pull my wrist from her grip. "Because," I say, my voice so soft it's nearly swallowed up by the trees, "I'm standing here, telling you how much you hurt me, and you can't hear it." Tears fill my eyes. I've lost the strength to hide them. "You broke my heart, and you didn't even notice. How can I . . ." My throat closes up, and I look away. "How could I ever trust you to put the pieces back together?"

Veronica is silent after that. I glance up to find her watching me, but she doesn't speak.

I don't expect her to. There's nothing left to say. I turn again to leave.

"This conversation isn't over."

My response sticks in my throat. I can't even look at her. "Yes. It is."

6

THE CONFRONTATION WITH VERONICA leaves my nerves jagged and raw. I ignore my parents' attempts to talk about it, choosing instead to spend the rest of the weekend locked in my room, blasting what to others may seems like a bizarre array of music. To me, it's like comfort food, warm and soothing. My playlist shuffles from screaming heavy metal to heartbroken show tunes to forlorn pop ballads. I listen to my favorite breakup song over and over, sobbing until I can't breathe. Until Mom begs me to play something else. Anything else.

That's when I switch to headphones and throw my pain on a canvas, not caring how much paint splatters all over my clothes.

My hands are still covered in vibrant colors on Monday, and it takes forever to scrub my skin clean as I get ready for work. At some point last night, my insides shifted and rearranged, replacing pulsing pain with boiling rage. I cannot believe Veronica cost me an entire month of training *and* got me banned from this week's lesson. She knows how much I've been dying to learn the next phase of magic. I bet she doesn't even care.

The smell of coffee lures me into the kitchen, but I grab an energy drink from the fridge instead. Coffee may smell great, but it tastes like dirt. When I plop into my chair at the dining room table, Mom shoves a plate of scrambled eggs and buttered toast in front of me.

"Long shift today?" Dad asks as he sweeps into the dining room with his coffee thermos. He's dressed for court, trading in his usual goofy ties for a slate-gray one. He's had a full caseload since his boss, the district attorney, went on maternity leave, spending more time than usual in court.

"Uh-huh." I wonder if Dad's cop buddies have any theories for him about the weekend's bonfire. My phone alert goes off, a five-minute warning before I need to be out the door. I take another bite before swallowing the first.

Dad kisses Mom goodbye. "Have a good day," he calls as he heads for the door.

And then it's just Mom and me. Goody.

She tries for small talk, asking about my art and my plans for the week, but I lob one-word answers in response.

"I really wish you'd stop with the sulking." Mom sips her coffee, her eyebrows raised as she waits for my answer.

"I'm not sulking. I'm eating." My phone beeps again. If I don't leave in two minutes, I'll be late. "Sorry, Mom. I have to go." I shove the toast in my mouth and deposit the plate of half-eaten eggs on the kitchen counter. I almost make it to the door before Mom calls out to me.

"Hannah. Wait."

I wait. But not patiently. "Mom, I'm going to be late."

"I just . . . I know this was a hard weekend for you." Mom's face softens for the first time since my grandmother's punishment. "Lady Ariana's lessons may seem harsh, but everything she does is for the good of the coven. She loves you."

"Was your old high priestess this tough?" Mom used to belong to a smaller coven in a coastal town a few hours from Seattle.

She moved to Salem for a job at the university, and when she fell in love with my dad, she stayed.

Mom pauses, too long to be telling the truth.

"Never mind. I have to go." I slip out the front door just as my final alarm rings on my phone.

I drive to work in an angry haze. I'm not oblivious. I get why we need strict laws—exposure would be catastrophic—but I wish my parents could stand up for me once in a while. I wish my grandmother was more like Gemma's, someone who'd bake me sweets and host sleepovers. A grandma who'd spoil me rotten, let me stay up too late, and make all my favorite foods.

With that particular pang of jealousy souring my hastily eaten breakfast, I arrive at the Fly by Night Cauldron. The lights are on, but the CLOSED sign still faces out.

"Lauren?" I call to my boss as I push through the already un-locked door. Tightness constricts my chest when she doesn't reply right away. "Are you in here? Should I change the sign?"

A chair scrapes somewhere in the back of the shop. I tense, and my magic flares, reaching for the air around me. I shove the magic down, burying the impulse. "Lauren?"

"I'm with a customer. Go ahead." Lauren's voice floats through the shop like incense on a gentle breeze, and the power swirling under my skin finally relaxes.

I flip the sign to OPEN and head for the register to clock in. I punch in my four-digit passcode as a curtain to my left flutters, then rips open. Lauren stands on the other side with a man, his back to me. I can't hear what he says, but it elicits a blush from my boss. Lauren gestures toward the door, and the man turns.

Shit.

Detective Archer. At my work. *What is he doing here?* As the detective passes the register, his gaze lands on me. Recognition lights his face, but he merely nods to me and continues out, the bell above the door jingling his departure. When my heart rate returns to normal, I look to Lauren. "What was he doing here?"

"Hmm?" Lauren fusses with her hair, the wide sleeves of her dress falling to her elbows. "Oh, Ryan? He's new in town. I guess he's introducing himself to all the local business owners." She sighs and leans her hip against the counter.

Something doesn't add up. "What was he doing in the back?"

Lauren's face flushes even redder. "I offered him a tarot reading. On the house."

"Anything interesting?" Maybe something came up about the bonfire. Not likely but not impossible either, especially since the detective was investigating it so recently.

"You know I can't discuss a client's reading, Hannah." Lauren may look like a ridiculous cliché—with her old-fashioned black dress, dark hair hanging well past her shoulders, and a pentacle the size of a baseball swinging from her neck—but she's a professional through and through. She isn't some Reg playing dress up, either; she's the real deal.

Well, sorta.

Lauren wasn't born to the Witch Clans, but she's a legitimate Third-Degree Wiccan High Priestess. She's studied Wicca for over a decade, advancing through the stages of initiation, learning all she can about the magical properties of herbs and moon phases and crystals and the rest of the natural world. Providing counsel to her own initiates and those who come to her for guidance.

She's almost like a Caster Witch, brewing potions and weaving spells. The same thirst to always learn more.

But that's where the similarities end. Lauren isn't a Caster. Her magic has nowhere near the reach. The immediacy. The strength. And yet there's no denying the power she does have.

"I will say this, though," Lauren continues, glancing toward the door to make sure Detective Archer isn't lingering on the premises, "that man is going to be good for Salem." She sighs, a soft, dreamy sound, and then seems to realize I'm still standing next to her. "Why don't you dust the shelves while we wait for Cal to arrive."

"Cal?"

Lauren nods. "He interviewed yesterday and was eager to get started. When he gets here, can you teach him the register? I've got back-to-back appointments most of the day."

"Sure," I say, reaching behind the counter for the dust cloth and Lauren's homemade cleaning spray, a mixture of water, vinegar, and lemon oil. I'm fairly certain she blesses each batch under a full moon for good measure.

I start with the counter, then move to dusting the tops of the mirrors and picture frames that hang along the back wall. Customers always get a kick out of Lauren's *Shoplifters Will Be Hexed!* cross-stitched sign.

The bell above the door jingles, and I turn to herd the day's first official client back to Lauren's private reading room. Most of our customers are drawn to the shop by Lauren's reputation with tarot, and today is no exception. I lead a short man in a crisp black suit to the back of the shop, where Lauren has candles and incense burning to cleanse and prepare the space. When I head back to the counter, there's someone drumming their fingers along the glass.

"Can I help you?" I ask, trying to keep the annoyance out of my voice. I just finished cleaning that.

The drumming stops, and the guy turns with a wide grin that immediately puts me at ease. He's about my height, his blond hair shaved on the sides and longer on top. He's wearing dark jeans and one of our Cauldron T-shirts. "I'm Cal. I'm supposed to start work here today." He gestures at our matching purple T-shirts to illustrate his point.

"Hannah," I say, shaking his hand. "Lauren's busy, so she asked me to show you the ropes." I gesture for him to follow me behind the counter. "Did she give you a code for clocking in?"

Cal nods, reaching into his back pocket for a small moleskin notebook. He flips it open and riffles through a few pages. "Yup. Right here."

I pull up the clock-in screen on the register and have Cal punch in his code. "Are you new in town?" I ask as he finishes up. "I haven't seen you around before."

"It depends on how you define 'new.' I just finished my first year at Salem State. I'm from Boston initially, but I decided to stick around and earn some extra cash while I get ahead in my courses." Cal gestures to the register. "Mind if I try?"

"Sure." I return the ancient register to the cheesy early 2000s home screen and watch as Cal brings up the clock-in function. "Why do you have to get ahead?"

"College isn't cheap," Cal says, like it's an obvious answer. "If I can finish my computer science degree in three years, I'll save an entire year of tuition and housing costs. What about you?"

"What about me?"

"What are you studying in college?"

My cheeks warm, but there's something so earnest about how Cal asks that I don't mind telling him the truth. "I'll actually be a senior at the high school this fall. Veronica's going to college this year, though. She's going to study journalism at Ithaca College in New York."

"Who's Veronica?"

My heart skips a beat when I realize what I've done. I thought this stupid reflex, this subconscious need to include Veronica in every part of my life, was broken. Dead. Gone.

"She's my ex," I whisper, my stomach clenching as I wait to see how Cal responds. Coming out is always nerve-wracking, no matter how many times I do it. And now that Veronica and I are broken up, there's an added sting of loss along with the rest of the anxious emotions.

Cal pauses a moment, considering me. Then he lets out a knowing sigh. "My first boyfriend broke up with me a few months before he went to college, too."

"Yeah?" I ask, instantly feeling a tighter kinship with my new coworker, like seeing a familiar face in a crowd of strangers. "What happened?"

"Some of it was the usual stuff, like not wanting to juggle a relationship while we went to separate colleges. Mostly, though, I don't think he wanted to date a guy." When Cal sees my confused expression, he clarifies. "I'm trans. I came out senior year."

"Oh," I say, trying to hide my surprise. "I'm sorry he dumped you."

"It's fine." Cal smiles wide, his pale cheeks flushing. "My new boyfriend is a much better match. He's home in Brooklyn for the summer though."

I offer my condolences on the long distance and walk Cal through the most common functions on the register. As we work, we swap stories about our exes. Cal groans sympathetically when I tell him about the public shouting match that ended my relationship, and I pester him for details about how he met his current boyfriend.

"This is the least intuitive register system I've ever seen. How old is this thing?" Cal asks, interrupting his own story. We're in the middle of a practice return, and the register keeps making angry beeps at him.

"You'll get the hang of it. Sometimes it helps if you smack it."

"That doesn't actually—"

I hit the register with the heel of my hand, and Cal cringes at the shuddering clang the old machine makes. "Try now."

Cal eyes me suspiciously and runs through the steps again, glancing at the notebook where he wrote the instructions. This time, the return goes through fine.

"Told you." I grin, and Cal smiles back. It's nice having some fresh blood around here. Lauren is cool and all, but she's still the boss.

The bell above the door rings, announcing a new customer. Cal plasters on a smile so wide it rivals Lauren's best customer service grin and offers a hearty, "Welcome to the Fly by Night Cauldron!"

His enthusiasm is infectious. I turn to greet the newcomer, too, but I freeze when I see who it is.

Evan.

I hardly recognize him at first. Gone is the goth kid who came into the shop before the bonfire. This new Evan's face is free from makeup. He's wearing dress pants, a white collared shirt, and a name tag with the Witch Museum logo.

What is he doing here?

"You good?" I ask. When Cal nods, I follow Evan down the candle aisle. I cross my arms, all my customer service training forgotten. "Can I help you?" I snap, my tone more hostile than my words.

Evan raises a brow. "Uh, hello to you, too, Hannah. And I'm fine. I know what I need." He disappears down another row, and the clinking of glass tells me he's looking through our vials of magical herbs.

A war rages inside, leaving me frozen in place. Evan's a Reg. His actions shouldn't concern me. Lady Ariana's words echo in my head: *It's not our place to save them from themselves.* If Evan wants to sacrifice another animal and risk the consequences of that kind of magic, that's on him.

And yet . . .

By the time I glance back at the register, Cal is cautiously ringing up the first of Evan's supplies. Crystals and candles, most of them black. Evan isn't by the counter, probably searching for something else. I peek down the herb aisle, but it's like he's disappeared. He's not in the book aisle either. I turn to help Cal at the register and smash into someone.

"Shit. I'm sorry." I look up. Evan. He's carrying vials of blood root and hemlock. I'm suddenly feeling much less apologetic. "What are you doing?"

He stiffens under my stare, and his expression becomes guarded. "That's none of your business," he snaps, and shoves past me to the register, where Lauren has appeared to help Cal. She shoots me a look as she rings up the rest of Evan's purchase, but I can't tell whether she's upset by his collection of supplies or my lackluster customer service skills.

With her, it could really go either way.

Evan pays and heads for the door. As he draws near, I step in his way. "What'll it be this time?" I ask, hands clenching into fists. "Another raccoon? Or are you going after something bigger?"

"I don't know what you're talking about," Evan says, holding my gaze like he's daring me to accuse him again. "Get the hell out of my way."

"Or what?"

Anger flashes through Evan's eyes. "Or you'll be next." He stalks around me, his arm jostling my shoulder, and he's out the door a second later, the chime a discordant crashing in my ears.

"What was that about?" Cal asks, coming around the counter when Lauren heads back to her office. "You okay?"

I nod, too busy fighting the angry thrum of magic in my veins to speak. Evan does not get to threaten me and walk away feeling smug. He's a *Reg*. Whatever power he feels, whatever rush he got from his ritual—and given his reaction, I'm almost certain it was his—that's nothing compared to what I can do. Less than nothing.

"Tell Lauren I'm taking my break," I say. "I'll be right back."

Locals and tourists mix and mingle along the narrow sidewalks as I slip out of the shop. I spot the crisp white of Evan's shirt as he turns the corner and hurry after him, weaving through pedestrians with a string of apologies in my wake.

A pack of middle schoolers clog the sidewalk, and I step into the street to hurry around them. A car horn blares behind me, and I jolt, pushing back onto the sidewalk and knocking into the gaggle of sixth graders.

"Hey!"

"Watch it, weirdo!"

"Out of the way, loser!"

When did preteens get so rude? I was terrified of seniors when I was their age. I consider tripping them with a crack in the side-walk, but I shake the thought away. Elementals don't interfere with the lives of Regs; only Blood Witches do that. Besides, Lady Ariana would skin me alive if she found traces of magic some-place with such a heavy Reg presence. I'm not letting my training get pushed back another second, especially not because of some snotty middle schoolers.

Up ahead, Evan crosses the intersection and heads for the Witch Museum—the one with those creepy wax figures that ex-plain the witch trials—and I hurry after him. On second thought, maybe preteens have always been little shits. Abigail Williams was only eleven when she turned an entire town on its head.

Thankfully, the light is red as I race through the intersection at top speed. I ignore the people who give me strange looks and reach for Evan before he passes the small crowd in line for tickets. "Evan, wait."

Evan jumps, startled, and pulls away from my touch. The Cauldron bag swings from his hand as he spins to face me. "What do you want?"

"You—" I suck in a lungful of air, my chest heaving. I am *so* not a runner. I press my hands into my thighs and double over, which totally ruins the fierce vibe I was going for. "You do *not* get to threaten me and walk away like it's nothing," I say when I finally catch my breath.

"Whatever." Evan rolls his eyes, dismissing me.

"I'm serious," I hiss. "You don't get to hurl curses as threats." My magic flares with my temper, kicking up a breeze in the cramped square. I press the reflex down.

"I told you. I don't know what you're talking about." He glances at the tourists around us and leads me away from the line by the elbow. His thumb digs painfully into my bicep.

"Get your hands off me," I snap, but I catch myself keeping my voice low, like I'm afraid to cause a scene. I tear my arm from his grip and shove a finger toward his purchase. "That bag is full of cursing supplies. Whatever you're doing, it has to stop. And you're sure as shit not going to curse me or I'll—"

"Or you'll do what?" Evan raises an eyebrow at me, and I *hate* that I can't show him the magic I could unleash if he tried to hurt me.

I force myself to take a deep breath and switch tactics. "I've worked at the Cauldron since I turned sixteen." I pause as a woman drags two young children past us. Only when they're out of range do I continue. "I know the beginnings of a hex when I see one. Hurting people is not the way to get what you want."

"Some people deserve to be punished." His eyes flash, glimmering in the sunlight. His voice is thick with hurt. "Some people deserve to watch their lives fall apart. Why shouldn't I be the one to make that happen?"

His question catches me off guard, and I don't have an immediate answer beyond *that's not how life works*, and somehow I doubt that will suffice. I search for a Wiccan explanation, hoping all his time in the Cauldron means he gives a shit about more than the magic. "Whatever evil you conjure, the Law of Return will send it back three times worse. Are you willing to risk that?"

"That's all I'm trying to do, make sure he gets what he deserves." Evan curls his hands into fists, squeezing so hard his arms shake, but he doesn't clarify who *he* is. "I don't care what happens to me."

"Evan—"

"Does your boss know you're here?"

"I . . . uh . . ."

"Didn't think so." Evan steps closer, until I have to crane my neck to meet his stare. "Leave me the hell alone, Hannah, or I *will* stop coming to the Cauldron. And I'll tell your boss *exactly* why she's lost my business."

This threat actually lands. I can't lose my job. As much as I complain about the tourists, the Cauldron is the only reason I can afford my clunker of a car and the insurance to keep it on the road. The extra cash pays for art supplies and midnight diner trips with Gem and even my half-assed excuse for college savings. "You wouldn't."

"I don't want to. Your boss has the best supplies in town." Evan's eyes go hard; he leans in close. "But I'm not going to let you harass me every time I walk through the door. Stay out of my business."

I really want to tell him to go screw himself, but the thought of getting fired and losing my only source of income—meager though it may be—silences my tongue.

"Understood?"

"Fine." I cross my arms and return his stony glare. "But don't say I didn't warn you."

"Whatever." Evan acts tough, but he can't hide the tremor in his voice. He may be desperate enough to break one of the fundamental tenets of Wicca—harm none—but he clearly knows he's playing with fire.

I lean against the rough exterior of the Witch Museum and watch as Evan slips inside. I consider asking Lauren why she even stocks the supplies for hexes and other negative spellwork, but I can practically hear her response in my head. Something about balance and the importance of letting people make the mistakes necessary to find their true path. Nonsense, really. Lady Ariana would never allow so much freedom.

There is no room for mistakes in the Clans.

A warm breeze drifts past, pulling strands of hair across my cheeks and rustling the low bushes beside me. I glance down.

It can't be . . . I jolt away from the building, my heart hammering against my ribs, adrenaline preparing my body to run. Lady Ariana said we were safe. She said there was no Blood Witch here.

She was wrong.

On the side of the Witch Museum, behind a row of bushes, shines a series of runes.

Drawn in blood.

In an instant, I'm transported back to a tiny apartment. Bloody runes cover the walls, and a girl with blue hair is desperately scrubbing them away, trying to erase them before the magic can take hold.

And then I'm in Central Park, where the Blood Witch finally finds me. Where she wraps her fingers around my throat—

Laughter cuts through the memory, bringing me back to myself. Behind me, a small child toddles down the sidewalk, squealing with delight as their two dads chase after them. The trio passes the Witch Museum, and the taller of the dads scoops up the curly-haired kid and reaches for the other man's hand. The family walks across the street to where a row of food trucks is serving lunch.

I smile after them and find the courage to study the runes more closely. Nothing bad will happen to me around all these people. I recognize *Jera*—two interlocking capital *L*s, twisted on a diagonal—and *Peorth*, which looks like an hourglass tipped on its side with the top missing. I don't recognize the other runes, but I know *Jera* deals with time and change while *Peorth* refers to things hidden. Usually magical things.

What is the Blood Witch trying to do? As the question presses to the front of my mind, I know I'm right. This wasn't a Reg.

I may not know much about blood, but I understand paint. There's a confidence to these runes, a sureness to their creation. If a Reg drew these, there'd be imperfections in the lines where they hesitated and consulted their guide. No. These runes look *exactly* like the ones in New York, complete with the impressions of two fingers in each stroke along the stone wall. A Reg couldn't do this. They wouldn't be this precise.

Was I wrong about Evan? He's clearly up to something, but maybe he wasn't the one who killed that raccoon. Maybe the same witch who drew these runes was out in the woods with us.

My hands shake as I reach for my phone. *How did they do this without getting caught?* This isn't exactly a quiet street. Even now, people in line are giving me weird looks for climbing through the bushes to take a photo. I doubt even Lady Ariana could test the wall for magic without being seen, so how did the Blood Witch—

It doesn't matter. I just need proof so Lady Ariana will believe me and take care of the intruder. She'll keep us safe.

I snap pictures of the runes with my phone. My parents should be able to identify the rest and tell me what they mean. In case that isn't enough to prove this wasn't a Reg with access to Google, I grab a receipt from my other pocket, soft and worn from going through the wash once or twice. I cringe as I swipe the thin paper along the markings, careful to avoid skin contact. I know firsthand what happens when a Blood Witch takes an Elemental's blood.

I'd rather not find out what happens if I touch theirs.

7

I'M HYPERAWARE OF THE blood in my back pocket when I return to work. Cal shoots me a panicked look as the register beeps at him, and I hurry over to help ring up a pair of tourists purchasing matching amethyst necklaces.

After my shift, driving home is an unexpected challenge. I keep picturing the bloody receipt pressing against me, and the thought twists my stomach into knots. I've never gotten out of my car faster than when I pull into our driveway.

My parents aren't back yet. Of course. The one time I actually want them to beat me home from work, they don't. I rush upstairs, set a clean tissue on my desk, and lay the receipt on top. It almost looks innocuous, like it came from a paper cut, but the bloody runes are seared into my mind. I may have to burn these pants.

I slip out of my jeans and throw on a clean pair. The ick factor is still there—I wiped *blood* off a wall—but there are more pressing concerns.

"Hannah?" Mom calls as the front door slams shut. The greasy smell of fried chicken trails up the stairs. "I brought home dinner."

I pick up the edges of the tissue and gently carry the bloody receipt out of my room. "Mom? I need your help."

There must be an edge of panic to my voice, because Mom comes rushing out of the dining room. "What is it? What's wrong?"

"We need the grimoire."

Mom raises a brow at me. "Why?" Her gaze falls to the receipt in my hands. "What's that?"

"It's evidence. I need you to test it." I squeeze by Mom on the landing. "I found runes on the side of the Witch Museum, written in blood, and—"

"And you think it's *Blood Magic*?" Air whips through the house, pulling the tissue from my grip. Mom uses the wind to float the receipt onto the coffee table and kneels beside it. "What were you thinking, bringing something like this into our house?"

"I'm sorry. I just—"

"Ooh, something smells good," Dad calls from the front door and wanders into the living room. He stops cold when he sees us, his boring gray tie halfway undone. "Do I want to know what's going on?"

"Your daughter thinks there's a Blood Witch in town. Again." Mom rolls up her sleeves and flicks her fingers, creating fire out of nothing. Jealousy presses at my skin. I cannot *wait* to learn how to do that.

"Hannah, you heard Lady Ariana. We're the only coven in town." Dad sighs and sinks into his recliner while Mom grows the fire in her hands.

"Then explain this." I pull out my phone and open my photos. "These were drawn on the side of the Witch Museum."

Dad takes the phone from me and zooms in on the picture. He studies the image for a moment before his eyebrows shoot up.

"Marie? Have you seen these?" There's an odd note to his voice. It's higher than normal. Strained.

"What is it? What do they mean?"

"Let me see." Mom leans over while Dad holds out the phone. Her eyes go wide as the fire in her hands turns blue. "Do you think?"

"I don't know." Dad moves onto the floor beside Mom, conjuring a wind that lifts the bloody receipt into the air.

"Will someone *please* tell me what's going on?" I pace the living room while my parents weave magic I don't understand. "Is there a Blood Witch here or not?"

Mom shoots me a look, her eyes reflecting the now-purple fire. "That's what we're trying to find out." She nods to Dad, who guides the receipt into the flame. The receipt catches fire and burns a bright turquoise. In a flash, it's gone.

"Is that it?" The whole thing took, like, two seconds. "What does that mean?"

My parents stand and share a look. It feels like a hundred years pass in the span of a few moments before either of them speaks. Finally, Mom sighs. "The test was negative. There was no magic in the sample."

"As your grandmother already said," Dad adds, "we are the only coven in Salem. We have been for a very long time."

"Are you sure? What about the runes?" They looked so similar to the ones I saw before. They have to be real.

Dad shrugs. "The runes seemed legitimate, but a Reg must have copied them from the internet." He leads us into the dining room. "The coven is safe. I promise."

I try to feel relieved, but mostly, I feel confused. How could I have been so wrong?

Dad and I follow Mom to the table, where she turns her curious gaze on me and studies my face. "What's with this sudden obsession with Blood Witches? You've never worried about them before."

"I—" All my secrets threaten to spill out, but I swallow them down before they make it to my lips. I've already lost a month of training because of these fears. If I tell my parents what happened in New York, if *anyone* finds out, the Council will come for me and Veronica. They'll come and they'll strip away our magic piece by piece until we're nothing but hollowed-out shells. Until we're nothing more than Regs. Worse, even, since we'll know how much we've lost.

"I don't know," I finally say, unable to find a suitable lie.

"We know the breakup with Veronica has been hard for you," Mom says, her words cutting straight to my heart. "But you have to find a more productive way to channel your frustration. Looking for monsters that don't exist isn't a healthy way to spend your summer."

"That's not what this is." But her words strike a chord. Maybe she's right. Maybe I am looking for villains to distract myself from the Veronica Situation. And Evan is clearly up to something. He works at the museum. The runes could be part of whatever pagan curse he's casting. Maybe he practiced at home until he perfected them. That would account for the lack of hesitation marks.

"Channel whatever 'this' is into your art. Leave coven business to the adults." Mom grabs one of the smaller boxes. "Biscuit?"

"Sure." I take one of the now-cold biscuits and drop it on my plate. "You *swear* there was no magic in that blood?"

"Cross my heart," Mom starts.

Dad finishes the saying. "And hope to die."

-|-   ✳   -|-

I trust my parents.

I really do.

But day after day at the Cauldron, as I restock some of the same tools Evan bought for his bloody rituals, the worries pick at the back of my mind. What if my parents were wrong? What if they *lied* when they said the test was negative? It's not like I would know. They never explained the intricacies of their spell. Never explained what the different colors meant.

Or maybe a Blood Witch made Evan draw the runes for them. It's not impossible. A few years ago, Lady Ariana told us about the Blood Witch who instigated the accusations during the witch trials.

According to my grandmother's stories, a Blood Witch named Elijah grew jealous when the Caster woman he fancied fell in love with a Reg man. When Elijah's Blood Magic failed to make the woman he desired love him back, he turned to the most sinister parts of his power. Despite the growing dangers of Witch Hunters, Elijah sent children like Abigail Williams and Elizabeth Parris into fits until the town was in such a frenzy he could accuse anyone he liked. Elijah started with the Reg man who had married the young Caster woman. In the end, when she still refused him, Elijah accused the very woman he claimed to love.

The Council, which up until that point had only gone after Witch Hunters—a secret society of Regs who had discovered the Witch Clans and sought to destroy us—decided something had to be done about Elijah. They sent agents to Salem to strip the Blood Witch of his dangerous magic, but he resisted. In the end, the struggle killed him, and his crimes led to the creation of the

Council laws we live by today. After the witch craze in Salem ended, and the rest of the living Caster families fled, the Council banned Blood Witches from the town and stationed a handful of Elemental families here. Our coven, and our family, descended from those first Elementals.

I was fourteen when Lady Ariana told that story, a little over a year after I passed my first initiation and no longer had to wear a binding charm to suppress my magic around Regs. I had nightmares about Blood Witches for weeks.

A sigh spills past my lips as I restock the candles. I hate that there's no one to talk to about this. Normally, I'd call Gem, but she has no idea magic is even real. My parents think I'm projecting breakup issues, and my grandmother is a little on the scary side.

There's no one to confide in. No one to help make sure my parents were right about those runes. No one except . . .

Nope. Not an option. Not even a little bit.

I spend the last two hours of my Friday shift trying to focus on other things. Like the creepy customer buying supplies for a love spell or the hipster teen who tries to slip a baggie of incense into his pocket. I even help Cal reshelve the books to distract myself. But no matter what I'm doing, the option that's not really an option?

Yeah, that keeps winding its way through my brain.

By the time I clock out and head for the parking garage, my stupid idea has turned into my last beacon of hope. I pull out my phone and stare at the blank text. *Screw it.* I punch in her number and hover over the keypad. It takes three tries before I can hit send.

HW: I need your help.

Ellipses bounce below my message.

VM: Where are you?

This is a bad idea. I should tell Veronica it was a mistake. Pretend I meant to text Gemma. Or Benton. Or literally anyone who isn't her. Instead, I lean against my car and type my response.

HW: Meet me at my place. Twenty minutes. Bring the book.

I unlock my car and slide in the front seat.

VM: I'll be there.

My skin flushes as I pull out of my space and drive down the winding parking structure. This was a mistake. A terrible, irreversible mistake. But it's also my only hope of putting these Blood Witch worries to rest.

Veronica is waiting for me when I get home, leaning against my front door.

Stay strong. You can do this. I cut the ignition and climb out of my car. "I want to make one thing clear before we go inside."

Veronica raises one eyebrow. "And what's that?"

"This isn't a social call. We're not getting back together."

"Then why am I here?" Veronica starts toward me, but I put up one hand and she stops.

"I need your help." I step away from my car, ignoring how incredibly exposed I feel. "Did you bring the book?"

Veronica raises her purse in response. It swings like a pendulum as I walk up the driveway and unlock my front door. My ex follows me inside and up the stairs. When we're shut in my room, I turn to explain, but Veronica isn't looking at me. Her attention is trained on the newest additions to my walls.

"When did you do this?" She's stopped in front of my latest piece. I started it a few days after we broke up, a self-portrait of a girl betrayed. Yet with each layer it morphed into something almost resembling strength. Freedom. "You look so . . ." she starts and trails off.

"So what?"

"Broken."

I stiffen. "I didn't bring you here to criticize my work. I can't stop worrying that there's a Blood Witch here. Even if it's not the girl from New York, there are others."

No one—except perhaps the Council—knows exactly how many witches are in the US. Lady Ariana says that for every ten Elementals, there are probably seven Casters and only two Blood Witches. They're uncommon, even for witches, but they're still very much alive.

And some of the most powerful among us.

Veronica finally turns away from the drawing. "Hannah, there's no Blood Witch. Lady Ariana said so."

"Then explain this." I pull up the pictures of the bloody runes and hand the phone to Veronica. Her eyebrows inch up her forehead as she examines the photos.

"This looks like the apartment in Manhattan." A tremor shakes her voice. "Where did you find this?"

"The Witch Museum."

She glances up from the images. "Here? We have to tell someone."

"I already showed my parents." I take my phone from her and slide it into my back pocket. "I even got a sample of the blood. They say it's nothing."

Veronica's whole body seems to melt with her exhale. "Why didn't you lead with that? If your parents tested it, then it's nothing. Why am I here?"

"Because you owe me."

Her sharp burst of laughter fills the room. But when I don't relent, Veronica studies me. "Wait. You're serious?"

"I stood up for you in the woods and had to skip this week's lesson for my trouble, so yes. I'm serious. At least humor me. Help me make sure our coven is safe." I motion for her to wait and slip downstairs. I return with a large bowl and bottle of water from the kitchen.

Veronica's sitting on my bed now, her legs crossed underneath her. She gives me an unamused look. "What do you think you're doing?"

"You and I are going to scry for the Blood Witch." I pour the water into the bowl and set it on my desk. "That's why I had you bring your grimoire."

"This is ridiculous." Veronica reaches into her bag and pulls out her personal Book of Shadows. "Why can't you be a normal ex and post angry poetry online?"

I ignore her question and reach for the grimoire. I wish I had all day to pore over these pages. They're full of magic Lady Ariana keeps hidden until we're at least eighteen. After our final initiation ceremony, our weekly classes end. Instead, we have one-on-one lessons with our high priestess whenever she deems us ready for more power. Newer skills. That's when we're permitted to copy spells from the coven grimoire. Under supervision of course.

When we were still dating, Veronica told me she felt something as she copied over the words and diagrams exactly. This pressure in her head that would build and build until understanding finally clicked into place as she finished the final strokes of her pen.

About a third of the way through Veronica's grimoire, after all our history and the intricate family trees for each of the twenty-three extended families with ties to our coven, I find the section on scrying and skim the pages. "It looks like we need something for contrast in the water."

Veronica breathes out an exaggerated sigh, like she's resigning herself to this process. "Lady Ariana taught me to use black ink, but Mom sometimes uses food coloring in a pinch."

"Would paint work?" I head for my art supplies on the other side of the room.

"I don't know. We can try." Veronica extracts herself from the bed and comes to stand beside me. "Add enough so that it can swirl around and make patterns."

I squeeze the paint over the water. It turns cloudy, and shapes start to form. "Now what?"

"Now you step back and let me do this."

"Uh, no." I return the paint and stand beside Veronica. "I'm doing this with you."

"You're not eighteen."

"And I don't get to learn this on my eighteenth birthday, because of *you*. I'd say this falls under the you-owe-me category."

Veronica groans. "Fine. But when it doesn't work right, don't blame me." She places her hands on either side of the bowl and instructs me to do the same. "First, we need to warm up the water."

"How do we do that?"

"If you'd stop interrupting, I'd tell you." Veronica shoots me a look before closing her eyes. She takes several deep breaths, and I do the same. "Show us yes," she instructs the water, opening her eyes to observe.

The bowl grows warm beneath my fingers, and the water spins clockwise, the paint inside swirling and dancing along the magical current.

"Show us no," Veronica says, and the water falls completely still before spinning counterclockwise.

"This is so cool." My words come out in a rushed, yet reverent, whisper. I can't believe I have to wait even longer before I'm allowed to do this on my own. "Now what? Can we ask about the Blood Witch?"

Veronica shakes her head. "First, we ask known questions to make sure everything is working as it should," she says, smiling up at me. She knows how much this means to me, to be doing this kind of magic. "Why don't you try? Ask something you know the answer to. Empty your mind of everything except your question."

My mind goes blank, and I have no idea what to ask. "Umm . . . Is my name Hannah Marie Walsh?"

"Really? That's the best you've got?" Veronica asks, but I barely hear her. I'm too busy staring at the water before us as it spins a lazy clockwise circle inside the bowl. This is working. It's really working. We can do this.

"Can we ask about the Blood Witch now?" I prompt.

"One more question first." The water stills between us, and Veronica closes her eyes. The bowl warms beneath my hands as she silently asks her question. The water spins counterclockwise, indicating a no.

"What did you ask?"

Veronica glances up at me, looking smug. "I asked whether you're really over me. Looks like you aren't."

I yank my hands away from the bowl. "Liar."

"The water never lies."

"I wasn't talking about the water," I snap. "You must have spun it yourself." Heat creeps up my neck. I should have known better than to trust her. "I didn't ask you here to play games. I'm serious about this Blood Witch. How can we scry together if I can't tell when you're messing with me?"

Veronica pauses, considering me, her hands still on the bowl. "Fine, fine. I'll be good. Now come on. What are we asking exactly? Our thoughts must be in sync."

"I suppose we start with the most basic question: Is there a Blood Witch in Salem?" I step forward and slowly re-place my hands on the bowl. If Veronica messes this up . . .

"Right." Her voice is solemn now, no longer teasing, which is a good start. "Just like before. Hold that question in your mind and push it into the water." Veronica closes her eyes and exhales slowly.

I follow her example, breathing deep and slow as if I were meditating. *Is there a Blood Witch in Salem? Is there a Blood Witch in Salem? Is there—* My eyes fly open as the bowl burns hot between us. The paint inside swirls round and round. Clockwise.

Veronica's hands tremble and she pulls them away from the

bowl. She looks up at me, her eyes wide. "I can't believe it. You were right."

"Who is it?" I ask the water. "Who's the Blood Witch?" The swirling stops. The water falls still. But then nothing. I look to Veronica. "You have to help me."

"We have to tell Lady Ariana." She backs away from my desk. "I can't believe this. Everyone said we were safe. My parents—"

"Veronica, focus. We need more than a simple yes from a scrying bowl. We need real proof before we bring this to my grandmother. Without it, we risk getting in trouble for meddling. I don't want to wear a binding charm again. Do you?" When Veronica shakes her head, I reach for her hands and bring them back to the bowl. "Help me do this."

I expect Veronica to say no, to pull away from my touch, but she nods her head. This time, the water trembles and the paint shifts like moving clouds. A figure forms at the center, standing alone. I'm about to ask Veronica if she knows what that means when two more figures emerge, standing behind the first. The water shifts again and shows the Blood Witch standing among a crowd.

Veronica jerks away, knocking over the bowl. Water and paint spill onto my floor.

"Dammit, Veronica! That's going to stain." I grab hold of the water's energy, drawing the liquid out of the carpet and back into the bowl. Unfortunately, it leaves the paint behind. "What's wrong with you?"

"Did you see how many witches there were?" Veronica collapses onto my bed and pulls her knees up to her chest. "There were twenty. At least!"

I shake my head. "I don't think those were all Blood

Witches." Though I can't back up my claim, my gut tells me I'm right.

The series of figures runs through my head again. One. Three. Many. I grab my sketchbook and a bit of charcoal and re-create the details before I lose them. "I think the first image we saw *was* the Blood Witch we were looking for. The extra pair in the second image felt farther away." I sketch them in the background of the main figure, trying to re-create the same perspective of distance I saw in the bowl. "It's like they're not as involved. Maybe they were the witch's family? Or they're part of a small coven?"

Veronica shakes her head. "Blood Witches don't have covens, not the way we do."

I run my hands over my face. "Are you sure we didn't do something wrong with the scrying? Those figures could mean anything."

"Don't blame me. This was your idea."

"I'm not blaming you." I let out a breath to the count of ten to keep the irritation from rising. "Walk through this with me, please? We know there's at least one Blood Witch in Salem. That first image was so close." I glance at my sketch, running my fingers along the outline of a slender person.

"These other two are farther away," I say, pointing to the smaller figures I've sketched in the distance. "Maybe they're on their way to Salem? Or maybe they're related to the Blood Witch in some way? Parents or siblings or children or something? Who do we know that fits that description?"

I turn the page in my sketchbook and work on the final image, the one with the Blood Witch surrounded by a group. The memory is already hazy, but I capture the positioning of each person as best as I can.

Veronica slides her grimoire back in her bag. "I don't know, Hannah. That description could apply to almost anyone. Maybe someone new to the area?"

"Maybe," I muse, thinking of Cal. He's the only new person I know. But he's so genuine and nice. There's no way he's a Blood Witch. "I think we should include Evan, too. He was at both the sacrifice and the runes. I'm pretty sure he's an only child, and he works with crowds at the museum. That could fit for this last image."

My ex seems less convinced. "You think *Evan's* a witch? And how exactly are we supposed to prove that ridiculous theory?" She slips her purse over one shoulder. "We can't cut him and see if his skin magically heals. If he's a Reg, that's both super weird and possibly criminal."

"I don't know, Veronica. But we have to do *something*."

The room falls silent between us, broken only by the buzz of my phone.

GG: Hannah!!! The girls at dance are dragging me to a party tonight. Come keep me company. Please please please!

Gears loosen and turn in my head. We'll have to break just a few more rules, but if we can catch the Blood Witch, it'll be worth whatever punishment my grandmother has in store for us. Who knows, she might even be grateful enough to reverse the one she's already levied.

I turn to Veronica, the final pieces clicking into place. "I have a plan."

8

MUSIC SHAKES THE FLOOR of Nolan's front porch as Gemma and I step up to the house. Students spill into the yard, balancing cans of shitty beer with plates of salty snacks while clusters of recent grads tip back Solo cups inside the foyer. Gem and I break through the wall of sound and officially enter the party.

I adjust my shorts and brush imaginary lint from the too-tight tank top Gemma talked me into wearing. Her mom gave us a weird look when she walked past the open bedroom door and caught Gem giving me a once-over to approve the outfit. Gemma didn't notice—she never notices—but I'm going to have to avoid her parents for at least a week now.

A quick glance around the party helps me refocus, and I shake the memory of Mrs. Goodwin's discomfort away. I need to find Veronica and borrow her mom's crystals. Veronica will amplify the stones' vibrations, making it impossible for anyone we see to resist our questions. If there's a Blood Witch at this party, we'll find them.

Gemma loops her arm through mine and leads me into the packed living room. I scan the crowd but don't see Veronica anywhere. *She'd better show.*

"Asshat at three o'clock," Gemma yells over the music, and gestures with her head.

About time. I turn to look, but it's not Veronica. It's Nolan. He's standing in front of the fireplace with a can of PBR in one hand, holding court over the soccer team while keeping an eye on the rest of the guests.

"So, what's the plan?" Gemma asks as we make our way to the kitchen for drinks. "Dance until we can't see straight?"

"I never see *straight*," I say, and Gem rolls her eyes at my pun. I'm about to remind her that I don't dance when two girls half stumble, half glide in from the backyard, their arms around each other's shoulders as they approach the table.

"Gemma!" The shorter girl brightens when she sees Gem, and I realize where I've seen her before: the dance studio. She looks different without her hair pulled into a high bun. Younger. More carefree. I don't recognize her red-haired friend, but her perfect posture and the slight turnout to her steps shout *dancer*.

The redhead's pale face blushes a soft pink, accentuating the dusting of freckles across her nose and cheeks. "Hey, Gemma. Who's your friend?"

"This is Hannah. The super talented best friend I told you about." Gem raises her brows suggestively, and I'm afraid to know what she told this girl about me. "Hannah, this is Morgan Hughes. She just moved to Salem."

Morgan grins at me, her gaze sweeping across my tight shirt, down to the shorts that hang low on my hips, and then back up again. Gemma introduces the other dancer, but her name doesn't register in any meaningful way. I'm too distracted. Morgan steps forward, all grace, curves, and long lines.

She holds out her slender hand and waits for me to take it. I slip my hand in hers, and I'm certain my face is redder than her hair.

"Nice to meet you," she says as I hastily drop her hand.

"You too," I say, my skin tingling where it touched hers. "Will you be at Salem High in the fall?"

"Yeah." Morgan runs a finger along the rim of her empty cup. "Nice of my parents to move me in time for my senior year, huh?"

"Promotion at work?" I guess.

"Something like that." Morgan fusses with her hair; her crystal-blue eyes never leave my face. "At least I have dance this summer to meet people before school starts. My first day shouldn't be too terrible." She glances away, and the beginning of a smile pulls at her lips. "Especially if you're there."

I freeze. Is she . . . No, she can't be. Gemma would have told me if there was a queer girl in her dance class. But Morgan glances back at me, smiling. Is she actually . . .

Flirting.

With me?

Oh god. What do I *do*?

I shoot Gemma a panicked look.

Thankfully, she notices and gives me a quick nod. "Come on, girls. Let's dance." She drags Morgan and the shorter dancer toward the living room with her.

Morgan turns as they near the doorway, spinning with a ballerina's grace. "Hannah, want to come with?" Her voice is light and full of promise, her vowels slightly Midwestern. Something about it turns my insides to mush.

I shake my head, but I can't keep the smile off my face. "You three go ahead. I'll meet you in a bit." When they're gone, I press a cold water bottle to my face.

Someone slow claps behind me. "Well, that was embarrassing." I turn and find Veronica leaning against the back wall,
wearing a short dress with a plunging neckline and kitten heels.
"A stunning reminder of why you'll be single forever."

"Grow up." I cross the room to my ex, hoping my face isn't as
red as it feels. *How does she always manage to make me feel so underdressed?* "Do you have them?"

Veronica pushes off from the wall and balances a hand on her
hip. "Could you sound more like a junkie? I'm not your dealer."

"You know what I mean." I pull her toward the corner of
the room, out of the flow of people. With the heels, I have to tilt
my head up to meet her gaze. "Did you get the crystals from your
mom?"

Something flashes in Veronica's eyes. "Who was that?"

"Why? Jealous?"

"Of her? Please." Veronica examines her nails, freshly manicured after last weekend's incident in the woods. "I'm not jealous
of some skinny ginger."

She says *ginger* like it's a bad thing; I happen to have a special
place in my heart for redheads. But I don't tell Veronica that. I
still need her help. "Do you have the crystals or not?"

Veronica reaches into her small clutch and pulls out a silver
chain with two stones dangling from the end. "There's chrysocolla
for honest communication," she says as she undoes the clasp on
the necklace. "And rose quartz to make you irresistible." Veronica
reaches to put the necklace on for me, but I step back.

"I'm perfectly capable of doing it myself, thank you." I grab
the thin chain and clasp it around my neck. "And rose quartz
won't make me 'irresistible.' It'll just encourage people to open up

to me. Promote trust and empathy." I grip the stones; their power pulses slow and deep. "Did you already activate them?"

"Yeah. They're good to go." Veronica cracks open a beer and takes a long drink. "You're welcome, by the way."

"Thanks," I say, weighing the crystals against my palm. *I hope this works.*

"Whatever. I still think this is a terrible idea." She takes another sip of her beer. "I saw Evan out back by the fire pit. Go chase your Blood Witch. I'm going to find Savannah."

"Are you going to question her? Do you have enough crystals?"

Veronica glares at me. "Savannah is not a witch. And even if she were, I wouldn't need magical help to convince her to share her secrets. People actually like talking to me."

Her words sting, but she's swallowed up by the crowd before I can unstick the witty retort at the back of my throat. I choke it down and slip outside. As I near the small fire, everyone seems hyperaware of my presence. They greet me with wide smiles, stepping into my path to say hello. It slows me down, but at least I know the crystals are working.

I manage to extract myself from the growing crowd as Evan walks past. "Evan, wait!" I hurry after him, one hand gripping the crystals, willing their power to reach for his retreating form. "I need to talk to you."

Either the rose quartz is working or Evan isn't the angsty goth kid he wants everyone to think he is, because he stops. Turns. Gives me an exhausted look. "What do you want, Hannah?"

The crystals grow warm in my touch. People wave to me as they pass, which makes Evan jumpy. I'm on edge, too. It's possible Evan's a Blood Witch, and if he is, he could hurt me. Faster than

I could conjure a defense. But unless he calms down, this interrogation won't go anywhere. "Do you mind if we go someplace quieter?"

Evan looks suspicious, but he lets me lead him to the edge of Nolan's property. Here, at least, we shouldn't be interrupted.

"Well, what is it?" he asks when I don't speak right away. "Here to harass me about my purchases again?"

"I wasn't," I say, clutching at the stones around my neck, hoping the rose quartz will loosen his tongue. "But since you bring it up, let's talk curses. I know you're the one who killed that raccoon at the bonfire."

"I didn't—" he starts, but his words die in his throat as the chrysocolla burns hot in my hand, choking away the lie. He tries to deny it again, but the sounds stick in his throat. Finally, he gives in. "How did you know?"

"In truth, I didn't know. I had a solid hunch though," I say without thinking. *Oh no.* I drop the stones, horrified. They aren't supposed to pull out *my* truth. It isn't supposed to work this way. How did they—

Veronica. Of course. I bet she messed up the spell on purpose. For a brief, sickening moment, I wonder if she faked the scrying today, too, like she did with her question about my feelings. Was the whole thing an elaborate ruse to humiliate me?

But she seemed so scared when the water confirmed there's a Blood Witch in Salem . . .

"Why did you cast the curse? What were you trying to do?" I ask, steering the conversation back on track. Imperfections aside, the crystals are drawing out the truth, and that's something I could sorely use.

"I don't want to talk about it." Evan pushes past me, his

strength knocking me back a step. My mind races, searching for signs of his magic. Was that the strength of a Blood Witch? Or simply a guy with more height and weight than I have?

"You have to tell me." I reach for his wrist, holding him back. I focus all my attention on the warm thrum of the rose quartz in my other hand, willing him to trust me.

"Why?"

"Because I'm scared!" The words tumble out, and the truth of them rings in the air around us, puncturing whatever bravado kept Evan so tense. "I've been so scared since that night, and if I knew what happened, if I knew what your plan was, maybe I could sleep better at night."

"Hannah." Evan's voice dips low, and he runs a hand through his hair. "I never meant for anyone to see it. I wasn't trying to scare you. Or hurt Savannah."

"Then what were you doing?" I ask.

Evan glances over his shoulder, but between the music and the distance to the nearest partygoer, there's no danger of someone overhearing. "It's about my dad."

"Your dad?"

Evan blows out his breath in a big rush. "You have to understand, my dad is not a good person. He's cruel and controlling. I've spent half my life terrified of him. My mom has, too. He was never violent, not physically, but nothing we ever did was good enough for him."

"Shit, Evan. I'm sorry," I say, and though this isn't the time or the place, though it feels incredibly selfish, I'm suddenly extremely grateful for my dad. For his kindness and his unending support. "What were you trying to do? Get him to leave you alone?"

"He already left. Took off a few months ago with the office

manager from his law firm." Evan makes a disgusted sound. "She's barely older than I am. She has no idea what kind of monster my dad is. He took everything. All my parents' savings. My mom can't keep up with the payments on our house."

"I am so sorry." I apologize again, because I don't know what else to say. This isn't the kind of conversation I was expecting. "But then . . . What's with all the spells? Are you trying to curse your dad?"

Evan scowls, and his voice goes harsh. "I'm not asking for anything he doesn't already deserve."

The chrysocolla burns hot against my chest. He thinks he's telling the truth, but he's not. He's doing too much. "I'm sorry you're hurting, but the kind of magic you're using—"

"I know," he says, cutting me off. "I know it's dangerous. I know my mom would never approve, but he deserves it, Hannah. He really does." Evan's pain crashes into me, channeled through the crystals at my neck, and it's so heavy. Years of hurt all bubbling up to the surface.

"But what about the runes?" I ask. "What were you trying to do with those?"

"Runes?" His voice is pitched with confusion. "I've only done that one ritual in the woods." Evan runs a hand through his hair, his face crumpling. "I just want my family to be okay. I didn't know what else to do." His breath hitches in his throat.

Before I realize what I'm doing, I reach out. Evan steps forward and lets me wrap him in a hug. His arms come around my back, pulling me close. He shudders, and I realize he's crying. *How long has he been holding all this in?*

I'm not sure what else to say. Guilt gnaws on my ribs, twisting my insides. I shouldn't have forced Evan's truth to the surface with magic, but I don't know how to apologize without outing my Clan. I want to tell him everything will be okay, but the chrysocolla won't let the lie past my lips. I never should have asked Veronica for these crystals, even if it has answered one question.

Evan is *not* a Blood Witch.

-|-　※　-|-

After Evan's confession, I head back to the house feeling like a judgmental asshole. When Evan came to the shop before the bonfire, I should have guessed something big was going on. He was never one to rock the goth look in school. And people often turn to Wicca—or any religion for that matter—when the rest of their life is falling to shit.

I glance over my shoulder and find Evan leaning against the fence. A smile quirks up one side of his lips, and he raises his hand. I wave back, but even from here I can see the sadness that deepens the lines in his forehead, can see the way he's lost in thoughts he'd rather not have.

Guilt latches around my ribs and tugs, trying to yank me back to the fence. I can't believe I suspected Evan of being a Blood Witch. Can't believe I used magic against a Reg. Veronica was right. This whole thing was a bad idea.

"Oh, hey. It's Hannah, right?" Morgan greets me when I make it back into the kitchen. She grabs the last hard lemonade. "Want anything?"

I shake my head. "I'm driving tonight." I stay firmly on my side of the table and steal glances at the ballerina before me. She's about my height, maybe an inch taller. Her red hair cascades past her shoulders, glimmering in the bright kitchen lights. Though I know it's pointless, I look for clues—anything to help me determine whether she was flirting earlier or simply being nice.

Morgan opens the lemonade and tosses the cap in the overflowing metal bucket on the table. "I feel like I already know you. Gemma talks about you all the time."

"Yeah?" *Funny, she never mentioned you.*

"Sure. Gem thinks you're hilarious. She also said you make the most amazing desserts. I'd love to try them sometime." Morgan comes around to my side of the table. She rests a finger on my necklace; the stones pulse with heat as she nears, matching my quickening heartbeat. "This is beautiful."

Flirting, she is *definitely* flirting. Or maybe not. Shit. I don't know. *Be cool, Hannah, be cool.* "Thank you," I whisper, barely able to push the words past my lips.

Morgan steps closer, well within my personal bubble. The heat of her body so close to mine presses against my skin. "Are you dating anyone?"

I can't speak. Her fingers linger on my neck, her touch the only thing my mind seems to grasp. Finally, I shake my head. "No, but I—"

She doesn't wait for me to finish. Morgan leans forward and presses her lips to mine. Her hand cups my face, fingers weaving through my hair.

It takes me a second to realize what's happening, but when I do? My heart dances in my chest, and I return the kiss, sinking into her warmth.

The stones at my throat pulse with heat, thrum with the very *rightness* of this moment. Morgan's lips are soft against mine, her hands warm at the back of my neck. Everything about this kiss is tender and soft and full of promise. Morgan tastes sweet from the lemonade, and my heart pounds in time with the heavy bass pumping through the house.

"All right! Now it's a party!"

Morgan and I flinch apart. Nolan stands in the entryway, his phone aimed at us.

"Aww, come on. I only caught, like, two seconds." He stabs at his phone and the light turns off.

"You were recording us?" I see red, and I'm ready to throttle him. "Delete it."

Nolan ignores me and watches his phone. "Not likely. This shit is hot."

I could kill him. I could actually kill him, the fucking perv. "Delete the video, Nolan, or so help me—"

"Relax, Hannah. Geez." He glances to my right. "Who's your friend? I don't think we've met." He steps forward and offers his hand to Morgan. "I'm Nolan. Soccer captain. Class president. Single." He grins. "Welcome to my party."

Morgan ignores his outstretched hand and folds her arms across her chest.

"Anyway . . ." He lifts the phone again. The light flicks on as he starts recording. "Just pretend I'm not here."

I block the lens with my hand. "Get the hell away from us."

"Uh, last I checked, princess, this was my house." A pause. "Fine, I won't record it." Nolan lowers the phone and shoves it in his back pocket. "You ladies want to add some testosterone to this little party?"

"Fuck off, asshole."

Nolan glares at me, but before he can say anything else, someone steps between us. All I can see is his height and dark hair. "Back off, Abbott."

"It's not my fault they're so—" Something shatters in the other room, drawing Nolan's attention. He casts a final glare at the three of us before storming away. "You better not break anything!"

The guy turns to us. "You okay?"

I'm relieved to see a familiar face. "Yeah. Thanks, Benton." The heat in the crystals fades, and a sinking feeling pulls at my gut. *Oh no.* Panic bubbles up my chest. *Did the crystals make Morgan kiss me?* Shit, shit, shit.

Morgan fidgets beside me and won't meet my eye. "That guy, Nolan, he has this video on his phone . . ."

Benton scowls. "I'll take care of it." He offers a brief smile before hurrying after Nolan.

With the boys gone, Morgan and I find ourselves alone in the kitchen. The energy in the room has shifted, an uneasiness settling in the space between us, and I don't know how to bridge this gap. How do you ask someone about their hobbies after your magically induced make-out session is interrupted by a future frat bro?

Thankfully, Morgan's braver than I am. She breaks the almost unbearable silence. "Do you think your friend will be okay?"

"Benton?" I nod. "He'll be fine. He actually earned his black belt a few months ago. Nolan's the one who should worry."

"Good." Her tone is harsh, and her hands clench into fists. "I hope he kicks his ass."

"He probably won't have to," I say, watching the way her anger makes her arms shake, like she's ready to deck Nolan herself. "Though I do agree with you. He totally deserves it. He actually got punched in the face last weekend for being an ass."

"Really?" Morgan lights up at the idea, but then her brow furrows. "If he's such a jerk, why did so many people come to his party?" She nods toward the living room, where a horde of teens balance cups of beer while they dance.

I point to the hard lemonade in her hand. "The free booze?"

"Fair point." Morgan flushes, her cheeks turning an adorable shade of pink as she traces her finger along the lip of her bottle. "I'm sorry, by the way. I swear I'm not usually that forward." She shakes her head, like she's confused by her actions. "I've never kissed someone without asking first. I have no idea what came over me."

"It's okay." I try to smile, but her words are a reminder of my guilt. I never should have asked Veronica for the stones. They've done nothing but mess with innocent Regs. I don't know why I thought it was a good idea to try to find a Blood Witch on my own. Mom was right. I'm not ready.

Besides, there may not even *be* a Blood Witch in Salem. The scrying with Veronica seemed to prove there was, but I should have known better than to trust her. She probably faked the whole thing. Besides, Evan admitted to the animal sacrifice. That was a Reg ritual, just like my grandmother said.

But what about the runes?

"I mean, it's really not okay, but I'm glad you're not mad." Morgan's words pull me from my runaway thoughts. She fusses with the simple metal ring on her middle finger, twirling it round and round. "So . . . I realize that dipshit ruined whatever vibe we had going on, but I'd still love to get your number."

"My number?"

Morgan's cheeks flare red. "Yeah. I mean . . . Gemma said you dated girls. I thought maybe we could go out sometime." When I don't immediately answer, Morgan backpedals. "Or we could be friends. I'm new here and it'd be good to have friends before classes. And I—"

"Morgan?" I say, interrupting her.

"Yeah?"

I can't keep the smile off my face when she looks up from spinning her ring. She's flustered and rambling and it's adorable. I just hope whatever's happening between us is still there when these damn crystals are gone. "I'd love to go out sometime."

Morgan hands me her phone, and I add my name and number. I want to say something witty, but my brain won't cooperate. Instead, it plays back an endless reminder of how much I fucked up today.

"So," Morgan cuts in, fighting through the awkward silence a second time. "Should we go find Gemma? Or maybe someplace quiet to talk?"

My heart sings at the possibility of spending more time with her, but I need to get rid of these crystals first. Before I can respond, power shimmers across my skin. Bright and angry.

Morgan turns back toward the living room. "Do you smell smoke?"

The energy in the air brightens at her suggestion. Fear rips through me, puncturing a hole in my chest.

"We have to get out of here."

9

SMOKE FILLS THE HOUSE. I can't see the flames, but the fire's gleeful hunger ripples across my skin. It's somewhere above us, spreading fast along the second floor.

"This way." I reach for Morgan to lead her into the backyard, but she darts forward into the living room.

"Gemma! Kate!" Morgan's voice is full of fear as she slips around the corner and disappears into the smoke.

I chase after Morgan, searching through the haze for her red hair and Gemma's blonde curls. Everyone is crammed together, pushing to get out the front door. They shove each other, bodies packed tight, but the narrow door slows them down. I don't see Gemma anywhere. *Please be outside already.*

The smoke thickens, and I cough. Without thinking, my magic flares to life, reaching for the closest element. A pocket of clean air swirls up from around my feet, making it easier to breathe. Though all magic is technically forbidden around Regs, this type of reflexive magic is rarely punished.

Above me, the fire's energy dips low, mostly extinguished, then flares bright again, growing faster than before. I turn, confused by the drastic shift in the fire's strength, and catch Veronica and Savannah rushing down the stairs. Fear climbs up my spine like ivy. Veronica's gaze meets mine, only for a second, and I know what she's done. Did Savannah see Veronica calm the flames enough for them to escape? Has Veronica exposed us to a Reg?

Glass shatters, and the fire roars upstairs, emboldened by the magic Veronica must have used to restart the flames and cover her tracks. I search for Morgan, desperate to get out of here, and am finally rewarded with a flash of red hair.

"Morgan! Over here!" I shout over the crowd's panic and the growing roar of the fire. "This way." I lead her back to the kitchen.

Drunk partygoers rush into the backyard, but Morgan pulls me to a stop just before the door. "What about Gemma and Kate? We can't leave them in here."

"I won't, I promise. But we have to go." I reach for Morgan's hand. "Do you trust me?"

Morgan pauses, but after a beat, she nods and lets me lead her into the backyard. She coughs as the fresh air hits her lungs.

"Come on." I race around to the front of the house, Morgan at my heels. Fire in the windows casts an eerie red-orange glow on the windshields of cars parked along the street and Nolan's silver SUV sitting in the driveway. I search the growing crowd for Gemma's face, and thanks to her height, I spot her near the back. "Gemma!"

Somehow, she hears my voice over the noise and turns. Gem shoves her way through classmates to get to me, the shorter dancer from before—the one I assume is Kate—following behind her. "Thank god, Hannah! I thought you might still be in there."

Gem crushes me in a hug, and then we watch as flames spread through the top floor of Nolan's house.

"Do you see that?" Morgan points toward the far right window on the second floor. "It looks like someone's still in there."

Gemma grabs her phone. "I'm calling the fire department."

While Gem dials, I follow Morgan's gaze up to the window. The curtains flutter, but that doesn't mean someone's inside. "I don't see anything."

The second the words leave my lips, a shadow appears before the window. The figure pushes back the curtains and throws open the window.

Morgan gasps. "Someone's trapped!"

Those closest to us shout and watch as one of our classmates leans out the window like he's judging the distance to the ground.

"Someone call nine-one-one!"

"Don't jump, dude!"

"He'll never make it!"

Morgan's grip tightens on my arm, hard enough that I flinch. "Isn't that the guy who helped us?"

Before I can look, someone behind me cries, "It's Benton!"

Benton glances directly at the crowd, and even from here I can see the panic. The fear. The soot and sweat covering his face. He's running out of time. I pull from Morgan's grip and step away from the crowd. *Mom is so going to kill me.* And I don't even want to *consider* what Lady Ariana will do.

"I'm going in."

"You're what?!"

"I can't leave Benton trapped in there." The fire's energy spikes, driving my pulse up with it. I need to hurry or this blaze will be beyond my power to control. "Stay here."

"You're going to get yourself killed!" Gemma says, ignoring the phone pressed to her ear. "Hannah, wait—"

But I don't. There isn't time. I call upon my magic, nurture the thrum in my chest, and race around the side of the house, heading for the kitchen door. I gather as much clean air as I can, hold it tight around my face, and dive back inside the burning house.

The smoke is near black now. Thick and roiling. The smell acrid and choking despite my makeshift mask. I get as low as I can and hurry through the house. The fire hasn't made it downstairs yet, but I still have to move fast. I have to get to Benton before the flames do.

The fire's power, infused with Veronica's magic, is so bright that it numbs my senses.

I pick my way through the halls and around disarrayed furniture, trying to follow the same path back to the living room where the stairs lead to the second level. The smoke makes it hard to see, and I stumble into an overturned chair and nearly fall on my face. It would be so easy to command the air, to clear the smoke out of my way, but with dozens and dozens of Regs on the front lawn watching eagerly through the windows, I can't risk it.

Finally, I reach the stairs and drop to my knees, keeping low to the steps as I follow the smoke upward. The fire's will sings against my skin. *Come. Play with me.* Fear prickles at the base of my spine.

"Benton! Where are you?"

Above me, Benton coughs. "Is someone there?" He sounds weak. Nearly breathless.

Power surges through my veins as I reach for the heart of the fire's power. *Calm now. You've done enough.* I try to soothe the flames climbing up the walls beside me, eating away at the striped wallpaper, but they resist my magic.

You've done enough. It's time to rest.

In the distance, barely audible above the roar of the fire, sirens wail.

They're bringing water, I tell the fire, pushing my will against its hunger. *Will you let them tame you?*

The fire recoils from my words. Then it pushes back and burns hotter. Its defiance growing stronger, more terrifying.

Above me, Benton coughs again. Wheezes in a staggered breath. He feels farther away now, like he's backed into a shrinking corner of fireless space.

"Benton! Can you make it to the stairs?" I shake off the panic seizing my chest and hope he can hear me. "Come on! We have to get out of here."

After a moment of silence, his voice breaks through. Hoarse and weak. "I can't. There's too much fire."

Shit. We're running out of time.

I inhale most of what remains of my oxygen and let power coil in my veins. I reach for the center of the fire's power, squashing it, dampening it, but it holds strong and pushes back against extinction. Flames bite at my legs, and though my skin will never burn, the hem of my shorts starts to smoke.

The sirens are louder now, but not close enough. They won't get here in time to drown the flames, not before my air is gone and I pass out. Not before Benton meets the same fate or worse, trapped in a room on the far side of the floor. I tug at the air again, searching for signs of Benton's wheezing breath. But it's gone.

He's not breathing.

I panic and make one last attempt to grab hold of the fire's energy, to bend it to my will, but when it resists, I let go.

And steal all the oxygen from the room—from the whole damn house—instead.

My lungs fill and my head clears as the fire suffocates and

dies away, leaving ash and charred wood, crumbled carpet and dripping wallpaper, in its wake. As soon as the fire dies, I exhale, returning the air to its proper place. Power hums in my veins. I feel like I could do anything. *Be* anything.

Sirens outside interrupt the thought. A higher, less primal fear pulses through me. I need to get out of here before someone finds me and realizes what I've done.

"Benton?" I rush up the stairs and search the rooms, finding him in the last one on the right, slumped in the corner with sweat coating his face. He's still not breathing. "Benton, come on." I shake him, but that does little good.

I glance behind me, making sure we're truly alone. When I'm positive no one can see, I hover a hand over Benton's nose and mouth, pushing magicked air into his lungs.

Benton gasps. His eyes shoot open, and I drop my hand. "You okay?"

He looks at me, eyes wide, and nods his head.

"We have to go. Come on." I help Benton to his feet and guide him down the stairs. Something crashes up ahead, and I freeze. *Is it the Blood Witch?* I shove the thought away. No self-respecting Blood Witch would attack an Elemental with fire. But that knowledge doesn't soothe my fears.

Whoever is in here must have seen the fire disappear.

Which means I am beyond screwed.

Before Benton can object, I set him on the bottom step and race down the wrecked hall. Movement flashes out of the corner of my eye. A shadow slips into the kitchen. A door slams. I have to know who it was, how much they saw. I pump my legs faster, flying around the corner into the kitchen.

It's empty.

A string of curses spills from my lips. If they make it to the crowd of students out front, I may never figure out who they are.

As I grab the door, a shadow falls over me. Huge and looming. I reach for my magic, ready to attack, but it's like stretching a pulled muscle. I hiss in a pained breath and tense as the shadow grabs me by the upper arm and drags me out of the house.

"Is anyone else in there?"

I look up and find a fireman attached to my arm, and I let out a relieved sigh. "Benton. He's still inside. On the bottom step." I force out the words, but the rest of my brain curses myself again. I shouldn't have put out the flames completely. How will the fire department explain that?

The man beside me repeats Benton's location into his radio and shoves me toward the front of the house. He deposits me in the back of an ambulance. "Stay here."

I'm fine. But I can't very well tell him that. The paramedics shove an oxygen mask on my face and shine a light in my eyes. They take my blood pressure and search my exposed limbs for burns. When they're convinced I'm okay, they wrap a blanket around my shoulders and take the mask away.

"Miss Walsh," a deep voice says. "Why am I not surprised?"

I look up. A man in a smart gray suit steps into view. "Detective Archer? What are you doing here?"

He ignores me and turns to the EMTs instead. "Is she all right?"

The paramedics nod. "Seems fine, sir," the taller one says.

"Good." Something flashes in the light of the ambulance. Cold metal encases my wrist. Clicks tight. "If you don't mind, Miss Walsh, I need you to step out of the truck." He helps me out of the ambulance and tugs my arms behind my back. The coldness encircles my other wrist.

And then my brain registers what's happening.

Those are handcuffs.

Detective Archer puts a hand on my shoulder and leads me away from the ambulance. "Miss Walsh, you're coming with me."

"What?" I ask, heart hammering, mind racing. "Why?"

Detective Archer guides me forward. "Arson."

The crowd stares in silent judgment as Detective Archer leads me to his car in handcuffs. Flashing lights illuminate classmates whose expressions range from shocked disbelief to devastated rage. Nolan stands with his friends, leaning against his SUV. A murderous look shadows his face when he notices my arms cuffed behind my back.

I search the crowd for Gemma. For Morgan or even Evan. Anyone who will see me and know this fire was not my doing. Instead, I only find Veronica at the front of the crowd, standing beside Savannah and a few of their friends from cheerleading. Veronica's eyes are wide, and her lips shape into an apology, but she doesn't try to help.

If she had checked to make sure there weren't any Regs upstairs before she used her magic to calm the flames, if she hadn't tried to cover her tracks by restarting the fire, none of this would have happened. Benton's lungs wouldn't be filled with smoke. I wouldn't be in handcuffs. She had better hope Savannah didn't notice anything strange.

Like an entire house fire going out in a matter of seconds . . .

Shame and worry and not a small amount of panic fight for dominance in my head. How am I going to explain how the fire died? My grandmother will murder me if she finds out—she reminded me just last week not to interfere with Regs. While I can't agree that I should have let Benton die in there, I understand more than ever why that's always been her rule.

I should have done something with *water*. Given the choice between literal magic and an unlikely but non-witchy explanation, Regs never jump to the mystical, not in any serious way. But I didn't leave the firefighters any clues for a reasonable explanation.

My inner monologue continues in a stream of self-loathing curses as Detective Archer leads me to a dark sedan and helps me into the backseat. My arms protest, my shoulders straining from the awkward angle the cuffs have forced them into. There's no way I'll be able to put on my seat belt like this.

As if that matters right now. At all.

The detective closes my door and heads for the driver's side. He's so tall he practically has to fold himself in half to fit into the front seat. He watches me a moment in the rearview mirror before pulling out of the Abbotts' driveway.

"Miss Walsh," he says as houses zoom past the windows, "care to explain why you tried to burn down that house?"

"I didn't." The urge to elaborate, to share more of the truth, is gone. Veronica's lingering magic in the crystals must be fading. I shift in the backseat, but it does nothing to alleviate the strain in my shoulders. At least he's asking about how the fire *started* rather than how it went out.

Detective Archer watches me in the mirror, so focused he nearly misses his turn. At the last second, his GPS reminds him to take the next left, and he jerks the steering wheel, slamming me into the door.

"Watch it," I snap.

The detective has the audacity to look apologetic. "Sorry. I don't know the town all that well yet."

"Don't you have to call my parents before you talk to me? I'm a minor."

"Sixteen?" he asks.

"Seventeen."

In the front seat, Detective Archer taps the steering wheel but doesn't say anything.

"Don't you have to read my Miranda Rights before you actually charge me with anything?" I might not be an expert in police procedure and legal protections, but my dad *is* the ADA. Miranda Rights are kind of a big deal.

In response, the detective glares at me and flips on the radio, drowning out my thoughts with classic rock. But despite the noise, the shadowy figure consumes my mind.

The fire could have been an accident, someone dropping a cigarette on the floor or spilling their beer on an active outlet. In which case, the person I saw running away was probably lost inside, unable to find a way out because of the smoke. But what if it was intentional? Who was the target? Every teen in Salem was there, more or less. Maybe someone trapped Benton upstairs intentionally. Or maybe someone was pissed at Nolan and wanted revenge.

By the time Detective Archer swings his cruiser into a parking spot in front of the police station, I still haven't come up with any answers. He helps me from the car, and fresh air assaults my nose. I cringe; my clothes reek of smoke. In the station, officers swivel to look at me as the detective leads me past. Their noses crinkle at the smell. Some narrow their eyes, a silent judgment for what they think I've done. But the ones who recognize me because of my dad? Their eyes go wide with shock.

Detective Archer deposits me in a small room. Stains cover the once-white walls, scuff marks and dark splotches that remind me of blood.

The thick metal table in front of me boasts dents and scratches from violent arrestees. My chair wobbles on uneven legs, and the light above sways as the bulb flickers and buzzes, struggling through the last days of its life. Panic curls in my gut like a sleeping lion trying to ignore the pesky fly that is my *stay calm* mantra.

As if this space didn't scream *Interrogation Room* enough, a dull mirror covers the upper half of the wall across from me. I wonder how many people stand on the other side, watching me, observing me, deciding my fate long before I have a chance to defend myself.

Who knows what kind of bullshit motives they're concocting to explain why I torched a classmate's house. They'll probably cast me as some jealous wannabe lover. I smirk at the absurdity of the thought. Me and Nolan? Excuse me while I vomit. I glance at my reflection, and even I have to admit I look a little guilty with my hair a mess, skin covered in soot, and a self-satisfied smile plastered on my face.

The clock behind me ticks on and on. Minutes stretch into hours. I shift in the chair, my shoulders aching from the way my wrists are still pinned behind my back. I glare at the mirror where I imagine Detective Archer would stand, just to his right of center.

"Did you want to chat at some point today? I do have a curfew to keep," I say, calling back to my excuse last week after the bonfire.

Silence is my only answer.

Okay then . . . "Has anyone called my parents? Or a lawyer? Pretty sure you're supposed to do that."

The door swings open, and Detective Archer finally walks in. He sets a folder on the table in front of him. "Why? Do you need a lawyer?"

I scowl. "I don't know. Are you charging me with anything?" I try to lean back, but it hurts my arms too much. "Can we not with the cuffs? My shoulders are killing me."

The detective sighs, like he's already exhausted by me. As if I'm the one who wants to be here so late. He stands and unlocks the cuffs, but he relocks them in front of me.

"Really?" I wince as my muscles adjust to the new position. Every inch of me is sore from putting out the fire. "It's not like I pose a physical threat."

"Let's talk about the fires," Detective Archer says, ignoring me. He flips open his folder and spreads write-ups and pictures in front of him.

"Fires? Plural?" I glance at the upside-down pictures before me, and it's almost like the detective is reading my tarot cards. Except instead of images like the Tower or the Fool, he's reading my fate in the mangled remains of a raccoon.

The detective nods, his eyes never leaving my face. "Two fires so far. We found you tampering with evidence at the bonfire last week. Tonight, a fireman found you inside a previously burning building, completely unharmed." He leans forward, eyes narrow. "Care to explain yourself?"

I search for a plausible lie, but putting out the fire has left my body exhausted and my brain foggy. "Explain what?" I ask, reaching for a suitable truth instead. "I wasn't the only one at both parties." *Besides, Evan's the one who killed that raccoon.* But I don't say anything. Evan has enough problems without the police showing up at his house.

Detective Archer slides four photos so they're faceup in front of me. He taps one on the left. "Look at the damage your little prank has done to this family."

Even though I didn't start the fire, I can't help but examine the image. It looks like it might be Nolan's parents' room. They've hung picture frames along the walls, all of which are broken and charred. Their bedframe has cracked in half, and the mattress and comforter are mostly ash. I swallow down the lump in my throat, waiting for the detective to ask a question I can't answer, to ask how the fire went *out* instead of how it started. "I feel bad for Nolan's family, but I don't get why you think I did this. I have an alibi."

"An alibi. From another teen who was drinking underage?" The detective raises a brow. "I'm sure you can understand my skepticism about the reliability of your friends." He sighs and picks up a pen, holding it over a yellow legal pad. "Whenever you're ready, Miss Walsh."

"First of all, I haven't been drinking. You can test that however you want." I shouldn't snap at him, but his dismissive attitude is getting on my nerves. "I was in the kitchen when the fire started, talking with Morgan." I try to remember her last name. Haggerty? Huewe? "Hughes. Morgan Hughes."

Detective Archer's eyes go wide. After a pause, he jots down her name and writes *possible alibi* next to it, as if he's not convinced my story is true. "If you were in the kitchen with Miss Hughes when the fire started," he says, his voice catching on her name, "then why did a firefighter find you inside the house? There's an exit through the kitchen." He pulls out another photo, this one of said kitchen layout, and sets it next to the rest.

Before I can respond, there's a knock on the door.

"What is it?"

A young officer cracks open the door and sticks his head through. He glances at me before settling his attention on the detective. "We have a Mr. and Mrs. Walsh here to collect their daughter."

Mom . . . Dad . . .

"We'll be done in a moment," Detective Archer says in a tone clearly meant to dismiss the officer.

But the young man doesn't budge. "Mr. Walsh . . . He's . . . uh . . . He's the assistant district attorney. He's really insistent, sir. And since you haven't entered any charges . . ."

What? I stand and lean my bound hands against the cold metal table. "I'm not under arrest?"

Detective Archer glares at the officer, but the way his face pales makes me think having an ADA for a father is handier than I knew. "Not yet, no. I just need you to answer a few more questions."

"Why? So you can trick me into admitting to something I didn't do? Don't think so." I thrust my hands toward the detective. "Take these off. Now."

We stand there, locked in a stalemate. The only sound is the buzzing of the swinging light above us.

The young officer fidgets by the door. "Detective?"

And with that, the spell is broken. Detective Archer reaches for his key and shoves it in the lock of the handcuffs. When they click free, the skin is red and painful underneath. "Don't leave town, Miss Walsh. And stay out of trouble." He turns to the officer in the doorway. "Take her to her parents."

"This way, Miss Walsh," the young officer says, opening the door wide and gesturing down the hall.

I spare one final look at the detective, take a deep breath, and head toward my executioners.

10

THE RIDE HOME IS SILENT.

Dad drives, gripping the steering wheel until his knuckles turn white. He's still dressed for work—an office day if his brightly patterned tie is any indication. Mom stares straight ahead into the dark night; she clutches her purse so tight I worry she might fuse it to her hands.

In their silence, toxic worries slither back into my chest. I was in a police station, being interrogated by a full-fledged detective. Never in my wildest nightmares did I think that was a possibility. Let alone the horror of my parents finding out about it.

I let out a shaky breath and wonder if Benton's okay. If his parents know what happened to him. Part of me wants to text him and make sure he's all right, make sure he doesn't realize *how* I saved him, but I can't risk Mom seeing the light of my phone and deciding to confiscate it.

The turnoff for Nolan's house is a block ahead, but Dad shows no signs of slowing. We pass the turn, and I twist in my seat to watch the road shrink in the distance. "What about my car?"

The air cools until I can see my breath, a sure sign Mom is pissed. But at least now I know my parents can even hear me. That I'm not a ghost haunting their car. They haven't acknowledged my presence, or spoken, since the passive-aggressive *thank you* Mom hurled at the young officer back at the police station. Their quiet is more unnerving than if they were yelling. I expected lectures and raised voices. Not this weird you're-dead-to-us silence.

Dad pulls into the driveway and cuts the engine. I'm prepared for fireworks, but I get nothing. We sit as still as statues, each second dragging longer than the last, until Mom cracks the plaster. She unbuckles her seat belt and leaves.

The car light dims, then goes dark. "Dad . . ."

"Talk to your mother." He sighs and hurries after said maternal figure.

I groan and lean my head against the back of the seat. The storm is coming. I have no doubt about that. Historically, it's been better to hit Hurricane Mom head-on, so I undo my seat belt and follow my parents into the house. The trail of lights leads me to the kitchen, where Mom is filling an exceptionally large glass with wine.

"Will somebody *please* say something?" I lean against the doorway that separates the kitchen from the dining room. "I am sorry . . ."

Mom chugs her wine and wipes her lips on the back of her hand. Finally, she turns and settles her attention on me. Fury lines her face, deep grooves that map my every disappointment. "Sorry for *what* exactly? For starting the fire? For wandering around inside a burning house, no doubt using magic so you didn't pass out from smoke inhalation? For agreeing to *talk to a detective* without bothering to call your parents?" She takes another huge gulp of wine. "What the hell were you thinking?"

"To be fair, I have witnesses that can prove I did not start that fire. And I'm fairly certain I told the detective we should wait for you."

Dad crosses his arms, scowling. "That is not the point."

"The point," Mom cuts in, "is that we explicitly told you to stay out of trouble. Lady Ariana warned you not to use your powers in public, but given the 'unusual' way the fire burned itself out before the fire trucks arrived, you clearly did not listen."

"What was I supposed to do? Let the house burn to the ground?"

"Yes," Mom says at the same time Dad says, "No," which earns him one of Mom's signature glares.

He deflates and leans against the counter. "We know you're not a bad kid. So level with us, Hannah. What happened tonight?"

"I don't even know where to start." I glance at Mom, but she just tips back her glass and reaches for the bottle. "Gem invited me to the party, and I thought it'd be a good distraction. So I went." *To investigate Evan.* Thankfully, I keep that truth locked inside. "I was talking to this new girl when the fire started. I got her out, then went back in."

Mom pinches the bridge of her nose. "Why would you possibly do that?"

"Benton was trapped inside on the second floor. I couldn't leave him there."

"Hannah." Dad sounds exhausted. But what is he going to do? Yell at me for not letting someone burn to death? "You don't have to be a superhero."

"I wasn't trying to! I just didn't want him to *die*."

Mom scrutinizes me, her eyes narrowing as her gaze sweeps across my throat. Her lips press into a thin line. "What is that?"

"What's what?" But my traitorous hands reach for the stones hanging around my neck.

"Hannah Marie Walsh, if those are spelled stones, so help

me . . ." Mom steps forward and holds out her hand, snatching the stones away the second I place them in her palm. She winds the metal chain around her hand, and the stones begin to glow. "Let's try this again, shall we? Why did you go to the party tonight?"

Heat pours into my chest, stronger and more demanding than the secondhand effects I felt at the party, and I'm delighted to answer. "To question Evan." The serene feeling evaporates the second the words leave my lips. Cold sweat prickles across my skin.

What did I do?

If Veronica's magic was even a fraction as strong as Mom's, Evan must have felt so violated. And Morgan . . . God, I'm a bigger creep than Nolan, messing with her emotions like that. She probably has no real interest in me at all. Even if she had a tiny crush when we first met, the stones probably forced it into something more.

I feel sick.

Mom squeezes the stones in her hand. "And why, exactly, did you use *magic* to question a Reg?"

Some small part of my brain protests, but the urge to tell my mom everything is too strong to ignore. I tell her all about Evan visiting the shop, both before the bonfire and the day I found the bloody runes. I tell her about scrying for a Blood Witch with Veronica. About how we thought it might be Evan.

Then the rambling really begins. I tell my parents about Veronica spelling the stones for me, about Evan's family troubles, and even the kiss with Morgan. I'm completely mortified as I listen to myself worry about how the stones violated Morgan's trust and how can I possibly hope to date her without apologizing but how can I apologize when she doesn't know magic is real.

And then I finally get to the smoke and the rushing, the moment I realized the fire couldn't be the work of a Blood Witch. My justification for diving back into the house to save my friend.

"I swear I don't have a hero complex, but I couldn't let Benton get hurt."

There's silence in our kitchen after that. Mom's second glass of wine stands forgotten on the counter.

Dad reaches for Mom's hand, takes the stones away, and sets them beside the bottle of wine. "Do we have to be worried about the detective? Does he know anything that puts the coven in danger?"

I shake my head. "I don't think so. He acted like he thought I did it, but he never filed charges." A humorless laugh escapes my lips. "He doesn't have any idea what's really going on."

Dad is less amused. "What did he ask about specifically?"

"He thought I was responsible for the animal sacrifice last week." I close my eyes and try to remember if there's anything else, anything that would give our coven away. "He was more concerned with who set the fire, not how it went out so quickly. I think we're safe."

My parents share a look, but it's guarded enough that I can't read its meaning.

"Are you going to tell Lady Ariana?" She's the *real* executioner, after all. If she deemed it necessary, she could petition the Council to strip me of my powers, and with them, everything that makes me an Elemental. Everything that makes me who I am.

Mom shakes her head. "We haven't decided yet. We're going to call Veronica's parents in the morning and make sure they're aware of her part in this." Mom nods to the crystals on our counter. "But I don't think involving your grandmother will be necessary. We're perfectly capable of dealing with your transgressions ourselves."

"But what about the scrying? Veronica and I—"

"You and Veronica are *children* messing with magic you don't fully understand." Mom reaches for her wine again and drains half the glass. "Scrying is more complicated than it seems. You saw what you wanted to."

"But—"

"Enough." Dad glances at the clock and sighs. "It's late, Han. You should get to bed."

"That's it? Just 'go to bed'?" Wasn't there supposed to be more yelling? More lecturing?

"Well, you're grounded until you're thirty, and your mother and I are going to discuss whether you'll be required to wear a binding charm, but that's enough for tonight." Dad points to the stairs, dismissing me.

I leave the kitchen, my palms sweaty with the thought of wearing a binding charm after four years without it, but Mom's voice calls after me. "And if you pull this crap again, you're quitting your job, selling your car, and living *here* until you're thirty."

-|-　　*　　-|-

There are a million texts waiting for me when I make it to my room. I ignore all of them except two. First, I text Benton to ask if he's okay. His answer is swift, assuring me he's alive and well, with promises to talk soon. Then I toss Gemma a quick *I'm alive, grounded but alive* text before I head for the shower. It's the longest yet least effective shower of my life.

My hair still smells like smoke the next morning, which is perhaps fitting given the way my phone is blowing up. Texts from Veronica I ignore. Notifications from trolls shouting about my new life of crime. Death threats from faceless users—probably Nolan and his friends—which is all sorts of fun. A few assholes even post blurry photos of Detective Archer shoving me into his sedan.

I remove the tags, but there's nothing I can do to take the pictures down. I hate that this crap will be archived somewhere when I'm trying to get into colleges this winter. I'm honestly relieved when my parents remember to take my internet access away.

Unfortunately, that sense of relief is short-lived. It dies when my parents hand me the binding ring I wore before my initiation at thirteen, with an added anti-tampering spell that'll make removal painful and impossible to hide. My magic protests, pressing against my skin so hard my hands shake as I slip the ring over my index finger. And then there's nothing. Just this hollow feeling in my chest where the constant thrum of magic used to be.

The only thing that manages to distract from the effects of the binding charm is the series of missed messages from Morgan.

I know they're from her for two reasons. One, the area code of the unsaved number is not from Massachusetts. And two, the messages are full of worry. *Please hurry. The roof looks ready to collapse.* Then all-caps panic asking if I'm okay and promising to send in help.

After that, nothing. Crickets. I assume she saw Detective Archer drag me to his car in handcuffs. My face burns at the thought. I'm sure that killed whatever interest she might have had in me.

If that interest was even real.

I wish I hadn't been wearing the rose quartz when Morgan kissed me. That makes everything so damn confusing. As if kissing a near-stranger wasn't already unusual for me.

By Sunday night I can't take it anymore. I have to know whether I've ruined my chance to get to know her. I swallow down my nerves and text her back.

HW: Hey, sorry. I'm alive and well. It's been a hectic weekend.

Every second after I hit send feels like an eternity. It shouldn't matter if she responds. I only met her once. She doesn't owe me anything, especially given how everything went down.

Yet I can't deny the way my heart dances when the three bouncing dots finally appear.

MH: Hey! Happy to hear the cops didn't lock you up for good. How's freedom taste? 😊

And just like that, the game of strategically timed texts and carefully placed emojis begins. We carefully avoid discussing our exes, but besides Veronica and my secret life as an Elemental Witch, I tell Morgan everything there is to know about me.

She teases me about my love of musicals—born out of Gemma's devotion to them and her dreams of dancing on Broadway—and I jokingly threaten to shun Morgan because of her soft spot for country music. We discover we're both too chicken to watch horror movies, and I convince Morgan—after much prodding and flattery—to send me a link to her dance videos. The way she moves is mesmerizing, and though I'll never tell my best friend this, I think she might even be better than Gemma.

Between texting Morgan and the discomfort of the binding ring, I end up falling asleep way too late. When my alarm rings in the morning, I almost wish my parents had made me quit my job. It takes every ounce of my resolve to roll into work on time.

I'm settled into my usual restocking rhythm—place and straighten, place and straighten—when the bell jingles above the door. Lauren is in the private reading room with a tarot client and Cal has class today at the university, so I abandon my shelves to greet our new customer.

"Welcome to the Cauldron, how can I— Evan? What are you doing here?" His face crumples when he sees me. "Is everything okay?"

Evan shakes his head. He looks like shit. His messy hair falls into his bloodshot eyes, and he hides shaking hands by crossing them against his chest. "Can I talk to you?"

"Of course." My mind races with possibilities as I lead Evan to a secluded corner of the shop. Was the fire at Nolan's another ritual to hurt his dad? I shake the thought away. Evan was outside when the fire started. He couldn't have done it. "What's wrong?"

Evan tips his head back against the wall. His chest heaves, and he looks ready to collapse. "It worked," he says, his haunted gaze turning on me. "The spells, they worked."

"The ones against your dad?"

"Yeah." His voice shakes, and he slides to the floor, wrapping his arms around his knees. "But I didn't mean for it to happen like this. I never wanted him to . . ." He trails off, unable to finish his thought.

I glance around the store to make sure Lauren is still in the back with her tarot client. When I'm sure we're alone, I sit beside him. "What happened?"

He's quiet for a long time, tears pooling in his eyes. I rest a hand on his knee, and he wraps his fingers around my palm. "He's in the hospital."

My body goes cold. I want to pull my hand away, but I force myself to hold it still. Inside, my magic battles against the binding charm on my forefinger, desperate to protect me from my own panic.

Finally, I force my lips to move, even though I'm afraid of the answers. "What happened? Is he going to be okay?"

"The doctors say he'll make it, but he was in a really bad car crash. Someone ran a red light and slammed right into him." Evan releases me and presses the heels of his hands against his eyes. "This is all my fault."

"You don't know that. Accidents happen all the time." But even as I say the words, they feel false, and I don't need a magically enhanced stone to confirm my fears.

"But it is. I wanted to hurt him. I'd meant his career and reputation, maybe have his new girlfriend dump his ass. He's a bastard, but I didn't want him in the hospital." Evan takes a shuddering breath and scrubs the tears from his cheeks. "Even the money part of the spell worked. I didn't know, but I guess my mom's been trying to sell our house. We got an offer within minutes of the crash. We'll have enough to pay off the mortgage and buy something Mom can actually afford."

"That still doesn't mean your spells caused this." I'm trying to be supportive, but even I have to admit that's quite the coincidence otherwise. "I'm sorry about your dad though."

"What am I going to do? You warned me. You said I had to watch out for the Law of Return. What's three times worse than getting hurt in a car crash?"

"I don't think magic is quite that literal." The bell jingles above the door, and Lauren's tarot client walks past the window. I stand and help Evan to his feet. "Come with me." I drag him toward the counter, where Lauren is adding cash to the register. "Lauren, do you have time for a new client?"

My boss looks between me and Evan and settles on a smile. "Of course. What's your friend in for? Tarot? A palm reading?"

Evan shoves his hands in his pockets and shoots me a panicked look before finding something immensely interesting to stare at on the floor.

"Evan needs some guidance. He's made some missteps, magically speaking, and doesn't know how to move forward." I don't get into the specifics. Those are for Evan to disclose.

Lauren turns her attention to Evan, and she's every inch the wise high priestess I expect from Lady Ariana. Lauren's only thirty, but I can see now why she's already a Third-Degree. She radiates wisdom and Wiccan power.

"Evan, is it?" she asks, and Evan nods. "Why don't you join me in my reading room? We can chat in private." Lauren heads toward her tarot room without waiting for an answer.

After a moment's hesitation, Evan follows.

I settle behind the counter to watch the store, but my thoughts get tangled like weeds on driftwood. Poor Evan. I hope his dad is okay, even if he is a total shithead like Evan says.

The bells jingle to announce our newest customer. I turn to greet them and smile wide when I see who it is, my worried thoughts pushed aside. "Hey, Benton. How are you feeling?"

"I've been better." His voice is hoarse, and the words send him into a coughing fit.

"Here. Sit." I grab the chair we keep behind the counter and pull it around front. Benton tries to wave me away, but I guide him into the seat. "You sound terrible. What are you doing here?"

Benton leans forward, elbows on his thighs, as another series of coughs wracks his body. "I saw some of the crap people posted about the fire. I wanted to make sure you were okay."

"I'm fine, Benton. Promise." I lean against the counter and glance down at him. At the dark circles under his eyes. "Why aren't you in bed? You need to rest."

"I can't sleep." Benton rubs his neck and leans back in the chair. "Every time I close my eyes, all I see is fire."

"Is there anything I can do?"

Benton shakes his head. "You totally saved my ass. I'm sorry you're getting so much shit for it."

"It's fine," I say with a nonchalance I don't feel. "It'll blow over in a few days."

He glances around the store to make sure no one is nearby and leans toward me. "Do you have any idea who did it?"

The question catches me off guard. "Not a clue. I assumed it was an accident." Benton scoffs, which sends him into another coughing fit. I raise an eyebrow at him. "You disagree?"

"I'm obviously biased, but that sure as hell felt intentional to me." Benton's jaw clenches, and he squeezes his hands into fists. The severe expression cracks when he falls into another round of coughing. He wipes the back of his arm across his mouth. "Whoever it was, I'm going to find them."

"You're what?"

"I'm going to figure out who did this." Benton looks up at me, his eyes wide and full of hope. "But I'll need your help."

"Benton, I . . ."

"I won't be able to sleep until this guy is behind bars." He reaches for my hand, and I bury the urge to remind him the culprit could also be a girl. Or someone who isn't either of those genders. "Please, Hannah."

"Why me? I don't know the first thing about investigating accidents. Or crimes." I add that second bit when Benton gives me an unamused look. I don't know why he's so convinced, but he clearly is. If I hadn't spent the better part of the past two weeks thinking a Blood Witch was after me, I might call him paranoid. But even I'm not that much of a hypocrite.

"Come on, Hannah. I almost *died*. I have to know who's responsible for that, even if it was an accident." He gives me his best puppy-dog look, his hazel eyes wide and glittering. "Please? Even if we don't find the bad guy, it'll still be fun to hang out before I go to college."

That final bit wins me over. I'm slammed with an overwhelming feeling of nostalgia, and he hasn't even left for Boston yet. "Fine, fine. I'm in. But I expect to get some serious pool time out of this."

Benton laughs. "You can come over every day if that's what it takes." He uses the counter to pull himself out of the chair and wraps me in a hug. Like me, he still smells faintly of smoke. "You won't regret this." He pulls out his phone and checks the time. "When does your shift end? We could meet at my place to go over what we already know. Make a game plan."

"I can't."

"But I thought you said—"

"My parents grounded me. They weren't super understanding about the whole almost-getting-arrested thing."

"Ah. Yeah, that complicates things."

The curtain in the back of the shop swings open. Lauren and Evan head toward the counter, still deep in conversation.

"We'll figure something out." Benton reaches for the door. "I'll see you soon." He pivots on his heel and is gone before my boss makes it back to the counter. I hurry to my place behind the register, my mind already spinning with wildly convoluted explanations for the fire.

"Everything go okay?" I ask Evan when Lauren disappears down the book aisle.

Evan nods. He still looks shaken, but there's a little more color in his face now.

Lauren returns with a copy of *Wicca for Beginners* and a set of altar candles. She rings up the order, applies the discount she gives all her students, and bags up the supplies. "I'll see you back here in a week. Be prepared to discuss the Wiccan Rede with a special look at the Threefold Law and the tenet of harm none. In the meantime, I'll light a candle for your family."

"Thank you." Evan offers a cautious smile to both of us and leaves with a very different type of supplies than he ever bought before.

"Is he going to be okay?"

Lauren nods. "He's made some missteps, and he has a long road ahead of him, but his life isn't over. He'll be okay."

11

THE RICH SCENT OF bubbling chocolate fills the kitchen with warmth. When the timer ticks down to the final second, I turn it off before it can beep, grabbing a towel to pull the home-made brownies out of the oven. After checking them with a toothpick, I set them on a rack to cool.

My parents are both at work—Mom teaching summer classes at the university and Dad preparing to prosecute his next case. I have the day off, and I'm not about to squander it. I raced through Mom's mile-long chore list this morning and still had time to bake for the illicit visitor I'm expecting any min—

Our doorbell rings. Right on time. "Just a sec!" I hang up the towel and hurry to open the front door, smiling at my new detective partner. "Hey, Benton. Come on in." Behind him, his beast of a car sits in the driveway. The matte-black BMW looks ridiculously out of place beside my old-as-dirt Toyota, and I'm suddenly self-conscious about him being here.

Benton adjusts the messenger bag he's got slung over one shoulder. "Nice place," he says, but he's being polite. My house is a shack compared to his family's mansion. He perches his sun-glasses on top of his dark, choppy hair. "Where should we set up?"

"We can work in my bedroom. It's upstairs." I lead the way, Benton trailing close behind.

He circles my small space and comes to a stop before the

self-portrait Veronica said made me look broken. "I remember you starting this in class. It turned out great."

"Thanks." I fuss with the hem of my shirt. I don't think I'll ever get used to people looking so closely at my work—especially the pieces I do mostly for myself. "We should get started. You can use my desk."

"Sure." Benton clears his raspy throat and slips the messenger bag off his shoulder. He sets a notebook and pen on the desk before reaching into the bag again. This time, he pulls out a sleeve of Thin Mints. "I thought these might help us concentrate."

I settle onto my bed and flash a grin, accepting a trio of cookies. "Now, this is how you get on my good side. I have brownies cooling downstairs for later, too."

"Was I not on your good side before?" Benton mimes a dagger to the heart. "Hannah, you wound me."

"Yeah, yeah, laugh it up." I take a bite and groan appreciatively. The only thing better than chocolate with peanut butter is chocolate with mint, especially in the summer. "So," I say around bites, "where do we start?"

"I googled investigation tips, and everyone says proper notes are essential." Benton flips open the notebook. The first page is pristine. "We should start with what we already know."

"Did you buy a new notebook for this?" I shove the last cookie into my mouth and reach for more. "And here I thought Gemma was the biggest school supply addict in Salem."

Heat creeps up Benton's neck and flushes his cheeks. "What can I say? I like a fresh start." He writes *Arson Investigation* in large block print and turns the page. "Do we think whoever set the fire at Nolan's is the same person who killed that raccoon last week?"

"I don't think so," I say, shaking my head. "Evan was outside when the fire started, so he couldn't have done it."

Benton looks up from his page. "Wait, back up. *Evan* killed the raccoon? Why? How do you know that?"

My answer tangles up in my throat. I can't tell Benton that I used spelled stones to pry the answers from Evan, so I ignore the *how* part of his question. "He was going through some tough stuff with his family. I guess he hoped the ritual would help." Thoughts of Evan's dad, of his accident, raise goose bumps along my skin. I wonder how Evan's holding up, if his misguided spell has brought him any more heartache or trouble. "But like I said, he was outside when the fire started. He's not our culprit."

"Not Evan. Got it. So where do we look for suspects? There were tons of people at the party." Benton wiggles the pen between his fingers, his forehead creased with concentration. "There's no way we'll remember every single person there."

"Let's back up. You're technically a witness, right? Walk me through what happened after you followed Nolan." My head fills with the disgusting comments Nolan made when he caught Morgan and me kissing. Fury simmers somewhere deep inside. He's such a fucking creep. "You did get him to erase that video, right?"

Benton nods, which calms my rage. A little. "I caught up to him in the living room. He was yelling at a pair of sophomores for breaking his mom's antique vase. It took a little convincing, but he deleted the video."

"Was he upset? Enough to go after you?"

"You think this was Nolan?" Benton taps his pen against the notebook. "I don't know. I mean, how pissed do you have to be to set your own house on fire?"

"I'm guessing more pissed than he was," I concede, since I don't have anything besides a bitter loathing for the asshole to argue his guilt. There's no evidence against him, and if he was that pissed about a single vase breaking, I doubt he'd set fire to his home. "What happened after you left Nolan?"

Benton writes *Suspects* on the top of his page and starts the list with Nolan—followed by several question marks. "I went looking for a bathroom. Someone was puking in the one on the first floor, so I went upstairs."

"Did you see anyone?"

"Yeah, actually," he says, and looks up at me. "Veronica. She was arguing with Savannah. I couldn't hear what they were saying, but when I opened the door, they both looked really intense."

"They were in the bathroom together?"

"No. It was a bedroom. I found the bathroom on the other end of the hall." Benton writes both of their names on his suspect list. "There was definitely something shady going on between them."

"Veronica didn't start the fire. My ex is many things, but she isn't an arsonist." I doubt we even *have* a true arsonist on our hands, but I promised myself I'd humor Benton's theories. I'm more concerned about what Veronica was doing closed up in a bedroom with Savannah.

"What about Savannah?" he asks, crossing out Veronica's name without pressing further, which I appreciate.

"I don't know much about her. What's her motive?"

Benton grabs another Thin Mint and eats the whole thing in one bite. "Maybe she thinks Nolan killed the raccoon, which would make him the reason her wrist is broken," he says, his mouth still full. He swallows and continues, looking pensive.

"Maybe it wasn't about me. Maybe Nolan was the target."

"I don't know, Benton." I flash a grin and waggle my eyebrows at him. "Maybe there's something between you and Savannah I don't know about."

"I've only had one crush since I moved to Salem, and it wasn't Savannah." Benton's cheeks flush red, but his words make my stomach sink to the floor.

"Benton . . ."

He holds up his hands. "No, I'm sorry." His whole posture deflates, but the red in his face doesn't fade. "I shouldn't have said anything. I promise I'll get over it. I don't want to lose you as a friend."

I nod, but the awkward silence stretches between us, chipping away at the easy banter we usually have. "Let's take a brownie break," I say when I can't stand it any longer. Benton agrees, so I lead him downstairs to the kitchen and slice into the brownies, still warm from the oven. My phone buzzes in my pocket, but I ignore it. "Do you want a corner piece?"

He recoils. "Middle piece or bust, Walsh."

"Blasphemy," I say, mocking a gasp. A smile quirks up the corners of my lips as I pull out one piece from the dead center. I grab a corner piece for myself and hold it up. "Cheers."

"Cheers," he echoes, making a fake clinking sound when he taps his brownie against mine. "Here's to cracking the case, Detective Walsh."

I laugh and take a bite, the chocolatey goodness melting over my tongue. We go through another brownie each, chatting about investigation strategies. Benton suggests we split up the guest list and interview our classmates as witnesses. I begrudgingly agree, and we head back toward my room.

My phone goes off again, and I finally pull it out. "Hang on a sec," I say, unlocking my screen. There are three texts waiting for me. Two are from Gemma, but the first . . .

It's from Morgan.

MH: You busy tomorrow?

Warmth spreads through me, but I can't tell if it's excitement or nerves or something else entirely. Before I give myself time to overreact—Is she asking me out? Is this a friend thing?—I check Gemma's texts.

GG: Morgan is freaking out over here! What are you waiting for?

GG: Hannah. When the girl you have a crush on asks you out, it's polite to respond.

My face burns. So she *was* asking me out.

HW: Should I say yes?

"Everything all right?"

"Huh?" I glance up from my phone and find Benton staring at me. "Yeah, fine."

Benton finishes the last bite of his second brownie and wipes his fingers on his jeans. "What's that look about?" He tilts his head to one side. "You look all . . . embarrassed."

"It's nothing." I tuck my hair behind one ear, trying to avoid Benton's questioning stare. I don't want to rub this in his face, but we're supposed to be friends, right? We shouldn't have to dance around each other because of an impossible crush, one he's promised to get over. "It's that girl from the party. Morgan. I think she just asked me out."

"You think?"

Before I can respond, my phone lights up.

GG: OMG of course you should!!! You two would be so cute together.

I bite my lip and turn back to Benton. "You know that feeling when you're not sure if someone wants to hang out as friends or if they're asking for a date? It's like that, except it can be even more confusing when you're both girls."

"Ah." Benton runs a hand through his messy hair. "Yeah, that sounds complicated."

You have no idea. I open up Morgan's text, but my fingers freeze over the keys. Even with Gemma's endorsement, the *You busy tomorrow?* still doesn't seem super flirty to me. Did Morgan say something to Gem about how she feels, or is Gemma shipping us because we're the only queer girls she knows? Am *I* shipping us for the same reason?

"What's wrong?" Benton asks when my hesitation extends to ridiculous lengths. "Not sure if you like her back?"

"I barely know her," I say, which isn't entirely true. We've texted a ton, but I'm worried our easy banter won't translate when we're in person. Most of all, I'm worried that without the crystals I was wearing at the party, she won't be interested at all.

"Isn't that the point of a first date?" Benton asks, cutting into my thoughts. "To get to know someone?"

"I guess." My phone buzzes in my hand as a new message comes through.

GG: Hannah Marie Walsh! Stop stalling. Put the girl out of her misery and respond already!!!

Fuck it. It doesn't hurt to go out and see if we click. Even if we don't, another queer friend is always a good thing. Gemma's great, but she doesn't always understand everything I go through. She hasn't even noticed how much her parents have changed around me.

I glance up at Benton, who gives me an encouraging nod.

HW: Totally free. What do you have in mind?

I watch the screen, waiting for the three dancing dots to appear. Benton and I head for the stairs at the front of the house, and as we pass the big bay windows in the living room, there's a loud crash. I jolt away from the sound, raising my hands to cover my face, but I'm too slow. A sharp pain blooms across my cheeks and arms. My magic tries to protect me, but the binding charm keeps it locked inside.

"Hannah! Are you all right?" Benton catches me as I sway on my feet, dragging me away from the broken glass.

A brick lies on the floor, only a few feet in front of where I was standing. Our front bay window is in pieces across the living room. I'm afraid to look at my arms, my face, worried there's glass lodged in my skin.

"Benton," I say, my stomach clenching. "Can you see who threw it?"

He leaves me and runs to the window, which stands like a gaping mouth, a few jagged pieces of glass hanging on like teeth. "They're gone." Benton bends and picks up the brick. "But they left a message." He unties the note from the brick and hands me the crumpled paper.

YOU'RE NEXT.

------ ✳ ------

Benton calls for an ambulance, and I'm too shaken to protest. The paramedics remove bits of glass from my face and arms, disinfect the wounds, and bandage me up. All things considered, I'm not badly hurt, but Benton fusses over me like I'm on my deathbed. He refuses to leave until I call both my parents and tell them what happened. He also tucks the threatening letter into his bag so he can review it for clues.

I thought he was overreacting about the fire, but maybe it wasn't an accident. Maybe someone is after him. After *us*.

Benton leaves with only moments to spare before my dad makes it home. Dad, for his part, is furious that I didn't call him sooner and worries over me until I have to shout that I'm fine. Once he's sure, Dad goes into work mode, calling the police and the insurance company.

While he talks to the officer and grumbles about being on hold, I'm texting furiously with Gemma, desperate for a distraction from this nightmare. By the time the handyman has boarded up the window and ordered a replacement, Gem and I have concocted a plan to make my date with Morgan happen despite being grounded.

At dinner, I tell my parents Lauren asked me to pick up an

extra shift to cover for Cal's doctor appointment. They nod and remind me to be careful. Despite Benton's concerns for our safety, my parents don't think it's anything to worry about. Dad's positive the broken window was meant for him, that a family member of someone he sent to jail must have done it.

I'm less sure, especially since the brick flew through the window right as I was walking past, but I'm not about to argue the point. I try to ride my wave of good luck, casually asking my parents if I can take off my binding ring during tonight's weekly lesson with Lady Ariana. That request does *not* go over well. My parents decide to call my grandmother and fill her in on my infractions at the party. I still get to attend the lesson, but I'm forced to dust the altar while my peers work magic.

It's the worst lesson of my life, but at least I have a date to plan.

The next day, as I get ready in the Cauldron's tiny staff bathroom, I'm starting to think this wasn't such a good idea. There's approximately five billion butterflies causing havoc in my stomach. The patchwork of tiny cuts on my face is too fresh to cover with makeup, so my only weapon is a tube of lip gloss. I wanted to bring a change of clothes, but I forgot Mom's classes didn't start until noon today, and there was no way to sneak anything remotely cute past her when I left this morning.

My phone buzzes, the sound overly loud against the sink.

GG: No getting cold feet! Morgan is so excited.

HW: Is class done?

GG: We're on break. About another fifteen minutes left. Get over here!

My reflection in the mirror smiles back at me. Maybe this look isn't too terrible for a first date. I did manage to wear my favorite jeans, and the deep purple of the Cauldron T-shirt isn't too awful. At least it's not the highlighter-green fiasco Lauren tried out the first year I worked here.

The drive to the dance studio is brief, but my palms are sweating by the time I get there. I wipe them on my jeans after I park. *You can do this. It's just a date. With a cute girl. Who may or may not even like you without spelled crystals around your neck.*

My thoughts continue to spiral, and I have to fight to force them away. I take a deep breath, asking the air to calm my nerves, but the binding charm on my finger prevents the elements from offering even the slightest comfort.

I shove aside the guilt over disobeying my parents, exit the car, and walk the familiar path into the studio and down to Room C. Music pours into the hallway through the open door. I lean against the doorjamb to watch, and the music sweeps me away. The dancers are working on a pointe number. Gemma is the lead of the piece, and it's easy to see why. Her form is exceptional, her timing perfect.

But in the back row, the newest dancer is giving Gem a run for her money.

Morgan moves with a fluidity and strength unlike anything I've ever seen. The videos of her old recitals don't do her justice. Her hair is high in a tight bun, which makes her features look focused and intense. Every movement is so precise, so emotive, it's like she has complete control over every cell of her body. Every strand of hair. I can't look away.

As the music comes to an end, the dancers strike their final pose and the instructor notices me loitering in the doorway. She glares in my direction, and I scoot out of the way. A few moments later, a dozen zippers slide across gym bags as the dancers unwrap their point shoes from their ankles.

The swarm of butterflies from earlier flutters their wings in my stomach.

Morgan emerges from the room first. A large duffel hangs off one shoulder. Her cheeks are flushed, but that's probably from the class.

"Hey, Hannah." She stops short. "What happened?"

My fingers drift to my face. "Someone threw a brick through my front window yesterday. I'm fine though."

"Are you sure?" She steps closer, the tips of her fingers brushing along the edge of my temple. I nod, afraid to breathe with her so close, and she pulls her hand away. "I'm going to change. Are you up for getting smoothies after?"

"Sounds great."

Morgan glides down the hall to the locker room. Once she's out of sight, I lean against the wall and brush my fingers across my face. The healing cuts send a pulse of worry through my entire body. I trust my dad's instincts, but what if Benton was right? What if that brick was meant for us? Maybe I shouldn't be wandering around town, powerless from the ring on my finger.

Gem sidles up beside me, and I force my fear away. "Excited for your date?" she asks, waggling her eyebrows and shimmying her shoulders.

"Go away. Before she sees you and thinks you're giving me a pep talk," I whisper, and nudge Gem with my shoulder.

"Do you need a pep talk?" The teasing is gone from her voice. "How's your face feeling?"

"Is it that bad?"

"No! It's barely noticeable." Gemma pauses, the lie hanging between us. "Are you nervous?"

I fidget and avoid Gemma's gaze. "A little. I never had to do the whole 'first date' thing with Veronica. I knew she liked me before I even knew I liked girls. This is new."

Gemma straightens. "You'll be fine. Gotta run!"

"Wait, what?" I watch Gemma race for the front door, and when I turn back around, I see what caused her to bolt. "Hey, Morgan. That was an amazing rehearsal. You're really talented. Like, incredible. I've never seen anyone dance like that, and I've even seen *you* dance before, in those videos you sent." Someone please shut me up.

"Thanks. Those videos were from last year, so I'm glad to hear I haven't gotten worse." Morgan smiles, her lips freshly glossed. Her hair is down now, soft curls flowing past her shoulders. "Should we get out of here?"

"Sure." I follow Morgan to her mom's silver SUV, where she stores her bag. "So, smoothies, huh?"

"I'm not really a coffee person. Makes me too jittery." Morgan leads me down the street to the Squeeze Café. "Gemma said this place was one of your favorites," she says as she holds the door for me.

I thank her and pass into the cool air conditioning, a welcome relief from the hot summer sun. Morgan follows me in, and we wait in line in silence. I order a strawberry smoothie; Morgan orders a lemonade slushie. After an awkward stalemate over who should pay—we end up splitting it—we find a small table in the corner and settle across from each other.

"So," I start, but I don't know where to go from there. All my previous fears about our texting banter not translating to real life itch at my skin as the silence stretches between us.

Morgan takes a sip from her drink. "Sorry again about the impromptu kiss at the party. I feel like that's maybe contributing to this awkwardness."

Her frankness startles a laugh out of me. "I'm sure it would be awkward anyway. I'm not exactly good at first dates."

"Is anyone?" Morgan brushes her hair behind one ear. "And it's not like Disney ever showed us how to fall for another girl."

I nod, sipping my strawberry smoothie. "This is the part where I ask you all the stereotypical first-date questions, right? Like 'What brought you from Minnesota all the way to Massachusetts?' And 'How did you settle on Salem of all places?' Are your parents captivated by the witch trials like all the tourists here?"

"Is your family not? Why live in Salem if you hate its greatest attraction?" Morgan quirks up an eyebrow and swirls the straw through her slushie.

"My mom works at the university. She's teaching summer sessions this year."

"Really? My dad just transferred to Salem State, too. He teaches history. Or he will once classes start this fall."

"Is that why they made you move for your senior year?" I can't imagine having to leave my friends. An unexpected urge to reach across the table and hold her hand swells within me.

Morgan doesn't respond for what feels like forever, and I wish I could take back my question or say something funny to make her laugh. After a long sip of her lemonade, she finally meets my eye. "I don't love that we had to move. Dad gave us practically no warning. I left my friends and my dance academy back in Duluth."

"I'm sensing a 'but' in there somewhere."

"But . . ." Morgan stares at her cup, sneaking a glance at me before she continues. "Moving here was also an easy way to cut ties with an ex who didn't want things to be over."

"Why do I get the feeling Gemma spilled about my break-up?" My phone buzzes in my pocket, but I ignore it. It's probably said best friend, already desperate for details.

"Probably because she did, but I totally get it. If I hadn't left Minnesota, our summers might have looked very similar." Morgan reaches out and rests her fingers against mine, her move-ments cautious, yet so much braver than mine. "I have to say, I prefer this version. I could use a fresh start."

My skin tingles at her touch. My heart races. She definitely likes me. Even without the spelled stones around my neck. "New beginnings can certainly be a good thing." My phone goes off—a call this time. "I'm sorry. I know this is incredibly rude, but my phone . . ."

"No, no. It's fine. Go ahead." Morgan leans back, taking her touch with her.

"Thanks," I say with what I hope is an apologetic smile. By the time I pull out my phone, the call is lost. Instead, I have a series of missed texts from Veronica. "Ugh."

"Bad news?"

"The previously mentioned ex-who-doesn't-want-to-let-go. She's blowing up my phone." I ignore her texts without reading them and place the phone facedown on the table. "Did you have the same problem with your ex?"

Morgan fusses with her ring again, spinning it round and round. "Mine was more the show-up-at-my-house-at-all-hours type."

"Yikes." Though I'm sure it doesn't compare to the fear she went through, I shiver remembering the *YOU'RE NEXT* note that came flying through my window yesterday.

"Yeah. It was honestly kind of terrifying." Morgan shakes her head as if she's trying to disperse the memory. "I'm half-convinced Dad looked for jobs out of state as a way to escape. He was *not* pleased with Riley. And talking to Riley's parents was not an option."

"Riley's the ex?"

"Yup. He would not leave me alone. It was like he became this totally different person."

"I'm sorry," I say, trying to piece together what might have happened. "Did you date him before you came out? Is that why you broke up?"

"No, I came out in middle school. I'm bi." She pauses, considering me. "That's not a problem, is it?" she asks, her question more challenge than curiosity, and I hate that I've put her on the defensive like this.

"No, of course not. I'm sorry. I shouldn't have assumed." I take a long sip of my smoothie and hiss when I get a brain freeze. "How'd your parents handle your coming out?"

"They were fine. My dad's bisexual, too, so it's not like I had to explain any of it to them. They both understood, him especially." She picks up her cup as my phone goes off. For the billionth time. "Is that your ex again? Maybe you should answer it. Be clear with her you don't want to talk."

"You sure? I could turn it off."

Morgan waves me on and sips her drink.

I pick up the phone and pivot toward the wall. "What do you want?"

"Hannah. Thank god." Veronica's voice is hoarse. Something crashes in the background. "No one else is answering."

"What's wrong? What's happening?" I'm out of my chair in an instant.

"Someone broke in. I locked myself in my room." Another pound. Another shout.

"Did you call the police?" I whisper into the phone, but Morgan's eyes shoot up to find mine anyway.

There's another crash, and Veronica gasps. "I can't. I think you're right. I think it's the Blood Witch."

"What?"

"He hit me. My blood . . . I think my blood touched his skin. Hannah—"

"I'm coming. Hang on." I turn to Morgan. "I'm sorry. I need to leave."

She shakes her head. "It's fine. Go. Do you need me to call anyone?"

"I've got it covered." I rush for the door, but I pause and turn back to my abandoned date. "I'm really sorry."

And then I run.

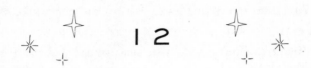

12

I DRIVE WITH RECKLESS abandon, my worries running on an endless loop. Nothing that's happened this summer makes any sense. Why would a Blood Witch start a fire at Nolan's house? Why not go after Veronica directly—like they've done now, I realize. The thought makes my whole body go cold.

No one's answering their phone, and I'm forced to leave coded messages—for my mom, my dad, Lady Ariana, even Veronica's parents—telling them to come. To hurry. I take a sharp left toward Veronica's street, cutting off a minivan, and dial my mom again. It rings and rings.

"Dammit." I throw my phone in the passenger seat when the voicemail picks up again. She must still be in class. If this isn't a good enough reason to convince my parents to teach me advanced air magic, I don't know what is.

Wait. Why didn't Veronica use magic to contact Lady Ariana? Even if her parents made her wear a binding ring, there are ways to take it off in an emergency like this. It's not like she'd have to hide the side effects from her parents. They would understand.

Maybe Veronica did reach out to Lady Ariana, but she's too far away to help. Or maybe this is all an elaborate lie to mess up my date. With Veronica, it's impossible to tell.

But her fear sounded so real . . .

When I turn onto Veronica's street, it's empty. Barren. There aren't even any kids playing in their front yards. I pull into her driveway, throw my car in park, and unbuckle my seat belt. The flutter of my heartbeat reminds me how dangerous this is. How spectacularly I failed the last time I faced a Blood Witch.

So long as he doesn't come in contact with my blood, he won't be able to bend my body to his will. He won't be able to stop my heart. So long as I don't bleed, I should be fine.

Hopefully.

I shake out my arms, like I can flick the fear off the ends of my fingers. The risks don't matter. I can't leave Veronica in there alone. I reach for the binding charm, bracing for the pain that comes with unauthorized removal, and rip the ring from my finger, gasping as a burning sensation twists across my skin. I drop the thin band of metal in the cup holder, my heart pounding as it rattles against the plastic.

I'm flooded with an awareness so intense it steals my breath. The air rushes in my open window, pulling Veronica's panic across my skin and threading it through my hair. Days of built-up magic thrums through my veins. I flex my hands, and my gaze catches on the red welts twisting down the length of my finger, already darkening to black. Irrefutable proof for my parents that I've broken their rules.

But I don't have time to worry about that. Every second I delay is a second more the Blood Witch has to hurt Veronica.

My car door creaks as I ease it open, and I try to shut it as quietly as possible. The element of surprise is one of the few advantages I have, and I'm not about to give it up. I race to the front door, but it's locked. Though the struggle inside is too quiet for the neighbors to hear, the air dutifully brings me every sound. Hiccupping sobs. A fist against her door. Muttered curses.

I slip around the house, looking for a way inside, but with each step my confusion grows. If the intruder is a Blood Witch, why hasn't he smashed through Veronica's bedroom door already?

A shadow moves past the window up ahead. I duck down. Press myself against the foundation. My heart beats so loud I can hardly hear myself think.

The Blood Witch.

He must have retreated downstairs. *Unless . . .* A sick horror fills my legs with lead. It climbs up my body, souring my stomach and threatening to stop my heart. There were three figures inside the scrying bowl. How many witches are in the house?

The shadow paces in front of the window, but I can't stay crouched here forever. I need a plan. Some way to distract the Blood Witch long enough to slip inside and launch a proper attack. I don't even need to win. Just buy enough time for our parents or Lady Ariana to arrive.

I wait for the Blood Witch to pivot in their pacing, and then I run to the back of the house in a half crouch. I'm low enough to stay below the edge of the windows, but I don't stop to look back. All I can do is hope the witch didn't see me.

When I round the corner, I stretch to my full height and inhale deep, drawing power from the air into my lungs. Energy shoots through my limbs, and a plan takes shape in my brain. It's risky, but I have to do something. Ex-girlfriend or not, Veronica is an Elemental. We're Clanmates *and* covenmates. I'm sworn to protect her as she is me.

I inch toward the sliding glass door on the back deck. It's

locked, no surprise there, but it's still my best way in. I just need a . . .

There. Mrs. Matthews edged her garden in heavy stones. I reach for the steady thrum of the earth's power and stretch my magic around the stones, lifting them into the air. Inside the house, something crashes. Veronica screams. Her fear grips my spine, and a few of the rocks fall. *Hang on, V. Just a little longer.* I sprint around the corner and send one of the rocks careening toward the side window.

Glass shatters, and I'm gone before I see whether the rock made contact with anyone inside the house. A bonus if it did, but at the very least it should provide a distraction. Three more rocks draw close to me, hovering around my hips.

I send the first through the sliding glass door. Careful to avoid cutting myself, I slip my hand inside and feel for the lock, my fingers just long enough to reach. It takes a couple of tries to turn it all the way, but then I'm inside.

The familiarity of this house picks at my heart. This place has been a second home my entire life. I know every inch of the sprawling floorplan, from the plush carpeting in the next room to the kitchen island half a dozen steps in front of me. I pick my way through the kitchen and peer around the corner.

Nothing. Shards of glass sparkle on the floor like crushed diamonds, and the rock I tossed through the window lies against the wall. I reach for it, my power wrapping around the hard earth and pulling it toward me.

The air screams a warning across my back. Before I can turn, something slams into me, sending me sprawling onto the floor. A hand wraps around my ankle. Panic burns inside, driving out every bit of training I've ever had. I fling the rocks blindly behind me, but fear makes my magic sloppy, and my only weapons bury themselves in the walls.

Focus. Focus, or you'll die.

I suck in a breath and push down the panic, flipping onto my back. This time, my kick catches the witch in the shin. He releases me, and I scramble back. The witch wears a mask and is dressed in black from head to toe. He's tall, at least from this angle, and he's holding what looks like the broken remains of the coat rack that normally sits by the front door, wielding it like a staff. This certainly isn't the petite Blood Witch from New York, but does he know her? Is that what this is about?

He moves fast, twirling the long piece of wood and bringing it down toward my head. Air surges up around me, knocking the staff far enough off course that it smacks against the floor beside me.

"Veronica!" I shout, scrambling to my feet. Magic pulses through me, pushes against my skin, ready to escape the confines of my flesh. My whole body hums with power, and I let it free. The air whips around me, tugging at my hair.

The Blood Witch stares at me, his eyes growing wide beneath the mask. He recovers quickly and lunges forward, swinging the staff for my head. I duck, grabbing hold of the air and pushing it forward to separate us. He falls back a step and catches his foot on the edge of an area rug. The witch trips, tumbling into the wall.

I pin him there, pushing harder and harder with my magic, the rush of air growing stronger with each breath. Wind swirls around me like a cyclone, filling me with strength.

"Who are you?" I have to yell over the wind and the pulse of blood in my ears. "What do you want from us?" My cyclone tugs at his mask, at the black clothes covering every inch of his skin. I have to know who it is so we can stop him and whoever else he's working with.

My hands tremble, and a fresh wave of fear tugs at my heart. I've never used magic offensively like this, and my strength is fading. Fast. As the thought rushes through my mind, I feel it. The subtle dip in the wind's speed. The pain lancing up my arms as I push too hard.

"Veronica!" I yell up the stairs to my right. "Our parents will be here any second." It's a lie. I have no idea how long until the cavalry arrives, but I need the Blood Witch to think he's about to be severely outmatched.

I press forward, hoping my nearness will hide the way the wind dies bit by bit. With shaking fingers, I reach for the mask. I have to know who he is.

The Blood Witch curses, his voice deep and gravelly. Fast as lightning, he grabs my wrist, twisting it until my arm is pinned behind my back. I cry out in pain, and the wind falters.

This is it. He's going to kill me.

"Get the hell away from her."

I glance to my left and find Veronica, her brother's baseball bat clutched tight in her trembling hands. There's dried blood on her nose and lips. Tracks of tears down her cheeks. I've never been happier to see her.

She rushes into the room, bat raised, and then I'm shoved forward, tripping and falling onto my knees. Every muscle protests when I turn around, looking for the witch who shoved me, but Veronica doesn't need my help. She's already chased him out her front door.

My lungs ache, and I let myself relax onto the floor, trying to get the room to stop spinning.

Veronica kneels beside me, brushing tears off her face. "Are you okay?"

"Never better," I say, groaning as I pull myself into a seated position.

"What happened to your face? Did he hurt you?" Veronica reaches for my cheek, for the healing cuts from yesterday's shattered window. Dad seemed so sure the brick was about his work, but what if he was wrong? And if it was from the Blood Witch, why did he go after Veronica instead of me?

Before I can share these new worries, the front door slams open. "Hannah! Veronica!"

Relief washes through me as Dad spots us. He hurries over and kneels beside me on the floor, crushing me in a hug. "Your mom is on her way. Lady Ariana's two minutes out." He turns his attention to Veronica. "Where are your parents? Your brother?"

Veronica sinks to the floor beside me, leaning against the wall. "Mom's at a conference in Chicago with Dad. Gabe's at our grandparents' place for the week."

Dad nods and turns his attention on me. "Where is your phone? You can't call in a panic and then not answer."

I pat at my jeans and come up empty. "I must have left it in my car." I lean against the wall, my arms still shaking and my head woozy.

"Hannah? Tim?" Mom's voice cuts off whatever Dad was going to say next. She's beside us a second later. "Oh, thank god." She kneels and wraps me in a hug.

I pull away from her embrace and glance at my ex-girlfriend, dried blood on her face and tears in her eyes.

"Now do you believe me?"

13

WE'RE SITTING AROUND VERONICA'S dining room table when Lady Ariana arrives.

She sweeps into the house, surveying the damaged walls and broken windows. The air grows heavy with her power, an electric current that raises the hairs on my arms and the back of my neck. By the time Lady Ariana makes it to the dining room, she can't hide her familial worry behind her usual high priestess mask.

"Explain." Her single word is soft and full of emotion I know she'll never admit aloud.

I tell my grandmother about Veronica's call and how I broke into the house to scare off the Blood Witch. Dad asks where I put my binding charm while he removes the twisted marks from my finger. After explaining, I ask Veronica why she didn't remove hers, but it turns out she suffered a different punishment for stealing her mother's crystals.

Instead of forcing her to wear a binding charm, Veronica's parents placed a temporary binding tattoo at the base of her neck. There's no way for her to wipe it away and restore her magic, which means she was as powerless as a Reg when the Blood Witch attacked.

Even my grandmother cannot erase the binding rune, though she admits she might if she were able, given the circumstances.

Instead, Veronica will have to spend the next ten days without her magic, until the binding wears off naturally.

"Tell me more about the intruder." Lady Ariana sits at the table and motions for my dad to make tea, which he does dutifully. She hasn't admitted that the intruder was a Blood Witch. I don't know if it's doubt that stills her tongue or pride.

"He was tall. Slender. Athletic." I shiver at the memory and wonder at the witch's identity. Is it someone I know? Is it the same person who set the fire? I run through Benton's list of suspects from yesterday. Nolan's about that height and build, though I still can't see him burning his own house. The intruder clearly wasn't Savannah, but the scrying session I'm determined *not* to mention suggests the Blood Witch isn't acting alone. She could be involved. "He was strong, Grandma. Fast. I really think this was a Blood Witch."

Dad sets a cup of tea in front of my grandmother, who takes a deep breath and waves a hand over the tea, cooling it to the perfect temperature. She takes a sip and then settles her all-seeing gaze upon me. "I still sense no Blood Magic, but I agree that something is amiss. Let me handle this, Hannah. Have patience."

"Are you sure? Who else would be after our coven?" I look to my parents for backup but find none.

"I'm withholding judgment until I learn more." Lady Ariana turns her attention to my ex. "Pack a bag, Veronica. I won't have you staying alone until the intruder is caught."

Veronica scurries away, and Lady Ariana makes a grand flourish with her hands, spinning an air message before her. She speaks, so soft I cannot hear, and releases the magic. I glance to my parents, but no one says anything. I have so many questions, so many worries, but I'm afraid to mention any of them.

On the plus side, I'm fairly certain I'm not grounded anymore. At the very least, I doubt my parents will make me wear the binding charm while there's a confirmed *intruder* targeting Elementals.

A few minutes later, Lady Ariana is finishing the last of her tea when she tilts her head ever so slightly. She nods, and Veronica steps back into the room, pulling a small suitcase.

"Veronica, your parents are booking the first flight back in the morning." Lady Ariana stands and hands Dad her teacup. "You'll stay with Hannah until your family returns."

Veronica's eyes grow wide, and she glances from me to our high priestess. "Are you sure that's a good idea?"

Even though I'm thinking the same thing, I know it's the absolute wrong thing to ask.

"Of course I'm sure. Be grateful I'm letting you drive yourself." Lady Ariana turns and glides out of the room. The rest of us are still frozen in the dining room when the front door slams shut.

When we make it back to my house, Mom tries to lighten the mood by ordering pizza. My overstretched magic leaves me simultaneously ravenous and nauseated, so dinner is a precarious venture. Veronica excuses herself early, leaving me with my parents, who don't seem to know what to do with me.

Mom keeps trying to speak, but she swallows her words before they come out. It's like she wants to yell at me for being reckless, for removing my binding charm without permission, and yet she's obviously relieved I'm okay.

For his part, Dad tries to crack jokes and talk about the ridiculous case he's working on—as much as he's able to without violating confidentiality laws—but eventually he gives up and retires to his office to work on said case.

I help Mom clean up and head to my room, but I change my mind at the last second, knocking on the guest room door.

"Yeah?" Veronica's voice is soft. She sniffles once. Twice.

"Do you need anything?" I crack open the door and wait another second for her to compose herself before I come in.

It's weird to see her like this, in this room. Veronica has spent the night at my house countless times before, but she's never slept in the guest room. When we were little, we'd set up sleeping bags and little pop-up tents in the living room. As preteens, we'd camp out in my room and slip off our binding rings—the normal pre-initiation ones, rings without the anti-tampering spell that burned my finger—practicing harmless bits of magic I'm sure my parents knew about but never mentioned. Even after we started dating, Veronica never slept in here. My parents sent us back to the living room, sleeping on air mattresses as far away from each other as possible in a room without doors.

She shouldn't be in here. This room is for strangers. Distant relatives. Veronica isn't either of those things.

Veronica exhales a sharp sigh and wipes at her face. "What the hell is going on, Hannah?"

"I wish I knew." I sink onto the bed beside her. "If this is about New York, why is the Blood Witch going to such lengths to hide their identity? Why set Nolan's house on fire? Why not come for us directly?"

The bed compresses as she leans her shoulder against mine. "Maybe the fear is half the fun." A bitter laugh catches in her throat. "She's playing with us. She has us running scared until she swoops in for the kill." Veronica shudders. "I'm sorry. I don't mean to be so morbid."

"But why us? If it is her, and she's after revenge for what

happened in New York, why not go after the Caster Witches who started this whole thing?" My hand goes to my throat, and the smell of burning flesh fills my nose. "They're the ones who tried to strip away her magic. We were just in the wrong place at the wrong time."

Memories drag me under like the tide. I'm back in the cramped apartment in New York, forced to guard a bound and bleeding Blood Witch. The Casters caught her after she ambushed me in the park, and Veronica agreed to help them finish their potion. Even though I wanted nothing to do with their plans, when the Blood Witch got free, she still blamed me. Hit me hard enough to steal my blood and force me to my knees. And when the Casters realized she had escaped, they came after me, too.

I shudder. Veronica *still* hasn't apologized for the part she played in that nightmare.

"Maybe you're right. Maybe this has nothing to do with New York." Veronica pulls her knees to her chest and wraps her arms around her legs, her whole body shivering. "But whoever that guy was, wherever he came from, he has my blood, Hannah. You know what that means."

My muscles tense. Veronica and I haven't seen eye-to-eye since that weekend, but I wouldn't wish the pain of Blood Magic on anyone. "You'll be safe here. My parents won't let anything happen to you." I reach for her hand, and she squeezes back. "I'm sorry I took so long to answer the phone."

At that, Veronica pulls away. "What were you doing anyway?"

I was on a date . . . But I can't say that. I won't make her night any worse. "I was at the Cauldron. I'm not supposed to answer my phone at work."

Veronica shifts until she's facing me. Her eyes bore into mine. "Would you have answered faster if you weren't at work?"

"Veronica."

"I'm serious. Would you have answered right away if you weren't working?" She grabs my hands and won't look away. She barely even blinks, and it's like she thinks she can stare long enough to see back in time and know exactly what I was doing when she called.

I pull from her grip, picking at the threads in the old comforter. "I don't know. We've had a complicated few weeks."

Veronica scoots closer until her knees rest against mine. "But you came." She trails a hand down my arm. "You saved my life."

"What can I say? We Elementals have to stick together." I force a smile, but her closeness makes me uncomfortable.

Veronica laughs, the sound bitter and hollow. "God, this day. I really thought I was going to die."

"You didn't. You're fine." I blow out a breath. "I'm sorry about your house though. I broke a few windows."

"I don't give a shit about the windows." Veronica leans forward and brushes her lips against mine.

I flinch back. "What are you doing?"

"Isn't it obvious?" She leans forward again.

"Veronica, it's over between us. We have to move on." I slip off the bed as I speak, but Veronica follows a second later, closing the distance between us. The wall ends my escape.

She stops before me, tears spilling over her eyes. "I was wrong, Hannah. I screwed up. I was selfish and bossy, and I didn't listen. I can do better. I want to be better, for you." Veronica tries to kiss me, but I turn my head so she catches my cheek instead of my lips.

"You're scared. I get that," I say, even though my insides squirm with unease. "But that doesn't mean we work." I try to slip by her, but she blocks my path.

"Give me another chance." Veronica brushes the hair away from my injured face. "You and me? We're meant to be together."

"I can't do this with you. I'm not—"

Veronica ignores my pleas and presses her lips against mine. The pressure of her unwanted kiss slams a rusty nail in the coffin of my heart. I shove her away and escape to the center of the room. "Dammit, Veronica. I'm not trying to be an asshole, but you can't keep doing this. How many times do I have to tell you no before you stop?"

"You're not listening!" Veronica wipes at the mascara-infused tears running down her cheeks. "I'm trying to apologize. I want you back. I want forever."

I cross my arms against my chest and force myself to stand tall. "You can't have me back. I've moved on."

Veronica snorts. "How?"

Harsh words rise to my throat, but then I remember the blood on Veronica's face. See the bruise darkening along her jaw. I swallow my anger. "It happens."

Veronica considers me, her head tilting, her eyes narrowing. "Not this fast. Not unless—" She shakes her head. "Tell me you didn't."

"Didn't what?" But my chest constricts. She knows. I don't know how, but she does. The heat in my cheeks grows into an inferno. "You slept with someone else, didn't you?" Tears stream down her face, painting her cheeks with streaks of black. "How could you?"

"How could I? Veronica, we're *not together*. Who I have sex with is none of your business."

"So, you admit it. You did sleep with someone. Fucking perfect." Veronica swipes the ruined mascara from her face. "I'm such an idiot. I knew I couldn't trust you."

"Excuse me?" My magic tries to surge in my chest, but pain lances through me, and I shove it back down. "I've never done *anything* to betray your trust."

"Should we review who ended our relationship?"

"God, enough! Can't you see how unhealthy this is? Why would you want to be with me when all we do is fight?" I ask, and she doesn't have an answer for that. "Exactly. For the record, I did *not* sleep with Morgan. But if I did, that would be none of your damn business."

An angry silence permeates the room. "Who. The hell. Is Morgan?"

Shit. "No one."

But Veronica isn't having it. "Who is she, Hannah?"

I tip my chin up. I'm done letting Veronica intimidate me. She doesn't get a pass to hurt me like this just because she's scared. Especially since *I'm* the one who saved her. "The girl from Nolan's party. Today was our first official date."

My words hover in the air between us, but I don't realize their impact until Veronica's eyes narrow. She grabs her purse and throws her phone inside. "You weren't at work when I called, were you? You were on a *date* with some goddamn *Reg.*" She swipes her keys from the nightstand, the metal scraping across the wooden top. "Did it even occur to you that this Morgan could be the Blood Witch? She shows up in Salem and then all of a sudden we're under attack? I bet she's an only child, too. Isn't she?"

"That doesn't mean she's the Blood Witch. She clearly wasn't

the one at your house. She was with me when I got your call." I
roll my eyes, but Veronica rips open the guest room door. "Where
do you think you're going?"

"Anywhere but here." Veronica glares at me over her shoulder
then disappears out the door.

"Dammit, Veronica!" I chase her down the stairs. "You're
safe here. Where else will you go?"

Veronica doesn't look back as she heads for the front door.
She shoves her feet in her sandals and unbolts the lock. "I'll take
my chances with Savannah. I can't spend another second here."

"Stop acting like I abandoned you. I stopped the Blood
Witch. So what if I've moved on?" I follow her out onto the porch.
"Don't be stupid, Veronica. You know you're safer here than at
Savannah's house. For all you know, *she* could be a Blood Witch."

"Don't. Just don't." Veronica storms down the driveway and
stops beside her car. The streetlights at her back cast her face in
shadows. She glances at the front window, the one still boarded
up after a brick shattered it. "The Blood Witch already knows
where you live, Hannah. Maybe you're the one who should be
scared."

-⊦-　⁎　-⊦-

I wake to thunder.

Lightning flashes, turning my eyelids red as the fog of unconsciousness fades. Another rumble crashes above me, shaking
me in my bed. Pictures rattle on the walls. My jar of paintbrushes
crashes to the floor. I bolt upright. The shaking isn't the storm
outside.

It's a pissed-off Elemental.

Mom stands in the doorway with Dad a pace behind. There's a mixture of exhaustion and panic in her eyes, a combination that sets me on edge. She glares at me. "Where's Veronica?"

I wipe sleep from my eyes as I sit up. "She left. Spent the night at Savannah's house."

Dad follows Mom into the room. He rubs a hand over the stubble along his jaw. "What do you mean 'she left'? Your grandmother was very clear about where she wanted Veronica to stay last night."

"I'm sorry, Dad," I say, not sorry at all. "We fought. She got pissed and ran out. It's not like I could tie her to the bed to keep her here." I glance at the clock. It's barely after four in the morning. "Why are you up so early?"

Mom perches on the edge of my bed. "Lady Ariana called a coven meeting. You need to get ready."

"The sun isn't even up yet." I groan and flop back onto my pillows.

"She said it was urgent." Mom looks to Dad, and something passes between them, some unspoken worry they won't share with me. "Come on. We don't want to be late."

My parents leave the room, and I reluctantly drag myself out of bed. My body still aches from the run-in with the Blood Witch last night. My limbs are heavy and numb, my head stuffed full of cotton.

Outside, the wind rages on. At least the rain is a sign of good luck. When humanity was young, Three Sister Goddesses gifted humans with magic, each creating one of the Clans. The Middle Sister covered the world with storms, and those who felt no fear and danced in the rain earned the power to control the elements.

They became the Elementals.

I stand beside my window, the glass cool against my warm skin. Lightning flashes in the sky and droplets of rain streak past like celestial tears. I can't see how Lady Ariana would have good news for us already. Unless—

Has she found the Blood Witch?

"Hannah?" Dad knocks on my door. "We have to leave in fifteen minutes. We can't make Lady Ariana wait."

"Just a sec." I dress quickly, brush my teeth, and grab a hair tie. When I fling open the bathroom door, Dad is standing there with circles under his eyes, like he slept as poorly as I did. I follow him downstairs, putting my hair into a messy bun as I go.

Mom ushers us out the front door without even giving me a second to grab a soda from the fridge. The drive to my grandmother's takes less than ten minutes since there's precisely zero traffic at this absurd hour. Her home is on the edge of town, tucked inside the Salem Woods, along forgotten roads few locals travel. Her driveway is packed, and we pull in behind Veronica's empty car.

Mom cuts the engine, and for a moment, we pause. The storms have passed, leaving only a light drizzle as the sky lightens on the horizon. I don't want to leave the safety of the car. Once we do, whatever news my grandmother thought was urgent enough to get the coven out of bed before five will be real. Dad mars the silence first, opening his door and leading us around the house and into the backyard.

Dozens of worried faces turn to greet us, but before we can join our coven, we pause at the altar where a trio of pillar candles burns before a statue of the Mother Goddess. As always, the middle candle stands a bit taller and burns a bit brighter than the others, a small sign of gratitude to the Sister Goddess who chose us.

My parents work quickly, passing a hand over the center candle, adding a thin stream of their magic to the flickering flame. I linger at the altar. I'm not ready to face the rest of my coven, not ready to see their worry and wonder if I'm the one who brought danger to our home. I reach out, brushing the tips of my fingers against the flame. A dozen threads of power keep the small fire alive despite the drizzling rain. I wish, not for the first time, that the Sister Goddesses hadn't been banished from our world. It would be nice to know they were out there, watching over us. Keeping us safe.

I shake the thought away and add my strength to the center candle.

When I turn to follow my parents into the thicket of conversation, I spot Veronica out of the corner of my eye. She's the sole member of the Matthews family in attendance, but she's not alone. Sarah and Rachel Gillow stand beside her, whispering something I can't hear. Sarah rubs Veronica's back, while Rachel rests a hand on her small but growing baby bump. The couple announced their pregnancy to the coven last month, after struggling for over a year to find a suitable Elemental donor.

My heart aches to see them with Veronica. For the past year, whenever we saw the Gillows at these gatherings, I'd whisper my hopes for the future to Veronica. We'd pester Rachel with hundreds of questions about how they met and how she knew Sarah was *The One*.

The sting of betrayal courses through me, even though I have no right to be jealous. We're all covenmates. I have no more claim to Rachel and Sarah than anyone else here, including Veronica.

"How are you holding up, dear?" a soft voice asks.

I'm scooped into an embrace before I can respond. My muscles protest the tight hug Mrs. Blaise wraps me in, but my heart warms under her attention. Mrs. Blaise is one of the oldest members of our coven, second only to her husband. I spot him on the other side of the yard, nursing a cup of steaming coffee. Mrs. Blaise releases me and pats my still healing cheek with her wrinkled hand. "That's a brave thing you did for Veronica. Foolish, but brave."

"Thanks." I loop my arm through hers, leading her to the center of the yard where the rest of the families have gathered. I've often felt like Mrs. Blaise was more grandmotherly than, well, my grandma, and her presence beside me is like being wrapped in the softest blanket.

That feeling dies when I see the look on Lady Ariana's face.

A ripple goes through the earth, a silent call to order. The families form a semicircle around our high priestess. Our assembly is smaller than usual, some of the families with young children electing to send a single parent as representative. Twelve of the thirteen families who live in Salem are present. The last—the Leskos—flew to Colorado three days ago to visit distant cousins.

The coven is silent as death as we wait for Lady Ariana to speak.

Our high priestess turns once, meeting the gaze of each witch in attendance. I swear I see a subtle shift in her features when she looks at me, but it's gone before I can name the emotion there.

"I'm sure you've all heard what happened yesterday." No one speaks to confirm, but the air warms with our agreement. "Given the circumstances, I had no choice but to contact the Council."

Beside me, Mr. Blaise drops his coffee, his hands quivering. Still, no one says anything. The ground trembles with our unease until Lady Ariana shifts her stance, stealing away control of the earth and forcing it to still.

"The attacks against our coven are not the work of a Blood Witch." At that, she looks to me, and I feel both relieved and diminished. "The Council believes there is a Witch Hunter in town."

Whispered conversation erupts around me. Mrs. Blaise stumbles and grips my shoulder for balance. I hold tight to her elbow, keeping her steady, and glance left to search for Veronica. Her gaze finds mine. Fear drains the color from her face.

"That's not possible." My dad's voice finally cuts through the growing discord in the coven. "The Council destroyed the Hunters. There hasn't been a confirmed sighting in over fifty years."

Lady Ariana shakes her head, and with that simple motion, she seems to age a decade. "The Councilwoman I spoke with was quite sure. Their agents have taken out two Hunters in the last six months alone." She sighs, her blue eyes almost gray in the pale light of morning. "They went after a third, but he slipped away before they could catch him."

On the other side of the circle, Rachel places a protective hand over her stomach. "What do we do?"

"Does the Council think the third Hunter found his way here? Do we have permission to stop him?" Ellen Watson, a girl a few years older than Veronica, squeezes her hands into fists. The wind picks up around her, tossing her long, light brown hair over her shoulders.

Lady Ariana holds up her hands, and the coven quiets. "The

infiltrate than by masquerading as an ally?

Even Gemma—

No. That's where I draw the line. I would know if Gemma was a Witch Hunter.

Beside me, Veronica shifts uncomfortably. "I hate to bring this up, but what if it *was* your date? She's the only new person in town, Han."

Anger flares hot in my veins. "I already told you, it wasn't Morgan. She was with me when you called, and she's not a guy. Besides, she's not the only new person in town." But even the new people I do know—Cal and Detective Archer—have never spent time with Veronica. How would they know to target her?

"I'm not saying it's definitely her, but you have to be careful. She could have an accomplice." Veronica turns and looks out at the rest of our coven. "We can't trust anyone. Until this Hunter is caught, every Reg is a suspect."

14

WHEN WE GET HOME, my parents start the stress cycle of *Who can take the day off to watch the kid?* After I protest, multiple times, about being labeled a "kid," I finally convince my parents that I'll be fine. Dad heads into work to prepare for court, and Mom leaves for her classes after making me promise a million times to be careful.

Once I'm alone, though, my bravado fades. The Witch Hunters are back, and not back in a general, out-there-in-the-world sense, but *here*. In Salem.

I spend the morning in a cocoon of blankets, hiding from the reality of it all. I write and delete at least twenty texts to Veronica. It hurts that she's not messaging me. That she's not reaching out. A few months ago, this kind of news would have sent me rushing into her arms. Though I don't regret our breakup, I do miss having someone to lean on.

Instead, I'm alone, which is the last thing I want to be right now.

The sun climbs in the sky, and it's a scorching day. My weather app is promising a full day of sun and an unseasonable high of eighty-five when a text comes through.

BH: My parents are out of town. Care to collect on that pool day I owe you?

A smile creeps across my face, and I crawl out of my blanket cocoon. My fingers fly across the keys. This is exactly what I need. A distraction from the danger lurking around every corner. Yet before I hit send on my text, I pause. A day alone with Benton, with nothing to buffer this new weirdness between us, doesn't sound much better than hiding at home alone.

I exit the text and place a call instead.

She answers on the first ring. "Hey, Han!"

"You free today?" I ask, getting right to the point. "Benton invited me over. We're going swimming."

Gemma squeals, which I take as a yes. "Are you kidding? Benton in a swimsuit? Sign me up."

"He's a person, you know," I say, a teasing note in my voice, "not just a set of six-pack abs."

"Yeah, yeah. Pick me up in an hour," she says. I send Benton a thumbs-up emoji, change into my bathing suit, throw shorts and a tee over top, and head out the door after shooting my parents a quick text, complete with *It'll probably be safer to be around Regs while you're at work!* since Mom doesn't like changing plans last minute.

Almost exactly an hour after my call to Gem, I pull into Benton's driveway. Gemma lets out an appreciative sigh when his house comes into view. The place is so massive the word *house* doesn't do it justice. *Mansion* or *estate* might be a better fit. There's even a cursive metal sign that reads HALL over the tastefully furnished wraparound porch.

"Every time I see this house, it looks bigger." Gem sticks her head out her open window to take in the sheer size of the place. "He's so down to earth, you'd never guess his family was this loaded."

We park and climb out of the car. "The only thing about him

that screams money is his car," I agree, and bound up the marble steps. The front door is hand-carved mahogany, complete with an ornate brass knocker. I don't use it though, reaching for the door-bell instead. Deep chimes resonate throughout the house.

There's a series of metal clicks, and then the door swings open. Benton stands on the other side, clad in navy blue swim trunks and a white tank top. The smile painted on his face falters, just a bit, when he spots Gem.

"I invited Gemma to join us," I say, aiming for a blend of confidence and apology that won't offend him or hurt her. "I hope that's okay."

"Of course. The more the merrier. Come in." Benton recovers quickly and holds open the door, leading us inside.

The house feels like a museum, with art covering all the walls, but there's something homey about it. Despite the Hall family only moving to Salem three years ago, it feels like they've been in this place for generations. A series of six-foot oil paintings of middle-aged adults hangs along the staircase. At the top is an enlarged copy of Benton's senior portrait.

I stop at the bottom of the stairs, running my fingers along the beautifully carved railing. The few times Benton has hosted parties, we haven't been allowed in the main house. He keeps us sequestered to the pool house out back, which comes complete with two bathrooms and a fully stocked kitchen. "What, no oil painting for you? Is this your family line?"

Benton clears his throat, and when I turn to look at him, his face is tinged with pink. "Yup, five generations. I won't sit for the oil painting until the family decides I've made a 'significant mark on the world.'" He puts air quotes around that last phrase.

"Well, then. No pressure or anything," I tease, yet I can't

help but wonder what kind of expectations his parents put on him. I think they're both surgeons, something medical anyway. The last I heard, Benton was going to study bio in Boston, but I remember all the times he talked about majoring in graphic design and marketing. Did he decide to go the premed route, or did his parents force him?

I'm about to ask when Gemma calls from the other room. "What's all this?"

We follow her voice into the hallway, where dozens of trophies are displayed behind a glass case. The pink in Benton's cheeks turns a deep scarlet. "My mom insists on putting them here. They're from martial arts tournaments. I have another one coming up soon."

"Can you show us some moves?" Gem twirls a curl around her finger, easing into full-on flirt mode. I guess that crush from freshman year never completely died.

"You want to spar?" Benton asks, dubious, raising a single brow at Gem. She parts her lips to respond, but before she can, he scoops her up and drapes her over one shoulder. Her startled laugh fills the room.

I follow them through the house and out back. The sun is bright, stealing my view of my friends for a moment. I shield my eyes, and sweat prickles immediately along my back. It won't take long for it to slick down my spine.

"Wait, wait, wait!" Gemma shrieks as Benton nears the pool. "My phone!"

Benton sets Gem on her feet. He backs away and strips off his shirt, tossing it on a nearby lounge chair. I have to hide a laugh when Gemma freezes, her gaze tracking each of Benton's now-shirtless movements.

He gives her a curious look, completely oblivious to the effect he's having on her. "Did you want to put your phone someplace safe?"

"Right." She shakes her head like she's trying to dislodge the image of him and sets her phone on a table. I join her, dropping my bag there and pulling out my sketchbook. "Do you think he noticed?" she whispers to me.

"Noticed what? You staring? Definitely. Does he realize what that means?" I glance back at Benton, who flashes me a smile and dives into the pool. He surfaces and shakes his hair out of his eyes. "He seems pretty clueless on that front."

Gem slips the sundress over her head and plops it on the table over her phone. "Damn. I wasn't trying to be subtle."

I laugh, but for her sake and mine, I hope he catches on. They'd be cute together. Plus, if Benton gets involved with Gemma, maybe he'll stop being so weird around me. I slip out of my shorts and tank and settle into a lounge chair with my sketch-book and pencil.

"Not coming in, Hannah?" Benton asks, resting his forearms on the edge of the pool.

"I will. After the sun fries me to a crisp." I glance at him, noticing the soft pull at his brow. The sparkle of water in his hair. "Actually, could you stay right there? Don't move." I flip to a fresh page, past the now-irrelevant drawings from the scrying I did with Veronica, and sketch furiously, trying to capture the look in his eyes before it disappears.

Gemma dives in and swims up to Benton's side, laying her arms next to his. She traces her fingers along the edges of the triangle tattoo at his wrist, whispering something in his ear. He smiles, glances at me, and then whispers something back to Gem, making her laugh. Luckily, I've already finished his expression, so the new conspiratorial glint in his eye doesn't ruin my sketch. Gem pokes Benton in the shoulder, and he climbs out of the pool, dripping all over the patio.

"Hey, I wasn't done." I shield my sketch from his dripping limbs as he comes to stand over me. "You're blocking my sun."

"Yeah?" He's trying to keep a serious expression, but his lips keep curving up. "What are you going to do about it?"

I start to respond, but a second set of wet hands grabs my sketchbook and yanks it from my grip. Benton lifts me out of the chair like I'm made of air and tosses me in the pool.

My shrieks are cut off by the splash as I go under, and the warm water welcomes my presence. Magic flares to life inside me, the water's essence cradling around me, more reassuring than even the blanket fort this morning. In here, I feel safe. Worries of the Hunter melt away. I wish I could stay under for hours, leaving the stress of the past few weeks on dry land.

A hand finds mine and tugs. I open my eyes, the chlorine stinging, and see Gemma. I shoot out of the water and wipe my hair from my face.

"Oh, thank god," Gemma says, wrapping me in a hug while our legs kick to keep us afloat. "Why didn't you come up? I thought you hit your head and were going to drown."

"I'm fine, Gem. I know how to swim." I roll my eyes at her. "Serves you right for tossing me in though." I splash her and swim away, careful to actually *swim* and not use my magic to move through the crystal-clear water.

The three of us stay in the pool until our limbs ache, our fingers prune, and our stomachs growl. Benton orders pizza and extra spicy wings, and we stretch out on the couches in the pool house, swapping stories. After checking with me for the all clear, Benton tells Gem about our investigation into the fire at Nolan's house and the brick that flew through my window.

At first, she's upset we didn't include her from the start, but soon she's coming up with motives for every one of our classmates. While Gem spins an elaborate conspiracy theory that has the entire soccer team out to overthrow their captain, Benton makes a trip into his house to grab his yearbook.

"I've been working on the note," he says when he returns, dropping the *YOU'RE NEXT* message on the table between us. It's full of creases, like Benton has folded and unfolded it hundreds of times in the last couple days. "I couldn't find any fingerprints, so I've been trying to match the handwriting to someone from my yearbook."

"That's a great idea!" Gemma gets up from her spot beside me and sits next to Benton on the loveseat. She watches as he flips through to tabbed pages in his yearbook. "Do you have any solid leads?"

"A couple, though none of them are perfect." He flips to the first of a few tabs. "The handwriting looks a little like Veronica's," he says, shooting me an apologetic look, "though I'm guessing we still don't think she's the culprit?"

I shake my head. "Definitely not." *Besides, she has plenty of ways to hurt me without throwing a brick through my window.*

"Okay, moving on." Benton flips to the next tab. "Cameron and Taylor both have similar writing, here." He points to a hastily scrawled *Have a great summer!* on the left page and a *It was so great knowing you!!!* ♥ on the right.

"What's their motive?" I ask, unconvinced. I don't know either of them well. They're both on the soccer teams—Cameron on the boys' and Taylor on the girls'—which makes me wonder if Gemma's soccer conspiracy theory might hold some weight. "I don't think I've said two words to either of them outside of class."

Gemma reaches for the next tab and turns the pages for Benton, who blushes when she leans against him for a closer look. She squints at the pages. "What about that one?" She reaches for the threatening letter on the table and holds it next to the yearbook. "The *you're* looks similar."

"Wait, let me see." I perch on the loveseat's arm and peer over Benton's shoulder. There, in all caps, is a message written in oddly familiar handwriting. *YOU'RE THE SHIT. NEVER CHANGE. —NA*

My best friend sighs. "Nolan Abbott," she grumbles. "If he threw that brick through your window, I'll kick his ass." Though she doesn't say it, especially not in front of Benton, I can practically hear the *ugh, I can't believe I made out with that jerk* running through her head.

"I thought his handwriting looked the closest, but what's his motive? Do you think he blames you for the fire at his house? He must know you're not responsible." Benton glances up at me. "Right?"

At first, I shrug. If this is about what happened at Nolan's party, a cryptic message thrown through my window is a weird way to get revenge, but could he be the Witch Hunter? I considered as much this morning at the coven meeting, but why would he toss a brick through my window, declare me his next target, and then go after Veronica the next day? It doesn't make any sense.

Gemma scoffs. "Nolan might be angry enough to threaten you, but he'll never go through with it. Trust me, he's all talk."

"So, what do we do now?" Benton asks. "Call the police?"

I shake my head. "We don't have enough for that, and I doubt they'd care about a broken window."

"I don't know, Han. Whoever it was threatened the ADA's daughter. I imagine the police take that kind of thing seriously," Gem says.

"If we go to the police, I want to bring real evidence. We need more than an amateur handwriting analysis." After my interrogation with Detective Archer, I have zero interest in talking to the police. But if we can get better proof against Nolan, maybe Lady Ariana can get the Council to check him out, just in case he is the Hunter.

"Are there traffic cameras or something we could use? See if his SUV was in the area that afternoon? I can drive by his house and get the license plate number," Benton suggests, closing his yearbook and setting it on the table.

I leave my perch on the loveseat and flop back into the couch across from Benton and Gemma. "We don't have traffic cameras in Salem," I remind him. "But my neighbors have security cameras on their garage. Maybe we could use that."

"Do you think they'd give you the footage?" Benton asks.

My excitement deflates. The neighbors in question left a few days ago for a camping trip in the Adirondacks. They'll be completely unplugged until they get back in a few weeks. But then I remember a certain new coworker's skill set. "They're out of town, but I might know someone who could hack into the feed. There's this guy at work. Supposedly, he has some serious computer skill—"

"Oh my god, Hannah!" Gemma says, cutting me off and sitting up straight on the loveseat. "I'm the worst best friend in the entire universe. I completely forgot."

"Forgot what?"

"Your date!" She scrambles over to the couch and sits beside me. "How did it go? Did you click? Did you fall in *lurve*?" she croons.

"You're ridiculous." I laugh, but the feeling quickly dies. I glance at Benton, who's suddenly hyper-focused on his pizza. We probably shouldn't talk about this in front of him, but Gemma shows no signs of backing down until she gets the full play-by-play. "Actually, I kinda blew it."

Gemma falls still. "What do you mean? What happened?"

"Veronica kept calling and texting me." I stare at my hands, trying to figure out how to explain what happened around two Regs, especially since one of them has a rather unfortunate crush on me. "I had to leave in the middle of our date."

"You didn't. Please tell me you didn't." Gemma leans in close, bringing the smell of chlorine with her. "I thought you were over her."

"I was. I *am*. But . . ." *She was in trouble. A Witch Hunter tried to kill her.* "There was an intruder in her house. What was I supposed to do?"

Benton perks up. "Are you serious? Is she okay? Are *you* okay?"

"Yeah. I'm fine. We're both fine. She was a little shaken, you know? Her parents are out of town, so she stayed over at my place." Memory of Veronica's advances and accusations sours my mood further. "Or at least, she was supposed to. We got in a fight and she took off."

"Holy shit, Hannah. Why didn't you say something?" Benton wipes sauce from his hands and reaches for his phone. "Do you think this is connected to the fire? Could it have been Nolan?" He pulls up his notes app.

"Wait, we can get to that later." Gemma waves Benton's questions away. "Did you at least text Morgan to explain why you bailed?"

"Umm, no?"

"Hannah Marie Walsh," Gemma says in a perfect imitation of my mother's voice, "you need to apologize to Morgan if you want a second date."

"I know." I groan and flop back against the couch, staring at the exposed beams of the pool house ceiling. "But I can't just text her. That seems too small for what I did."

"Why not?" Benton asks. "A text is better than nothing."

Gemma ignores him. "We'll think of something perfect. A grand gesture that says 'I'm sorry' without looking like you're trying too hard."

"It has to be soon though. It's already been over a day."

"But why—" Benton tries, but we both shush him.

Gemma's eyes grow wide. A grin lights up her face. "I have just the thing."

+   *   +

When I go to work the next day, Lauren won't stop looking at me. A few days ago, I might have chalked up her interest as the worry of a highly perceptive boss. I couldn't muster my usual level of cheer when I clocked in this morning, and I'm sure the forced curve of my lips set off her Concerned Adult mode.

But now my mind goes to a more insidious place.

What if Lauren really is a Witch Hunter? It's possible she noticed Veronica spelling the air that day before the bonfire.

I shake the thoughts away and focus on my work. The display

of tarot and oracle decks is already meticulously ordered, but I adjust the angles again anyway, making sure they're perfect. I turn to work on the runes and nearly jump out of my skin.

Savannah stands before me, a hand cocked on her hip and a scowl on her face. She looks pissed, but I have no idea why.

"Hi, Savannah. I hope you weren't waiting too long," I say, my face flaming. "Can I help you find something?"

"You want to help me? Stay away from Veronica. You've done enough damage."

"Damage?" I have no clue what she's talking about.

Savannah rolls her eyes. "You heard me. She told me everything. How you flirted with her and got her hopes up just so you could reject her again. You humiliated her."

"But I didn't—"

"Save it." She comes in close, her flowery perfume overpowering. "If you don't leave Ronnie alone, I *will* hurt you."

There's nothing I can say to convince her she's wrong—Veronica clearly spun what happened to make me the bad guy—so I keep quiet. Savannah seems satisfied by my silence. She turns on her heel and slips out the front door.

"What was that about?" Lauren's voice startles me, and she reaches out a steadying hand. "I didn't mean to scare you."

"It's fine. Do you need me on the register?" The shop is busier than usual, and Cal casts a frazzled look our way as his line grows to five customers deep.

Lauren glances back at the front counter, a frown pulling at her lips. "Maybe in a minute. I wanted to ask you about something."

"Ask about what?"

Lauren fidgets, fussing with the pentacle she wears around

her neck. "Your energy is different today. Withdrawn." She steps closer and lowers her voice as a customer wanders past. "Is everything okay at home?"

"Home is the least of my worries," I say without thinking. I stumble over what to say next. It's not like I can tell her about yesterday's coven meeting or the threats hanging over us.

"Something else then?" she prompts. "If there's anything I can do to help, please don't hesitate to ask. I'm worried about you."

Her concern blossoms a seed of guilt in my chest for thinking she was a Witch Hunter. But maybe that's what she wants? I sigh internally. Being suspicious of everyone is exhausting.

The bells chime above the door, and I use the excuse to turn away. "I should really help with the register."

"Hannah."

"Hey, Lauren," a man says behind me. Chills run down my arms. I know that voice.

Lauren's cheeks flush pink. "Ryan. Hi." She brushes her hair out of her face. "I didn't think I'd see you until tonight."

Detective Archer smiles, his attention focused on my boss. He seems genuinely happy to see her, but I can't stop the bad feeling that crawls across my skin like a legion of bugs. What if he's the Witch Hunter? None of this started until he showed up in town.

"I was in the neighborhood. Thought I'd drop by and see if you were free for coffee." Detective Archer—who's apparently *Ryan* to my boss—rests one hand on his belt. The movement pushes his navy suit jacket back enough to display his badge. And his gun. He glances down, eyes narrowing almost imperceptibly. "Miss Walsh, I forgot you worked here."

"I do." I stare up at the detective who nearly had me confessing to witchcraft in an interrogation room. *Exactly the sort of thing a Witch Hunter would do.* Somehow, I doubt my presence here is truly the surprise he's pretending it is.

Lauren glances between us, a smile plastered on her face. "Hannah's a fabulous employee. She's always on time, and she's learned a ton since she started working for me." Lauren continues to gush, like she's a mother bragging about her child getting into advanced classes, which adds thorns to the blooming guilt in my chest. Finally, she takes a deep breath. "So, how do you know Hannah?"

Detective Archer shifts, his jacket falling forward to hide his weapon. He considers me a long moment before responding. "Our paths keep crossing around town." He smiles at Lauren, and his crush would be cuter if he wasn't such a likely suspect.

I clear my throat, interrupting the weirdly intimate staring contest they've got going on. "What the detective means to say is that he almost arrested me last week."

"He what?" Lauren's jaw practically hits the floor. Detective Archer glares at me, which only eggs me on further.

"He thinks I'm the one who tried to burn down Nolan's house."

"Oh, Ryan." Lauren puts a protective hand on my shoulder. "There is no way Hannah's involved in something like that. She's as good as they come."

The detective runs a hand through his hair. He heaves a sigh that goes all the way to his toes. "I can't talk about an open case, but it's a matter of public record that I didn't file charges against Miss Walsh. She was only in for questioning."

Lauren's eyes go wide, and when she looks at the detective

again, there's a hint of suspicion in the pull of her brow. "Goddess, Hannah. No wonder your aura is so subdued."

The bell on the front counter rings. The three of us turn to look. Cal nods to the growing line in front of him, his shoulders high and tensed.

"Hannah, why don't you help with the line? Ryan and I are going to talk in the back for a bit." Lauren practically pushes the detective toward the STAFF ONLY door, ignoring his protests. Her shoulders are set, her brows pinched together. She's in full-on mama bear mode. I should bake her thank-you cookies. Plus a sorry-I-thought-you-were-a-Witch-Hunter cake.

I weave my way through the cramped store and take over the register, doubling the speed of the checkout line while Cal bags up purchases.

Once we're through the line, Cal glances toward the back of the shop. "What's the deal with you and Detective Archer?"

"He's convinced I'm some kind of delinquent." I lean against the counter, but then something about Cal's question trips me up. "Wait, how do you know him?" I don't remember mentioning his name to Cal.

Cal shrugs, though his pale skin flushes pink. "The detective's in here a lot. I think he has a thing for our boss."

I don't understand the embarrassment riding high in Cal's tone. "Do you have a crush on him or something? I thought you already had a boyfriend."

"Eww, god, no. The detective is way too old for me." Cal pulls out his phone and flips through his pictures. "Besides, my boyfriend is way cuter." He shows me a photo of himself standing next to a considerably taller boy with dark hair, light brown skin, and a prominently squared chin.

"He's cute," I agree, "for a boy."

Cal laughs and tucks his phone away.

"Could I ask you for a favor actually?" I glance behind me to make sure we're alone. "If you're as good with computers as you say you are, that is."

"Depends." Cal considers me, his brow knit. "You don't want me to break into a bank or something, do you?"

"Nothing so scandalous, I promise." I fill him in on the brick incident. "My friends and I were hoping you might be able to get access to my neighbor's security camera and see if Nolan's car makes an appearance around that time."

"Couldn't you just ask your neighbor for the tapes?"

"They're out of town until—" The bell on the counter chimes, cutting me off.

"Excuse me? I'm looking for my best friend. Maybe you've seen her around somewhere?" Gemma says, and I turn around. "She's about this tall and suffers from a chronic case of sarcasm. It's very unsightly."

I roll my eyes. "Hey, Gem."

She grins. "Got a minute?"

"Umm." I turn to Cal, who nods. "And about the camera?"

"I'll think about it. Now go ahead. I'll ring the bell if I need you."

"Thanks." I lead Gemma down the book aisle where there's the fewest customers. "What's up?"

"Do you have everything ready for Operation: Apology Ambush?" Gem steps back and sweeps her gaze over my outfit. "Please tell me you packed a change of clothes."

"Of course I did." I'm not going to beg for forgiveness wearing the same work uniform I wore to the disastrous first date.

"And I finished my apology gift this morning. It's in my bag."

"Perfect!" Gemma reaches out and straightens my name tag. "How much longer do you have in your shift?"

I pull my phone from my back pocket and check the clock. "About twenty minutes."

"And you know what you're going to say when you see her?"

Not exactly. My apology works on a surface level—she can't blame me for being worried about an ex who was under attack—but if she digs into why I went to her house instead of calling the police, things get tricky.

"Hannah."

"I'll think of something," I say, not altogether confident in my ability to pull this off.

Gemma shakes her head. "This has to be perfect. Come on, practice on me."

"Do we have to?"

"Yes."

I groan, but we practice until my apology is perfect.

15

I HOLD A SMALL box tied with ribbons and stand immobile outside the dressing room door. I can't believe I let Gemma talk me into this. Tonight's the dress rehearsal for their spring dance recital, and Gemma thought this would be the perfect chance to surprise Morgan with an in-person apology. The grand gesture sounded exciting, but now I feel ridiculous.

The door swings open, and Gem sticks her head out into the hallway. Her blonde hair is pulled into a perfect dancer's bun with enough hairspray to set fire to the whole building. The exaggerated makeup looks cartoonish close up but will make her features pop when she's onstage.

She scowls at me. "Hurry up. We have to be backstage in five."

"Perfect. I'll be ready in ten."

"You're impossible." Gemma rolls her eyes and reaches into the hall. She latches on to my free arm and drags me through the door.

The toxic, too-sweet smell of forty kinds of hairspray assaults my nose. Dancers of all ages, from four-year-old baby ballerinas to high school seniors in pointe shoes, mill about the room.

Now that I'm here, the hustle and bustle of the dressing room seems like the worst possible place to apologize to someone for ditching them in the middle of a date.

"She's over there, with the level two kids." Gem gestures vaguely to the right and hurries off to a group of dancers whose bright-pink tutus match hers.

I glance in the direction Gem pointed, but I don't see Morgan anywhere in the crush of flustered parents. "Where?"

Gemma spins back to face me, rising into the air as she balances on the toes of her pointe shoes. "Over there. With the six-year-old tap dancers."

This time when I look though the scrambling masses, I spot kids in black sparkly costumes and tap shoes click-clacking on the hardwood floor. Among the older adults adjusting bows and tying ribbons, I spot a flash of red hair.

Gripping the delicate box harder than I should, I weave my way across the room to the energetic baby dancers. Their cheeks are flushed with an excitement that cuts through even the thickest coats of makeup. Halfway there, I catch sight of Morgan, and the air leaves my lungs in a rush.

Unlike all the other dancers in the room, Morgan's hair falls in waves past her shoulders. The jeans sitting snug on her hips mold to her curves, and the plain green tee looks comfy and well worn compared to the sparkling new outfits around her. Her face is free of makeup, and it makes her look real, almost vulnerable, amid dozens of dancers who wear blush like armor. She must have moved to Salem too late in the rehearsal season to perform in the recital.

Morgan glances up and catches me staring from the center of the room. Dancers and parents brush past me, but I'm an unmovable boulder stuck in a river's mighty current. Morgan raises one brow in a silent question. I lift my offering higher, into her line of sight.

The beginnings of a smile light her face, but then someone clears their throat. Loudly.

"All right, people." The director of the dance studio stands in the doorway, surveying the chaos. "People!" When no one responds, she claps her hands in a quick rhythm. Dancers and helpers alike stop what they're doing to repeat the pattern. Silence falls over the crowd. "Right then. Let's get this show on the road. Level five, you're up first. Level two is on deck. Parents, let's get our tap dancers waiting in the wings. Everyone else, I want you in the audience. Move out!"

Noise swells as dancers check their reflections in mirrors one last time and hurry out of the room. I lose Morgan in the rush for the door; the box falls to my side, the contents jostling. So much for Gem's master plan. I turn to leave.

"Is that for me?"

Morgan's voice washes over me like the mist off a waterfall. Gentle yet inescapable.

I pause, my feet rooting to the earth. I tuck a loose strand of hair behind my ear and wish I had done something more than a messy bun this morning. "Yeah." With a final breath to steady my nerves, I face the near-empty room. "There's a card, too."

"What's in there?" She approaches cautiously, and I hold up the box for her. With gentle, sure fingers, she unties the bow and reaches for the card. "Did you make this?"

Heat burns my cheeks, but I nod. "I thought that might last longer than real flowers."

Morgan traces a finger along the edge of the card I painted for her last night. The front is a scene of wildflowers, done in watercolors. I may have cheated slightly, using my magic to shift the colors around the paper just so. Inside, I painted the background in overlapping splotches of pink, purple, and blue and used a calligraphy set I got last year for my birthday to write in my fanciest script *I'm Sorry*.

"This is beautiful," she says, her words breathy. Then she tilts her head to one side, holding the card at arm's length. "Was the color choice intentional? It looks like the—"

"Bi pride flag?" I finish. "Yeah. The whole thing is an apology for bailing on our date, but I'm also sorry for assuming you couldn't be out and date a guy."

She nods and falls quiet, tracing her fingers along the edge of the card. Finally, she gives herself a small nod. "What's in the box?"

"Remember the first night we met? You asked me to bake for you." I lift the lid, revealing my favorite homemade chocolate chip cookies. "I figured now was as good a time as any."

Morgan smiles wide and takes the top cookie out of the box. "You really didn't have to go all out. A text would have been fine." She takes a bite and her entire body shudders with delight. "Not that I'm complaining. These are delicious."

Her approval warms me from the inside out as she finishes the cookie. "I'm glad you like them. I swear I'm not usually that flaky."

"I get it." Morgan takes the box from me, carefully securing the lid. "It's okay if you're not over your ex. I shouldn't have rushed you into something new."

"But I am. I swear. I'm totally over Veronica."

"Really, Hannah. It's okay. You don't need to make up excuses. If you want to be friends, I understand."

My heart sinks, falls straight to my feet, and plummets into the earth. "Is that what you want?"

"I don't know." She traces the top of the pastry box instead of looking at me. "The cookies and the card are great, really, they are. But when I'm with someone, I want to land the part of girlfriend, not understudy for an ex."

"It's not like that."

"Isn't it? She called you nonstop until you picked up. And when you did, you immediately ran out to be with her." Morgan crosses her arms. "What am I supposed to think?"

That same lock of hair falls free again, and I shove it back into place. I didn't want to bring this up, but I won't let Veronica ruin this for me. "There was an intruder in her house."

"What?" Morgan looks up, concern tightening her voice. "Is she okay?"

"Yeah, she's fine." I interlock my fingers and flatten my hands on top of my head. "We think he was there to rob the house and didn't realize Veronica was home. She startled him when she came out of the bathroom."

Morgan lets out a long sigh. "Wow. I'm sorry." She taps her fingers along the top of the box. "I feel like a terrible person."

"You didn't know."

Morgan looks up and meets my eye, holding my gaze with a challenge in her own. "So, you're really over her then? She's not your leading lady anymore?"

A flicker of hope burns inside me. "That spot is currently wide open."

Morgan blushes, and it's the cutest thing I've ever seen in my entire life. Second perhaps to the way she bites her lip when she tries to hide her smile. "Good to know."

All my earlier nerves fall away. "Does that mean I get a do-over? I owe you a much better first-date experience."

Morgan considers me. She taps her chin and stares up at the ceiling in mock consideration. "Hmm . . . I don't really believe in do-overs." She pauses long enough to let my heart ricochet around in my chest. Long enough for me to panic. "But you can take me out on a second date."

I have to restrain myself from breaking out into my horribly embarrassing happy dance. "You won't regret it. I promise." I smile so hard my cheeks hurt. I could give her a proper tour of Salem and show her all my favorite spots. "I just have one more question."

Morgan inches closer until we're sharing the same air, the same breath. "Ask me anything." Her words whisper across my skin, full of promise.

A wave of uncertainty crashes over me, but I meet Morgan's gaze and find my courage. "Can I kiss you?"

Morgan wraps her arms around my neck, the edge of the pastry box poking into my back, but I don't even care. "I thought you'd never ask."

She leans forward, and I pull her close, pressing my forehead to hers. The air tingles with power between us, sending shivers across my skin. I wait until I can't handle the anticipation a second longer.

When our lips touch, everything else fades away. All the worry. All the fear. Her lips are soft and warm against mine. She tastes like berry lip balm and second chances and endless possibilities.

I never want this moment to end.

-|-　＊　-|-

Morgan and I spend the rest of dress rehearsal in the back row of the theater. She provides commentary for the pieces, explaining the difference between contemporary and modern styles of dance and detailing the long routine of preparing pointe shoes.

I try to hold on to all the things she says, every last word, but when she kisses me again, language loses its meaning. Around hour two, I gather up the courage to hold her hand during a particularly moving piece by the modern group. Or maybe contemporary. They look so similar, and I've already forgotten the difference.

As rehearsal winds down, Morgan disappears to help out backstage and in the dressing rooms. She plants a kiss on my cheek before she goes, leaving me a blushing mess in my seat.

Gemma plops down next to me a few minutes later. She's replaced her costume with old jeans and a loose-fitting T-shirt. "Morgan seems in good spirits."

"I think it's safe to say she forgives me. She liked the cookies." She did, however, request a text next time something comes up, so she's not left worrying. She said she spent almost two days trying to figure out what she had said or done to send me running away without a word.

A niggling bit of guilt still gnaws at my insides over that.

Gemma nudges me with her shoulder. "You gotta give me more than that. This was *my* master plan, after all."

I lean back and stare up at the rafters of the auditorium. One of the lights flickers like it's about to die, fading in and out like a lightning bug. "You know I don't kiss and tell, Gem."

"Since when? I swear, I know more about your sex life than my own sometimes."

That gets a laugh, which I hasten to cover when a parent shoots a stern look my way. "This thing with Morgan . . . It's too new. I'm not ready to jinx it by blabbing." I stand and stretch my limbs. My phone buzzes. It's a text from Morgan, saying her dad's there to pick her up and we'll talk soon. "Are you ready to go?" We're at a recital hall in Beverly, and I promised to drive Gem home after.

Gemma reaches out a hand, and I help her to her feet. Her movements are as fluid as ever, but there's a cautiousness to her steps. She's clearly exhausted from rehearsal. We exit the theater together, night falling like a blanket to snuff out the light, and Gem has me walk her through every second of my apology. When I pull onto the main road, I have to flip my rearview mirror to keep the bright lights of other cars out of my eyes.

"So, what's the plan for your second date?" Gemma reaches for the lever and leans her seat back, sighing as she stretches out her long limbs. "Will you go the dinner-and-a-movie route? Ooh, or maybe you could take her to the psychic fair coming into town next week."

"I haven't really decided yet," I say, knowing there's zero chance I'll take Morgan to a psychic. I won't even let Lauren read my tarot. I turn onto the Essex Bridge to take us back into Salem. "What about you and Benton? How're your plans for a summer fling going?"

Gemma groans. "Terrible. The boy's hot, but damn is he dense."

"That bad, huh?"

"I mean, he's clearly an intelligent human being, but he hasn't picked up a single one of my hints." Gem turns to look at me, and a shot of guilt punctures my heart. "He's infuriating."

"That sucks, Gemma. I'm sorry." Behind me, someone turns

on their brights, burning my eyes despite the adjusted rearview mirror. "I feel like that's partially my fault. Apparently, Benton forgot I was gay and developed a bit of a crush on me."

"How do you forget someone's gay?"

"That's a great quest—"

Someone slams into us from behind. The seat belt digs into my chest as I jolt forward. I look in the mirror, but whoever it was isn't behind us anymore. "Are you all right?" I ask, my hands shaky on the wheel.

"Look out!"

A large SUV pulls up alongside us, the windows tinted too dark to see the driver inside. They swerve, smashing into the side of our car. We slam into the concrete-and-metal guardrail lining the bridge. Gemma's door caves in, and she screams, a bone-chilling sound that wraps around the base of my spine. Her window implodes, and there's a screech of tires. The SUV backs up, crossing two lanes of traffic, then jerks forward, gathering speed and slamming into us again.

They're going to crush us. They're going to kill us.

I reach for the bits of earth energy in the concrete barrier. I push with every ounce of my adrenaline-fueled magic.

Break. Please break.

At first there's nothing but Gemma's screams and the prickles of pain along my skin and the revving of the SUV's engine in my ears.

And then finally, an explosion of dust and debris as the concrete barrier gives way. Our car rushes through the gap and plummets into the frigid water below.

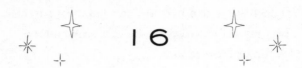

16

A SHOCK OF PAIN slams against my chest as the car lands in the river. Water pours through the broken window, the cold numbing my feet, my calves, my thighs. Gemma's screams fill my head, leaving room for only one other thought.

I don't want to die.

Magic surges beneath my skin, and I don't care if this sends me to the Council. I don't care if I lose my power. I'm not ready to die. I'm not ready to lose my best friend, especially not to a Witch Hunter. I reach a hand across the front seat and press against the broken window with my magic. The water moves fast, too fast, and I can't get a grip on its energy. Panic rises with the waves, the frigid water reaching my belly button, then my ribs.

"Hannah," Gemma says, her screams turning into sobs. "I don't want to die."

"I know," I say, pushing harder and finally, *finally* finding a hold in the river's power. "Just stay calm." I push with all my strength and the water stops rushing in through the window, rolling over the broken glass and continuing along the length of the car as we sink farther and farther beneath the surface.

Gemma leans away from the scene of my magic. "What's happening? How—" She turns to me, eyes wide, cheeks streaked with tears and mascara. "Is that you? How are you doing that?"

"You're hallucinating," I lie. "From the shock." I stare through my unbroken window, looking for a way out of this that protects my secret. I can't raise the car out of the water. I don't have that kind of power, and even if I did, there would be too many witnesses. The magic would be too obvious.

I unbuckle my seat belt and reach for the lever under my seat, pushing my chair as far back as it will go. We'll have to swim. Or at least make it look like we're swimming. I should have enough strength to pull us to the surface and back to shore.

If we can get out of this sinking car.

"What are you doing?" Gemma asks, her arms trembling from cold and fear and adrenaline.

"I'm making sure we don't drown." I reach into the water and unbuckle her seat belt. "Can you get out through your window?"

Gem tries to pull herself up, but she cries out and falls back, squeezing her eyes shut. "It hurts. Holy fuck it hurts."

"Where?" I reach my hands into the water, trying to feel for what might be wrong.

"My leg." Her hands disappear under the water. For a moment, she's silent. Then the tears start again. "It's trapped by the door." Sobs choke her, and she reaches for my arm. "What if it's broken? What if I can't dance?"

My panic rises to meet hers, and a thin stream of water breaks through my barrier. I force the worry away and throw more magic at the shattered window. I have to keep out as much of the water as I can until I have a plan. "Look at me, Gemma. Look. We're going to get out of this. I need you to hold as still as you can, okay?"

She nods, and I close my eyes, slipping my awareness into the water that's already past my elbows and halfway to my shoulders. The thread of magic slides along her legs, and my stomach clenches when I touch exposed bone. Jagged metal has torn through skin and muscle. I force my attention on the broken door, on the thin stream of water separating it from Gemma's body, and then I *push*.

Her screams pierce the small, cramped space between us, but the water's pressure bows the door back out, freeing her leg. The water turns pink. Then red.

"No, no, no, no." That's too much blood. Way too much blood. Gemma's eyes go glassy. Her words slur as she tries to speak, and then her head lolls back against the headrest. We have to go. We have to get back to the surface.

I can't climb over Gem without hurting her more, so I reach for the handle and shove my shoulder into the door. The pressure of the water rushing past keeps it closed. I scream, shoving harder and pushing the water inside the car against the metal, forcing it open. The entire door rips off at the hinges, floating away on the current. Water rushes into the car, faster than before, but it doesn't matter now. We have to go.

"Come on, Gem." I thread my arms under hers. "Deep breath." I inhale a lungful of air and tug us out of the car and into the current.

The water buffets us up and down, spinning us until it's hard to tell which way is up. Only the car's descent helps me find my bearings. I pull on my magic one more time, begging the water to carry us to the surface. Pain floods my body, screaming through bone and flesh and blood, but my magic obeys.

We burst above the waves, and I gasp for air, shivering and crying and afraid my toes are going to fall off from the cold. I pull one of Gemma's arms over my shoulders, and her head knocks against mine.

She's not breathing.

I swim toward the first land I see, the last of my magic pushing us swiftly toward civilization. Over the clinging scent of the water, I catch a whiff of fries and seafood as I pull Gemma onto the rocky shore. I can only hope the Hunter who pushed us off the bridge didn't wait around to see if we survived.

"Somebody help!" I scream, pulling Gem higher onto the rocks. Blood slides down her leg, coating the wet stones. "Please!" My vision swims, and I collapse against the rocks, knocking my elbow. The pain finally dislodging the tears I've been holding back.

There's a rush of movement. Strong arms lift Gemma and carry her up the incline. Hands help me to my feet and deposit me in a chair as a man lays Gemma flat on her back and listens for breath. I try to tell him she's not breathing, that she hasn't been, but before I can get a word in, he's pinching her nose and blowing into her mouth.

"Hannah?" A familiar voice calls over the growing noise around me. A figure darts forward out of the growing crowd.

I glance up. Lauren. With Detective Archer on her heels.

Fear forces energy into my limbs. I shoot out of my chair, backing away. "It was you." My mind races to keep up. They're the Hunters. Both of them. They have to be. Why else would they be here, lying in wait to see if their plan worked? To see if they managed to kill me.

"Hannah, what's wrong?" Lauren reaches for me, but I pull away.

I turn to run, but my wet shoes squeak against the ground. They slip. I fall.

The last thing I remember is Lauren and Archer standing above me.

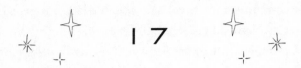

17

WHEN I WAKE, MY head feels stuffed with clouds and every inch of me hurts so much I'm afraid to move. Mom sits in a chair beside me, a book propped open on her lap. Machines beep in time with my heart. I glance down. Someone removed my clothes and put me in one of those flimsy hospital gowns. An IV needle is attached to the back of my hand, a second one in the crook of my arm.

"Hannah?" Mom sets her book on the little nightstand between us and comes to sit at the edge of my bed. "How are you feeling?"

"I don't know," I say, and try to focus my muddled brain. I wiggle my toes and force myself to sit upright in the bed. My muscles strain, stiff with overuse, but I think I'm still in one piece. "Okay, I guess. What happened? What day is it?" Bright sunlight filters in through the curtains.

A crease of worry appears on Mom's forehead. "You were in a car accident last night. Don't you remember?"

Memories burst forth, Mom's words like dynamite in a dam. I took Gemma to rehearsal so I could apologize to Morgan. Heat rushes to my face. We stole kisses at the back of the theater. But then there's the bright headlights and the giant SUV. The crunch of metal and the freezing cold water spilling through Gemma's window.

Gemma.

The machines around me race in time with my frantic heart. "Is she okay? What happened to her?"

"Gemma will be all right." Mom brushes my hair from my face and rests a hand on my shoulder. "She's resting. She was in surgery most of the night for her leg."

Her screams fill my head. Her fear. The blood staining the water as we sank. Tears pool in my eyes until my mom is a blur of color. "It was the Hunter," I whisper, my words coming out shaky and raw. "He ran us off the road. *They* did. The detective and Lauren. I saw them."

"Your boss?"

"She was there, Mom. Her and the detective. They found us at that restaurant. It has to be them." They must have doubled back after they shoved us over the bridge to make sure their job was complete.

Mom shakes her head. "Lauren's the one who called to let us know what happened. She and the detective were on a date. They were ordering dinner when your car went over the bridge." She shudders, and her eyes sparkle with unshed tears. "It wasn't them."

"But—"

"It's not them, Hannah. We will find the Hunter, I promise. Your father is at the police station right now, making sure we get answers and keeping the coven off their radar." She kisses my forehead and stands up from the bed. "There is something I need to ask you."

"What is it?"

"Gemma," Mom says, her eyes searching mine. "Does she know?"

The stupid heart rate monitor marks the fear quickening my

pulse. No one can know what Gemma saw, what I had to do in front of her. "She doesn't know anything. She lost consciousness when we hit the water."

Mom lets out a deep sigh. "Good. Okay. That's one less problem to worry about."

Guilt digs its jagged talons into my chest, working between my ribs. She was hurt because of *me*. And if anyone finds out what she knows, it'll only get worse. Instinctively, I reach for my phone so I can text her, only to remember that it's with my car, at the bottom of the river. "Can I see her?"

"Sure." Mom calls for a doctor to get me examined and approved for discharge. I'm told to get plenty of rest. My parents brought fresh clothes with them to the hospital, and I'm beyond grateful to slip into clean yoga pants and an extra-soft T-shirt.

Before we can leave for Gemma's room, there's a sharp knock on my door. Mom opens it, and Detective Archer steps through. He's wearing a slim-fitted black suit today, a far cry from the casual jeans and polo he was wearing last night with Lauren.

I reach for my mom's hand, pulling her close. "I don't want to speak with him."

"Hannah, we talked about this," she whispers. "It wasn't the detective."

"How do you know? He could have an accomplice."

Mom sighs and looks to Detective Archer. He nods. "Go ahead, Marie. You can tell her."

"Tell me what?" I step away from my mother. "Why does he know your name?"

"Hannah, Detective Archer is an agent with the Council." Mom's words rattle around in my brain like rocks spun in a can. "Your grandmother met with him and his assistant last night."

"But he's . . ." My words wander off, and I piece together every interaction I've had with the detective since he arrived at the bonfire in the woods. His interest in signs of witchcraft. His interrogation after the fire at Nolan's house. Was he searching for proof of an out-of-control Elemental? Was he investigating *me*? "I don't understand."

"I'm sorry for the deception, Miss Walsh." Detective Archer— who's really *Agent* Archer—takes out the little notebook from his inside pocket. "What can you tell me about the accident last night?"

I shake my head, trying to place Archer's Clan. He's not an Elemental. I would have noticed his power right away. The Council always has at least one Blood Witch among their ranks, sometimes two. Could that be him? Did he draw those runes to flush out the Hunters? Does Blood Magic even work that way?

Detective Archer looks up from his notebook. "I'm a Caster."

"Oh, I wasn't—"

"You were. Now please, Miss Walsh, last night?" He taps his pen on his notebook.

Annoyance flares inside me, but I force it down. This man is an agent for the *Council*. One wrong step and he could recommend that the Elders take my magic. So I tell my story, making sure to emphasize that Gemma saw nothing. That she's completely innocent in all this, a victim the same as me. More even, since she was hurt because of *my* affiliation with the Clans, something she knows nothing about.

What I don't say, despite it being heavy in my mind, is that this is *his* fault.

The Council is supposed to protect us from Witch Hunters. Where was Archer when that SUV ran me off the road? Where was he when a Hunter attacked Veronica in her home? Was he too busy making heart eyes at my boss to do his job?

"Can I see Gemma now?" I ask, directing the question at my mom. I'm anxious to see her, to see if she remembers what happened, and my stomach is growling. I don't know how many meals I've missed. Two at least, maybe three.

Detective Archer nods, like the question was meant for him. "Of course. I have to question her anyway."

"Can I have a few minutes alone with her?" I ask, hoping I don't sound as guilty as I feel. "She's my best friend."

He looks to Mom, who nods. "You can have five minutes, but then I will need to question her and see what she remembers about the crash." Though he doesn't specify, I know exactly what kind of memory he's searching for.

I follow the detective through the hospital, trying my best to keep my face neutral. Despite the soreness in my body and the onslaught of worries in my head, I keep pace with the Council's agent. He stops when we round a corner and gestures down the hall. "She's in room 408. I'll wait here. Five minutes, Miss Walsh."

"Thank you," I say, my words high and squeaky. Nervous sweat coats my palms as I inch down the hallway. Through the open door, I spot Gemma's parents, and my fear grows toxic. Mrs. Goodwin looks like she could be Gem's older sister. They share the same face, if separated by three decades of experience and stress. She sits on the edge of Gemma's bed, much like my mom did with me. Gemma's leg is wrapped in a bright-pink cast and suspended above the bed by cloth slings.

My heart lurches in my chest. She's alive. Mom said she was fine, but seeing her awake and sitting up with her parents sends tears rushing to my eyes.

Mr. Goodwin stands beside the bed. Where Mrs. Goodwin is grace and poise, her husband is solid and earthy. He's a burly man, clad in flannel and the thick hipster glasses he's had since forever. Well before *hipster* was a thing. He runs a hand over his beard, a nervous gesture I've seen before. He glances to the hallway.

And spots me.

His gaze goes hard, and I knock on the open doorframe. "Hey." The rest of my words dry up. How am I going to explain this to her parents? They've spent the last year afraid I would turn their daughter into a lesbian. Instead, the witch in me has landed her in the hospital.

"Hannah!" Gemma reaches for me, her eyes spilling over with tears. "You're okay. No one would tell me anything."

I step forward to embrace my best friend, but Mrs. Goodwin blocks my path. "I thought I told the nurses we didn't want any visitors."

"Mom," Gemma snaps, but the blow has already landed. I fall back a step, bracing an arm on the door.

"I'm sorry," I say. "I'll go."

"You're not going anywhere," Gemma says at the same time her mom says, "Good."

Gem glares at her mother. "Hannah saved my life last night. You can't just throw her out of my room. I'd be dead right now without her."

"I'm your mother," Mrs. Goodwin replies, voice so stern it makes me want to disappear. "I have every right to send away the girl who put you in danger in the first place."

"Oh my god, Mom. Stop it. I told you, someone hit *us*. It wasn't Hannah's fault."

"She's a bad influence on you. Always has been. I told you to stay away from her."

"That's bullshit, Mom, and you know it."

"Language, Gemma," Mrs. Goodwin snaps. She stands from the bed and rests her hands on her hips. "This is exactly the kind of thing I don't want you picking up from her."

"Are you sure?" Gemma's voice is deceptively sweet. "Or are you worried I'll catch her gayness?" The whole room goes dead. Silent. Frozen. "You used to love Hannah," Gemma continues, her voice soft. "And things have been weird since she came out. I went along with your new rules, because I thought you needed time to adjust. But you're not adjusting. You're getting worse."

"Gemma . . ." Mrs. Goodwin says, but she doesn't seem to have any direction for her thoughts.

"I'm sorry, Mom, but you need to get over yourself. Hannah's my best friend. I love her like a sister, and I'm not letting you push her away. Especially not right after she saved my life."

A strange feeling warms my chest. Relief, I think. I didn't realize Gemma noticed all the ways her parents have treated me differently over the past year. I didn't know how much I needed her to stand up for me like this.

But the relief doesn't last. Despite what she thinks, I *am* the reason she's hurt. My magic is the reason her leg is suspended in the air and her face is pale and mottled with bruises.

Mr. Goodwin reaches for his wife's arm. "Let's give the girls a moment alone." He steers her out of the room, and she lets him.

As soon as the door clicks shut behind them, Gemma's piercing gaze turns on me. "What the hell happened last night?" she snaps, her tone still sharp from her fight with her mother.

"I wish I knew." I sit on the edge of her bed and reach for her hand. "My dad thinks it might have been a drunk driver."

"Bullshit." Gemma hurls the word at me like a weapon. "That wreck was intentional. And then you . . ." She struggles to continue, and a sick feeling squirms in my stomach. "How did you do that?" Her tone tells me she remembers. Everything.

Which means I am so fucked.

Someone knocks on the door. Panicked, I blurt out, "Don't say anything. To anyone. We'll talk soon."

"But—"

"How are you feeling, Miss Goodwin?" Detective Archer steps into the room armed with his notebook. "Ready to give your statement?"

Gem stares at me. For a moment, I worry she'll spill everything, but then she sighs and gives me a shallow nod. "Sure thing, Detective. Hannah, let's talk later." The look in her eye leaves no room to disagree.

"Of course. As soon as you're out of the hospital." I thrust a thumb toward the door. "My mom's ready to take me home."

I don't wait for either of them to dismiss me. I hurry out the door, my heart threatening to burst from my body and flop onto the hospital floor.

-|- -*- -|-

Worry picks at my brain as we drive home.

I keep reaching for my phone to see if Gemma has texted yet, demanding answers to questions she shouldn't know to ask, only to remember that both of our phones met a watery end. Then I stress about Detective Archer and what he knows about my transgressions this summer. If he's guessed the things Gemma saw me do.

And then there's Morgan. I wonder if she messaged me. If she's at home, cursing my name for ghosting her right after I apologized for the first time I ran out. It's like the entire universe is conspiring to keep us apart. First, the Hunter interrupts our date by attacking Veronica, and then he runs me and Gem off the road moments after I apologize. At least I'll be able to message and explain my silence once I get to my computer.

Dealing with Gemma's questions will be a whole lot harder.

Mom turns left, and we near Veronica's neighborhood. A thought tingles at the back of my mind. I certainly don't trust her enough to mention what Gemma saw me do, but Veronica is the only other person who's faced the Hunter head on. She'll at least understand the worry picking at my mind.

"Can we stop by Veronica's house?"

"I thought you wanted to get lunch? It's after one," Mom says without taking her eyes off the road.

My stomach growls at the mention of food, but that can wait. "Please? I need to talk to someone about last night. Someone who's not my parents." I add that second part when it looks like Mom might object.

The turn for Veronica's street is four blocks ahead. Then three. Two. Mom sighs and makes the turn. "Are you sure this is a good idea, Han? The last time you girls were in the same room, Veronica stormed out of our house."

"I doubt she'll try to make out with me this time. I smell like dead fish."

Mom crinkles her nose. "I wasn't going to say anything, but yeah. You do." She laughs, and it's the first time she's even smiled since I woke up in the hospital. She pulls into Veronica's driveway and waves to Sarah Gillow, who's serving her shift of protection detail. Mom waits in the car as I climb out.

I nod to Sarah and hike up the three steps to Veronica's front door, my wobbly legs protesting each stair. I knock, but no one answers.

"Veronica?" I knock again and check the door. It's unlocked, so I ease it open. "Veronica?" The familiar house is silent and protests my intrusion. The air is charged with an energy I can't place.

The main floor is empty: kitchen, dining room, and living room. Even the laundry room is vacant, though I doubt Veronica ever sets foot in there. I find myself back in the front of the house with only the second floor left to search. The unusual energy grows stronger by the stairs. Worry creeps over my skin. "Veronica?"

Upstairs, the first two bedroom doors are open and empty. Veronica's parents are likely at work, and her little brother is still with their grandparents. I pause before Veronica's room. The door is only open a crack, just enough for the sounds of heavy breathing to reach the hallway where I stand.

My head fills with images of Veronica lying on the floor, bleeding out from the Hunter's second attempt on her life.

Veronica's voice comes through the door, broken and needy, pulling me from my thoughts. Her words lost to a gasp.

I slam open the door. It bangs against the wall, the noise too loud, too sharp in the otherwise silent house.

The scene before me doesn't compute.

Veronica gasps and reaches for the sheet, pulling it up to cover her naked body.

Hers . . .

And Savannah's.

"What the hell are you doing here?" Veronica snaps at me as she adjusts her covers, her already flushed face burning scarlet.

I stand there, staring like an absolute creep but unable to look away. To even blink.

Savannah's eyes fill with tears as she covers herself with the discarded blanket. "You can't tell anyone. *Please.* Promise you won't say anything."

Her panic shakes the numbness from my body, and I finally turn away, closing the door behind me. A deep hurt rises up from my core as I stumble down the familiar stairs, and I want to scrape the sight of them together out of my mind, burn the image away with acid.

How could she? After giving me so much shit about a simple first date.

"Hannah, what's wrong? Is Veronica hurt?" Mom asks the second I slide into the front seat. "Why are you crying?"

I wipe the moisture from my cheeks. I didn't realize I was.

18

I REFUSE TO SPEAK to Mom on the ride home. Tears coat my eyes, turning our sleepy neighborhood streets into a smear of color, like paints dripping down a canvas.

Our driveway is still empty—Dad isn't home yet and my car will never return. Mom swings into her usual spot and shifts into park. The car jostles as it settles to a stop, and the movement breaks the dam on my eyes. Something snaps deep inside and tears spill over. I reach for the latch and practically fall out of the car as the sobs catch in my chest. Mom calls after me, but I don't stop.

I am so done with this.

Veronica has hurt me too many times. She doesn't get to be part of my life anymore. I want a total annihilation of her presence. Wind whips around me as I head for the door, left unlocked in my parents' haste to get to me last night. Leaves rattle in the trees above me. The earth rumbles. The whole world trembles in the presence of my rage. But my magic cries out for more. Cries out for *fire*.

My fingers tingle with need. All it'll take is a spark, the tiniest ignition, and I can burn away every memory of the girl who broke my heart. I'm inside a second later, the door slamming shut behind me from a gust of wind. I know the punishment from Mom will be swift on my heels, but I can't stop. I race up the stairs and burst into my room. The air around me grows aggressive, tearing at my clothes, ripping at my room. The stack of sketches flies off my desk and sticks against the far wall. Picture frames shake against their hooks.

But it's not enough.

I tear into the closet. Dig through the discarded shirts on the floor and grab the shoe box where Gemma hid all my Veronica keepsakes. I dump the box on the floor in the middle of my room and pick through trinkets from a year of dating. Movie ticket stubs. Strips of photo booth pictures taken at the mall. Notes passed discreetly at coven meetings. It's all going to burn.

Back at my closet, I search underneath my small altar to the Sister Goddesses, tossing aside used candles and heavy crystals until I find the half-used book of matches. I return to the pile of memories, pluck a single match from its root, and strike.

The power is instant, rippling across my skin, sending shivers of desire across my flesh. I separate the fire and hold it in my hands. The heat grows, looking for something to consume.

I pick up the first picture in the pile. Our last trip to the mall before Veronica made her move and kissed me. Just days before I knew I was anything other than straight. I let the flame lick across the back of the photo, and then I *push*, burning a hole that consumes Veronica's smug face.

The front of the photo bubbles up and spits an acrid smoke into the air. The smell almost makes me gag. I grab the small garbage can from beside my desk and drag it to the middle of the room, letting the bits of charred photograph drop into the metal can instead of my floor. The fire jumps and dances, destroying every last bit of the picture then licking across my palm, like a dog looking for a second treat.

Every picture burns to ash. Every letter. Everything she ever touched. I'd burn the memories right out of my brain if I could. What else? There must be something else. I turn and scan the room. There! The stupid self-portrait I used to love. *She can't call me broken after this.*

I lunge for the frame, careful to keep the flames from catching on my wall.

"Hannah?" Mom slips into my room, a horrified look on her face. "Honey, don't destroy that." She eases the frame from my hand, and with a wave of her palm, extinguishes every bit of fire in the room.

Anger still burns inside, and I want to snatch the picture back. I want to tear it into a thousand pieces. But I don't. I can't afford to make this worse.

Mom surprises me. Instead of the reprimand I'm expecting, she sets the picture gently against my desk and sits on my bed. She pats the spot beside her. "Talk to me, Hannah. What happened?"

Cautious, I sit beside my mom, still half-worried a binding ring is in my future. "I found Veronica—" My words die in my throat, choked by a surge of emotion that comes out of nowhere. I burst into tears and bury my face in my hands.

Mom rubs little circles on my back, the way she used to when I wasn't feeling well as a kid. She waits patiently, letting me cry snotty tears into her shoulder. I try to explain, but through the hiccuping sobs I don't get out much more than: "Found her . . . sleeping . . . with Savannah . . ."

Somehow, Mom manages to understand. "I'm so sorry, baby. It's hard when the people we loved move on without us."

I swipe the tears away with soot-covered hands, and I'm sure I have smudges all over my face from burning Veronica's pictures.

"It's not just that. Veronica gave me so much shit for going on a date with this girl, Morgan. That's the reason she left the night she was supposed to stay here. She acted so upset, but the whole time she was having sex with Savannah anyway!"

Mom cringes, and I wonder if it's sympathy or simply the sheer awkwardness that is listening to your daughter talk about her ex-girlfriend's sex life. She pulls away and considers me. "Wait. What date? Who's Morgan?"

Ugh. This whole being terrible at lying thing is getting really old. "It was nothing, Mom. She's in Gemma's dance class."

"And she's a Reg?" Mom asks, even though she knows the answer. "Is this the girl from that party?"

"Mom," I groan. "You're supposed to be helping me feel better, not giving me the third degree about the girl I have a crush on."

"Right. We can talk about that later," she says, which isn't ideal but at least gives me time to come up with a good story about why I lied about the extra shift at the Cauldron. "How can I help? Does ice cream still heal all Veronica-shaped wounds?"

Warmth fills my chest. "It certainly won't hurt."

--- ✳ ---

I'm on lockdown for three days. My parents keep me home from work, and there's always someone in the house with me. Mom or Dad. My grandmother or another coven adult. Between the protection detail on Veronica's house and the extra company at mine, the coven is stretched thin.

At least my parents replace my lost phone, giving me some contact to the outside world. The first text I get is from Veronica, though, and seeing her number pop up makes me want to throw the new phone against the wall. I almost do, until I also get a text from Morgan. Gemma must have told her about the accident, and Morgan offers to come over and keep me company.

I decline, more than a little reluctantly, blaming the constant surveillance from my parents. We spend the days apart live-texting each other as we binge-watch cooking shows from our separate houses, salivating over the culinary masterpieces. Morgan asks to watch my baking skills in action, which gives me an idea for the date I'm planning—the one we'll go on as soon as I get out of this damn house.

Finally, on the fourth day after the accident, my parents lift quarantine. We're only going to Lady Ariana's house, but it's better than nothing. Our usual Tuesday lesson has been canceled, replaced by a full-coven meeting. Mom's hopeful there will be updates about the Hunter, but Dad isn't so sure. More than anything, he's glad Lady Ariana has agreed to let Detective Archer teach us some Council-approved self-defense.

Trees whiz by my window, the sun still bright in the sky. I hate the winter months, when the sun disappears before we've eaten dinner. I'm not sure how I feel about seeing Detective Archer again. I worry he'll take one look at me and know about the other texts I've been avoiding the past few days.

Texts from Gemma, counting down the seconds until she gets out of the hospital, until she can ask questions I'm not allowed to answer. I've been simultaneously strategizing for this conversation and convincing myself it'll never happen, but I'm running out of time. She could be released any day now.

Mom pulls the car into Lady Ariana's driveway, parking behind Sarah and Rachel's black hatchback. Veronica's car is parked along the street, on the other side of the driveway. I suppress a groan. She's the *last* person I want to see right now. I've glanced at her texts the past few days, but since not one of them contained an apology *or* any concern about my well-being, I've ignored them.

"Hannah? Is everything okay?" Dad pokes his head back in the car. I hadn't realized he and Mom already got out. "We don't want to be late."

"I'm fine. I'm coming." I unbuckle my seat belt and climb out. My body is still achy, though the worst of the soreness is finally gone.

My family rounds the corner to the backyard, and the scene is more familiar than the hushed gathering in the early hours of last week. Around the safety of the coven, the children have removed their binding charms. They chase each other across the wide expanse of the yard, laughing and throwing balls of water—held together by their fledgling magic—like Reg children might toss water balloons. Veronica's brother, Gabe, is back from his grandparents' house, and he's currently trying to use his earth magic to trip his cousin Sullivan.

Veronica, for now, is nowhere to be seen.

At the altar, I let my parents stop first, and they add their power to the trio of candles that represent the Sister Goddesses. When I'm alone, I do the same, my fingers lingering over the center flame. The Middle Sister's flame.

I wish you were still here. A deep longing swells up inside me, so suddenly it nearly knocks me off balance. What must it be like, to pray to a god you believe can hear you, a god who could answer your prayers if only you tried hard enough?

Because of the Blood Witches, we've never had that option.

After the Eldest Sister created Caster Witches and the Middle Sister made Elementals, the youngest of the Three Sister Goddesses grew jealous. Unable to create witches of her own, she stole into the Mother Goddess's garden and pricked her finger on a rose, sacrificing her own magic to create the Blood Witches.

The Youngest Sister's crimes should have cost her immortality, but the Mother Goddess took pity on her, the favorite of her daughters. Instead, she banished the Sister Goddesses, forbidding them from interfering with the affairs of Earth's mortals ever again.

"Can I talk to you?"

Veronica's voice jolts me out of my thoughts, and I flinch. "No." I stalk away from the altar, losing what little calm the short ritual had provided. Instead, my head is full of images I want to carve out of my mind. No one should have to see their ex with someone else, not like that. Not when all you wanted was someone to tell you everything would be okay.

"Hannah, please." Veronica chases after me, but I'm saved from responding when Lady Ariana sends a pulse of energy through the earth.

The children stop playing, and we all gather at the center of the yard. I spot Detective Archer, standing a few inches taller than anyone else, wearing his usual suit and tie. He waits a few paces behind Lady Ariana, showing her deference before the coven.

"Agent Archer and I have talked at great length about what you will learn tonight. It will be a difficult lesson, one that goes against the very nature of our magic. Unfortunately, we feel it is a necessary one." Lady Ariana glances behind her, and Detective Archer steps forward. "Agent, you wanted to say a few words before we begin?"

The detective nods, but he shifts on his feet and doesn't seem to meet anyone's gaze. "Yes, thank you." He clears his throat. Once. Twice. The usual comfort, the confidence I'm accustomed to seeing from this man, has all but vanished. "My assistant and I are working diligently to find this Hunter. We haven't been able to pinpoint their location yet, so it's vital that you each know what to do if you run into one."

To my left, Ellen Watson raises a hand but doesn't wait for permission to speak. "Do you at least know who it is?"

"We're investigating a few leads, yes."

Ellen shifts her weight and glances down the line of assembled witches. "So, you *don't* know then. It could be anyone in town."

A flush of color rises on the detective's face, though his expression remains stern. "We have strong reason to believe that a Hunter we faced a few months back has made his way to Salem."

"But how do you—" Ellen tries again.

"That's Council business, I'm afraid. I'm not at liberty to discuss such matters." Detective Archer clears his throat and turns his attention away from Ellen. "As for protection, your best bet against a Hunter is to fly under the radar. If they don't see your magic in action, they'll have no idea you're part of the Clans."

It's a little late for that.

Instinctively, I glance down the line at Veronica. That particular ship has already sailed for both of us, though I'm still not sure how the Hunter first learned of her. The magic she used at the bonfire was subtle. Who could have noticed?

"I know magic can be a little more . . ." Archer pauses, searching for the right word. "*Instinctual* for Elementals. Historically, the smallest bits of your magic have been acceptable in public.

That will no longer be the case. A single slip can put an entire family in danger. The Hunters know our gifts are hereditary."

At that, a murmur goes through the assembled witches. Parents clutch their youngest children close. A sick feeling coils in my stomach, heavy with dread. I don't know why I never considered it, not once in all the times I've stressed about the Hunter knowing about me. He knows about my parents, too.

"As such," Archer continues, "your high priestess has agreed to temporarily extend the age through which a binding charm is required. Until the Hunter is caught, all witches under seventeen will wear the ring."

The Nevins twins, who turned sixteen back in April, try to protest, but their parents hush them before they get out more than a single indignant sound. Detective Archer continues his advice, all of which is completely useless to my family. We're already known to the Hunter. We're already a target.

My phone buzzes in my pocket, but I don't bother looking. It's probably Gemma, with an updated countdown on when I'll have to break another of Detective Archer's rules. With a Hunter threat this immediate, a threat I never thought I'd face in my lifetime, it's more dangerous than ever for a Reg to know the truth. But I can't risk Gemma's life. I can't give her to the Council.

Detective Archer turns the meeting over to Lady Ariana, and though I didn't think it was possible, the night gets even worse. The magic she and Archer want us to wield goes against everything Elemental magic is supposed to be.

Instead of working along the natural currents of energy, they want us stealing air from lungs and finding threads of water energy inside blood in order to freeze it. The magic is supposed to be near invisible to onlookers, and the pain it causes will give us a chance to run for help, but it feels too close to Blood Magic for comfort. We're paired up to practice the techniques on vials of blood and old-fashioned fireplace bellows, but I don't have the stomach for it. For any of this.

Especially after we're paired off by age, which matches me with Veronica.

I gingerly accept a small vial of blood from Lady Ariana and follow Veronica to the side of the yard. She sets the fireplace bellows on the ground and turns to me. "Whenever you're ready. My binding tattoo hasn't worn off yet."

My phone buzzes against my leg again, and this time, with the adults busy elsewhere, I pull it out. "I'm not freezing blood. That's disgusting." I set the vial beside the bellows and wipe my fingers against my jeans, even though my skin only touched the glass. "Besides, it's too late for us. The Hunter already knows who we are. There's no point trying to be subtle. This magic is a waste of time." *Not to mention the stuff of nightmares.*

Veronica rolls her eyes at me. "The subtlety isn't for the Hunters. It's to make sure we have a defense if we're attacked in front of Regs. The last thing we need is further exposure."

Heat burns my cheeks, but I'm not about to admit she's right. Instead, I check my phone and find two messages waiting for me. One is from Gemma, no surprise there, but the other is from Cal. He must have gotten my number from Lauren. Maybe he needs to swap a shift.

"Oh, so your phone is working then." Veronica's voice is sharp, edged like a knife.

I glance up before I can read Cal's message. "What's that supposed to mean?"

"You've been ignoring my texts since Saturday. Savannah is freaking out."

"Forgive me for not giving a shit about your new girlfriend," I snap. "I've been a little busy. You know, recovering from nearly drowning."

Veronica sighs, and it's like all the fight in her deflates. Her entire posture shifts, but I don't trust the change. She's played this card before. "I'm sorry, Han. I never meant for you to see us, but Savannah isn't out yet. You can't say anything. She won't even talk to any of our other friends. She's convinced her parents are going to find out."

"And what? You thought I'd tell them?" Anger boils up inside me, and I don't care if the entire coven overhears us. "I would never do that, and fuck you for thinking I would." A few heads turn our way, but I don't back down. "And it's nice to know you're capable of saying sorry. Even if it's only when you want something from me."

"Hannah—"

"Did it even occur to you that Savannah might be one of the Witch Hunters?" I ask. The shock on Veronica's face, the quick denial that rises to her lips, stokes the embers of my rage. "She knows where you live. She's been cozying up to you ever since the bonfire, and Lady Ariana said the Hunters would try to get close to us. I bet she saw you dampen the fire at Nolan's party. I bet that's when you screwed over the entire coven. All because you think you're too damn good for the rules."

Veronica doesn't say anything. She purses her lips and lets tears slip down her cheeks, but I won't be swayed by her hurt. She brought this on us. It's her fault I almost died. Her fault Gemma knows about what we can do. Her fault everything is falling apart around me.

I turn away and check my phone again. The text from Gemma is exactly what I expected, an announcement that she's leaving the hospital and demanding I come over to explain. Guilt twists in my stomach. It may be Veronica's fault this conversation has to happen, but I'm about to break coven rules, too. I text my best friend back, promising to come over as soon as my *family thing* is over.

The second text, the one from Cal, makes my skin go clammy. It's not about work.

He managed to hack into my neighbor's camera feed. I click on the attached video and watch the fuzzy scene unfold with growing dread. The camera doesn't cover my house, but I see the SUV pull up across the street. Someone climbs out and walks offscreen with a brick in their hands. When they race back to the car, I catch a glimpse of their face. It's fuzzy, but I'm not at all surprised when I recognize the smug expression.

Nolan.

19

SEEING NOLAN'S FACE STOPS me in my tracks. I've almost made it to the safety of Mom's car, where I could hide until my parents came looking for me. Instead, I return to the backyard, searching for Detective Archer. He's on his phone when I find him, talking in fierce, hushed tones. He hangs up when he sees me.

I show him the video—carefully sidestepping how I came to be in possession of such a thing. Cal just did me a solid; I'm not going to rat him out to the police. Archer pulls out his little notebook, and I give him all the information I know about Nolan. When I'm done, the detective slips his notes back into his suit jacket. He doesn't seem convinced about Nolan's guilt, but he promises to look into it and sends me back to my parents to practice the blasphemous magic.

My parents rightly assume being paired with Veronica didn't go over well, and they walk me through the new magic. I'm terrible at it, partly because learning new magic is always difficult and partly because I don't *want* to be able to do such things. Mom coaxes me through the techniques, and I promise to try if she'll teach me to send messages with air magic.

She agrees, and when we get home that night—after I promise not to tell my grandmother—Mom lets me copy the explanation from her Book of Shadows, and I learn to create my first air message. This type of magic makes my bones sing with the very rightness of it. *This* is what the Middle Sister wanted for us, magic that works with the flow of nature. She didn't want us stealing breath or freezing blood.

With the basics of my new communication method intact, I convince my parents to let me visit Gem, despite the darkening summer sky. Even if something happens to my phone, I'll be able to get in touch, which is the fact that finally convinces them. Mom lets me borrow her car, and I'm on the road the second she hands over the keys.

When I finally get to Gemma's house, I stand outside her door, afraid to knock. I'm grateful that Gemma stood up for me in the hospital, but I have no idea how that's going to affect the way her parents treat me. Will they make a better effort? Will they be even more standoffish? My phone buzzes in my pocket. Gemma asking what's taking me so long, or maybe Cal checking in. I never got a chance to text him back, but I can deal with that later. I suck in a breath and knock.

There's movement inside, and the door swings open, revealing Mrs. Goodwin. After a moment of hesitation, she invites me in. "Gemma's upstairs in her room. You know the way." Her words aren't overly warm, but at least she doesn't remind me to keep the door open.

"Thanks, Mrs. G," I say, and slip past her. Walking up the stairs to Gemma's room has never been so hard. Even with days to prepare, I still have no idea what I'm going to say to her, but I have to say something. She saw me using *magic*, and she's made it very clear that she remembers every last second of what happened.

Guilt twists knots in my stomach. My grandmother would be furious if she found out what I'm about to do. She'd send me to the Council without a second thought, especially with one of their agents in our midst.

"Hannah? Is that you?" Something creaks inside Gemma's room, a sound I can't place until her door swings open. *Crutches.* She leans heavily on the supports, her entire right leg consumed by her hot-pink cast.

Tears spill over my eyes. Seeing her like this, here in her room, is a million times worse than the hospital. It makes this nightmare so much more real. "My god, Gem. I'm so sorry."

She glances down at herself. "I'm fine. Get your ass in here." Gemma closes the door behind us. "How did you do that?" she asks, cutting right to the point. "You stopped the water. You un-bent the door. How?"

Even though I knew these questions were coming, I freeze.

"Come on, Hannah, don't shut me out." Gemma maneuvers to the bed and props her leg up with pillows. "We've been best friends our entire lives. You can trust me."

"It's not about whether I trust you. Of course I do." I perch at the edge of the bed, resting my elbows on my thighs. "It's just . . . Would you want to know, even if knowing put your life in danger?"

Gemma points to her broken leg. "My life is already in danger." Her voice is thick, and it breaks a deep, hidden part of me to see her like this.

"I'm so sorry you got hurt." A shock of fresh pain wells inside. Gemma has only ever dreamed of doing one thing with her life. She was born to be a dancer, but now I see the life she's sacrificed so much for slipping out of her reach. "What do the doctors say?"

"Don't try to change the subject."

"I'm not." Okay, maybe a little. "I know you want answers, and I'm trying to figure out how to give them to you. But I also want to know how you are. How you *really* are. Not the optimistic spin you give your parents."

Gem reaches for my hand and squeezes tight. "I'm scared," she whispers, her voice barely audible as tears fill her eyes. "They had to put a metal rod in my leg to set the break. I'm going to need physical therapy, and I'll be out of dance classes for at least the entire fall. I don't know if I'll be recovered in time for auditions. And if I can't audition, I can't get into dance school."

"So maybe you take a gap year," I say, trying to be supportive, but it only makes Gemma cry harder. "Hey, it's going to be okay. If anyone can make a comeback, it's you." I try to wrap my best friend in a hug, but she pulls away.

"Enough stalling," she says, wiping the tears from her face. "I need to know what's going on. Are you a mutant? Are you telekinetic? Ooh, can you read minds? What am I thinking right now?"

I laugh and roll my eyes. "I'm not a comic book character."

Gem raises an eyebrow. "You didn't answer my question. Can you read minds or not?"

"No. I can't. And I can't move objects with my mind. That's not a thing."

"But you can do *something*," she insists. "I saw you."

Her words kill the humor in my heart. She watches me, eager for my answer, but I don't know what to say. Lady Ariana's voice is in my head, stern and terrifying as she spends my entire childhood reminding the coven what could happen if a Reg ever found out about us. I hear my parents' constant reminders to tell no one, not even Gemma. Detective Archer reminded us tonight of the dangers of letting our secret slip, even for a moment. There's no way I can tell her.

And yet, no matter how much I want to deny it, Gemma's a part of this now. The Hunter probably didn't know she was in my car, but that doesn't change the fact that he hurt her. How can I expect Gem to protect herself when she has no idea who or *what* she's facing?

I lie back against the bed and glance at the girl who's been my best friend my whole life, the only person who knows me better than Veronica. Or will, once she knows this final piece of me.

"Do you believe in magic?" The words hang in the air between us, and I cannot believe I'm doing this.

Gemma falls silent, like she's trying to decide if I'm being serious or still joking about comic book characters. Like she's trying to decode whether this is some sort of test, and if it is, which answer gets her what she wants.

Finally, *finally*, she speaks. "After what I saw in the car, yes."

"Okay."

"Okay?"

I rub my hands along my jeans to wipe away the nervous sweat on my palms.

"Hannah . . ."

"I know. I know. I just . . . I don't know how to say this. Technically, I'm not supposed to say anything."

"Holy shit." Gemma's eyes go wide. "Are you some kind of witch or something?" She falls back in the bed until she's lying beside me. "I knew it."

Her words echo in my head. They sing across my skin like slipping on the perfect pair of jeans. Like coming home. But my stomach's still a twisted, tangled mess.

I stare at the ceiling, bracing myself. *Just say it.* "I'm an Elemental Witch."

A stillness settles over the room. I hold my breath.

"Elemental." Gem tests the feel of the word on her tongue. "So, that's how you stopped the water? What about the metal door?"

A strange sensation buzzes in my chest, and I finally exhale. It's like I'm embarrassed and excited and terrified all at once, and I can't seem to fully inhale around so many emotions. "I didn't do anything to the metal. I used the water to push it back out. Elementals can only control the four elements—fire, air, water, and earth."

Gemma nods, like it's the most obvious explanation she's ever heard. "So, can you, like, create fire and cause earthquakes and . . . something with air?"

I shake my head. "Elementals can create fire after we turn eighteen, but we can only manipulate the other three. Like cooling the air. Moving earth or stone. Freezing water, directing it. But there are limits. I can't control the weather or anything like that."

"Interesting." She furrows her brow and brushes a stray strand of hair out of her face. "Controlling the weather would be a handy trick though."

"Gemma, this isn't a game. Magic isn't a 'trick.' If my high priestess found out you knew about me, if she knew I told a Reg—"

"A 'Reg'?"

"Regs are people like you. Non-witches."

Gemma raises one eyebrow. "Like Muggles or something?"

A smile pulls at my lips. "Yeah. Exactly."

Gemma pouts. "This is bullshit. How is it *you* got a real-life Hogwarts letter, and I'm a stupid Muggle?"

"There's nothing wrong with being a Reg. Trust me, being an Elemental isn't all sunshine and rainbows."

"Yeah, except when someone attacks you, you can actually defend yourself." Gemma points to her cast. "Did another Elemental do this to me?"

I shake my head. "No. We think there's a Witch Hunter after the coven."

That gets a brow raise. "Witch Hunter? Is that who's after you? Wait, are Nolan and Veronica witches, too? Is that why someone torched Nolan's house and tried to rob Veronica?"

That actually gets some semblance of a laugh. "Nolan is most definitely a Reg." My humor dies when I remember the fuzzy video on my phone. *Is he more than that though? Is he the Hunter?*

"Nolan's a Reg," Gemma says, her eyes narrowing, "but Veronica isn't."

Shit. This is what I get for coming unprepared. "It's bad enough I told you about me, Gem. I can't out anyone else in my coven."

"Coven? How many of you are there?"

"Not many. There are only about a dozen families currently living in town."

"Right. Not many," she grumbles like that number is huge or something. "How many people know about this?"

"You're the only Reg I've ever told. And it's technically treason to tell, so you're probably the only living Reg who knows."

Gemma flinches. "Please stop calling me that."

"Calling you what? A Reg?"

She shudders again. "Yes. That. It makes me feel pathetic. Like you look down on me or something. It's gross."

Heat flares to my cheeks. "Sorry."

"What about your parents? Do they know?"

"It'd be kinda hard to keep it from them since it's hereditary."

Gemma nods, her expression growing pensive. "So, you and your parents. Veronica and hers . . ."

"Stop." I hold up my hands to cut her off. "I'm sorry, Gem. But I can't tell you who this touches. I know it sucks, but if the Council finds out—"

She scoffs. "What would they do? Ground you?"

"Execute me," I say, and Gem flinches. "Or at the very least, they'd strip me of my powers, which almost no one survives anyway. And there's a good chance you wouldn't survive the Council either."

"Shit." Gemma sighs. "So what? There's a council that goes around killing witches?"

"Not exactly. Their mission is to protect our secret. By any means necessary." There's so much more to it than that, but Gem already knows too much. She doesn't need to know how each Clan has a voice on the Council. Hell, she doesn't even need to know Elementals aren't the only witches out there. "Which means you absolutely cannot, under any circumstances, mention *anything* about this. To anyone. Including my parents. Mom is already suspicious that you might know. I told her you were unconscious once we hit the water."

"Okay, fine. But you gotta help me out with this Hunter thing. He might be after me, too, so I need to know how to deal with that."

"I agree. Which is why I've said anything at all."

Gemma shifts and reaches for my hand. She squeezes tight. "What's the plan?"

$$\dashv \quad \ast \quad \dashv$$

Gemma and I spend hours going over various theories about the Witch Hunter's identity. I text Cal a thank-you for his help, send the video to Benton with a quick *meet me at work tomorrow* message, and show Gemma my proof against Nolan. Her face drains of color when she sees his SUV, and I can't believe I didn't make the connection before.

His car looks just like the one that pushed us over the bridge.

As Gem and I go over the evidence against Nolan, I slip up and mention that Detective Archer's an agent with the Council, which leads to a whole second explanation of Caster Witches. I stress the importance of the detective never finding out what she knows, and I leave with her promise that she won't do anything without me.

Once I'm home, Gemma goes completely radio silent. I tell myself she's sleeping, still recovering from her stay at the hospital, but a small part of me worries that she's not as cool with my lineage as she pretended to be. I know she'd never tell anyone what I am, but I don't want this to change our friendship. I don't want to lose the Gemma I know and love.

My worries turn out to be unfounded. Her first text comes through the next day while Mom drives me to work, and by the middle of my Cauldron shift, she's blowing up my phone.

The battery runs dangerously low from the constant vibrations. I ignore the latest message buzzing against my leg as I run a dust cloth over the collection of crystal balls and blackened mirrors that we keep in a back corner of the shop for scrying. Though Gem speaks in coded language like I taught her, the whole day has been a barrage of ridiculous theories about the identity of the Witch Hunter and demands for a demonstration of my Elemental power.

Gemma's request leaves me conflicted. My whole life, I've been taught to hide my magic at all costs. It's become this secret, personal thing. Yet the idea of finally showing Gemma my true self, showing her all of who I am, holds a thrill of freedom.

A shoulder knocks into mine, sending the crystal ball in my hand tumbling to the ground. My magic reacts, pulling up air to act as a pillow. I realize at the last second what I've done and force the air to dissipate. Glass shatters all over the floor, only a second later than it should have.

There's sharp laughter behind me. "Watch out, witchy girl. You could hurt yourself."

Dread creeps up my spine as I turn to see who pushed me, a shot of panic pushing adrenaline through my veins. "What do you want, Nolan?" I inject annoyance into my tone to cover the fear. This corner of the shop is hidden from the register where Cal is working. I'm all alone with the boy who threw a brick through my window, who possibly ran my car off the road.

Who is very likely a Witch Hunter.

Nolan cocks his head to one side, a predatory smile curving his lips. "Just stopping by to check on my handiwork." He runs a finger along the top of a crystal ball, his movements infused with the lazy patience of someone who thinks they hold all the power. "I wonder if any of those cuts will scar."

A million biting retorts rise to my lips before my brain remembers that I was afraid, that Nolan might be more than a pompous jock. The bell above the door chimes, and I latch on to the distraction. "I have other customers. I have to go."

"I'd wait if I were you. We have so much to talk about." Nolan steps in front of me, blocking my escape. "I know what you did at my house." He leans close, his voice a whisper against my skin. "I'm going to tell everyone your secret."

"I don't know what you're talking about," I say, trying to sound irritated, like his words are nonsense, but my voice breaks. I try to shove past him. "Get out of my way."

Nolan catches my wrist and holds me in place. His fingers dig in hard enough to bruise. "Not until you admit what you did."

"Let go of me." I rip my arm from his grip, my whole body shaking. He's still blocking my path back to the register. I try to remember all the things we learned last night, how to find the water energy in his blood and freeze it, but the memory slips through my fingers like trying to capture smoke with a butter-fly net.

He pulls out his phone. "Not until you admit your crimes on camera."

"My crimes?"

"Is everything okay back here?" Benton rounds the corner, sidestepping the broken glass, and glances between me and Nolan. "What's going on?"

"None of your business, Hall." Nolan tilts his head up, the edge of his jaw sharp. "Now, if you'll excuse us, Hannah and I have some unfinished business."

Benton looks to me for confirmation, and I shake my head. "No, you don't," he answers, planting himself between us. "I think it's time to leave."

Nolan's expression hardens. "Make me."

"Don't push me, Nolan. You know I can kick your ass five ways to—"

Fists fly, and before I can even track their movements, Nolan hits the ground. I'm fairly certain he swung first, but he's the one with blood dripping from his nose.

"Asshole," he says, holding his face.

"You'll want to put some ice on that," Benton says, totally nonchalant. Like punching people in the face makes for a completely average afternoon.

Nolan drags himself to his feet and brushes glass from his clothes. He still looks ready for a fight, but he doesn't seem to like his odds. "This isn't over," he says, and turns to leave, shoving a second crystal ball to the floor on his way out.

I don't release my sigh until the door slams shut behind him.

"Are you okay?" Benton turns to me and surveys the piles of shattered glass on the floor. "I can pay for the damage."

"You don't have to do that." I hurry to the back room and grab a broom. Out of sight, I let out a shaky sigh. My hands are unsteady, and I press the heels of my palms against my eyes to keep tears from spilling out. I can't keep doing this. I can't stand this new reality, with Hunters lurking around every corner. I hate feeling so afraid all the damn time, hate not knowing whether Nolan's a Hunter or if he's just an asshole.

I force myself to take several deep breaths, letting the air's calm soothe my anxious energy. I return to Benton, who I find directing an older woman away from the broken scrying tools. He takes the broom from me and sweeps up the glass. "Please let me cover the damages. At least one of those was my fault."

I start to object, but the look on his face has me nodding instead. Besides, it's not like the cost matters to him, not the way it would to anyone else our age. "Thank you," I say, and he smiles. I kneel to hold the dustpan in place, and from this angle,

I notice a bruise blooming along his jaw. "Did Nolan actually land a punch?"

"What?" Benton's hand goes to his face when I point. "Oh, this? No, it . . . I had that tournament a couple days ago. Took second place because of this hit."

"Second place is still pretty badass." I stand and dump the glass into the trash. "And thank you again. For helping with Nolan. You didn't have to do that."

"Anytime, Walsh." Benton nudges my shoulder with his, and I get the feeling things are finally back to normal, that he's finally moved on from his crush. "So, are we ready to go to the police? Between the video you sent and Nolan turning up here, that has to be enough evidence, right?"

I make a noncommittal noise, piecing together a different puzzle from the one Benton's working on. Nolan's the right height to be Veronica's attacker, and he's certainly athletic enough to be a Hunter. I need to update the detective about Nolan's visit and see if he's made any other progress in his investigation.

"Hannah?"

"Yeah?"

Benton tilts his head, considering me. "Is everything okay? I thought you'd be thrilled to catch Nolan."

"I am. It's just . . . I don't know. It's good to know who did it, but it still sucks that it happened at all, you know?" We take care of the last of the glass, and I lead Benton to the front of the store. "And you saw the SUV. That could be the same car that ran me and Gem off the road."

"How is Gemma?" Benton asks, his cheeks flushing a bit pink.

I catalog his reaction to share with her later. "Better. She got out of the hospital yesterday, but she's going to miss months of dance."

"She must be crushed. I'm glad she's okay, though. That both of you are." We squeeze by a tourist examining the shop's rune collection. "We should try to link the crash to his car, then the police won't have any reason not to believe us. We could drive by his place tomorrow and check for damage."

"Morgan and I are going out tomorrow, but if you want to go without me, we can meet up the day after to review?"

Benton smiles. "That'd be great. I think I'll stop by the police station tomorrow, too. I can hold off on telling them about Nolan, but I want to know if they've made any progress on the fire," he says, sounding more nonchalant than I'm sure he feels about his near-death experience. He reaches into his pocket. "But first, let me pay for this." He holds up the tags from each of the broken crystal balls.

I smile. True to his word to the very end. "Sure thing."

When we clear the shelves and the register comes into view, the line is three people deep. I slip behind the counter to help ring up purchases. Benton waits patiently at the back of the line, handing over the tags with a self-conscious smile once he gets to the front.

"I've got this." I send Cal to greet the new customers coming through the door and take the tags from Benton. "One ten twenty-eight," I say, and Benton swipes his card like he's buying a five-dollar coffee and slips it back into his wallet.

Lauren appears in my periphery, in deep blue robes today, leading her latest tarot client to the exit. She swings by the register on her way back through the shop. "How is everything going over here?" she asks, her eyes lingering on Benton, who's loitering at the counter without any obvious purchases.

"Great." I pump a proper customer-service level of enthusiasm into my voice. It's clearly artificial, but it'll have to do. "Benton was kind enough to pay for the crystal balls I broke." I shoot him a look, hoping he reads my request to hide the fight from my boss.

"She didn't break them. At least not on purpose." Benton turns and flashes Lauren a smile. "I startled her." He covers so seamlessly I could hug him.

Lauren returns the bright expression. "Well then, for your good deed, how about a complimentary tarot reading?"

The smile falls from Benton's face. "Oh, no. That's all right." He steps back, toward the exit. "I appreciate the offer." He checks his phone. "But I really need to head out. Maybe another time?"

"Of course." Lauren tilts her head as she watches Benton disappear through the front door. "You know, Hannah, if you ever want a tarot reading of your own, you've earned one. On the house." My boss turns away as a customer approaches. "Can I help you?" She follows the older woman to the wand case, pulling the keys from her pocket.

Cal slips back behind the counter. "How did those crystal balls really break?" he asks, raising an eyebrow. "I've been around long enough to recognize when you're spinning a story for Lauren. Are you okay?"

"I'm fine. You aren't going to tell Lauren I lied, are you?"

Cal shakes his head. "What happened?"

"Remember that video you sent me last night?" I ask, and when Cal nods, I continue. "The guy from the video, Nolan? He was just in here."

The color drains from Cal's face. "He was here? I'm so sorry,

Hannah. If I had noticed him come in, I would have . . ." He trails off, either unsure or unwilling to share what he would have done. "Are you okay? Did he threaten you?"

"Not really." Cal's been great these past couple weeks, but there are already too many Regs involved in this mess. I can't drag him in, too.

But Cal's not buying it. "'Not really' doesn't mean 'no.' Are you sure you're okay? Do you want me to say something to Lauren?"

A customer approaches, cutting off our conversation. We work together to ring her up, and when she's gone, I assure Cal that I'm fine. He presses me to tell Detective Archer, and I agree. He already knows about the video, and I was planning to update him anyway.

I need this Hunter caught so I can stop suspecting everyone I know of trying to kill me.

20

"ARE YOU REALLY GOING to wear that?"

"What's wrong with it?" I glance down at my outfit. I'm wearing my favorite jeans—well, second favorite. My *favorite* pair met an early death after that whole blood-on-an-old-receipt thing—and a black T-shirt with a Rubik's Cube design on it. "We're just going hiking."

Gemma leans heavily on her crutches and tilts her head to one side. Her eyes squint as she scrutinizes my outfit. "Take the shirt off. It's ridiculous." She maneuvers over to the closet and picks through my clothes. "Don't you have anything in here besides T-shirts?"

"Not much." I slide the shirt over my head and toss it in the corner with the rest of the clothes Gemma vetoed. "There are some plaid button-ups in there."

Hangers zip across the metal bar as Gemma picks through my options. "Would it kill you to buy something with a little structure?"

"I have a couple of V-neck tees. Does that count?"

"Barely." Gemma pulls out a soft blue V-neck and tosses it to me. It's one of the few shirts I own that doesn't have some sort of graphic on the front.

"Are you sure?" I ask as I pull it over my head. "Isn't it kind of boring?"

Gemma appraises me when I'm fully dressed, making me turn so she can get a 360-degree view. "Nope, it's perfect. Though we could have done a little more with your hair this morning."

I flop onto my bed and stare up at the ceiling. I'm starting to regret my decision to let Gemma help me get ready. "This isn't prom, Gem. It's a walk in the woods. I don't need to go all out."

"Ooh, do you think you'll take Morgan to prom next year? Are you going to rock a suit again like you did with Veronica, or will you both wear dresses this time?" Gemma falls silent for a moment then curses under her breath. "I'm sorry. I shouldn't have mentioned you-know-who."

"Veronica and I are old news. It's fine."

Gemma's crutches creak as she crosses the room to join me on the bed. "Wow. Look at you being over your ex. I guess meeting someone new will do that."

"Well, that *is* what the infamous They always say. But could we stop with the fanciful leaps into the future? Morgan and I have been on one date. Half a date, actually, since I had to bail to deal with the Witch Hunter problem." It still feels weird—and amazing—to be so open with her about the witchy parts of my life.

"Speaking of which, have you thought about what to tell Morgan?"

"What do you mean?" I ask, a clear warning threaded through my tone. Gemma knows I can't tell Morgan about any of this. I bend over and pull out the shoe organizer from under my bed, searching for a pair that'll be good for the hike but isn't hideous.

"Look, I know you can't tell her about the witch thing." Gemma says *witch* like I'm in some weird cult. "But she deserves to know someone might be after you."

"Gemma, we've talked about this." I stand and pace the room, avoiding my best friend's increasingly accusatory gaze. "Besides, I'd say the car crash is a pretty clear indication that someone is 'after me.'"

"I still can't believe your parents are letting you out of the house when they know about the Witch Hunter." Gemma adjusts her hold on her crutches and stands up, hopping a bit to balance on her good leg. "My parents almost didn't let me come over today, and they think the car thing was a freak accident."

"Actually, my mom doesn't know I'm going on a date. She had to take her students to Boston this morning as part of their art history class." Besides, I'm guessing Gemma's parents were hesitant because of more than just the crash. "But Dad still feels guilty about not believing me when I first thought something was wrong, so he was easy enough to convince."

It doesn't hurt that he's working from home today anyway, so he had no excuse to keep me from borrowing his car.

"Speaking of parents . . ." Gemma stares at the floor, leaning heavily on her crutches. "I'm really sorry about mine. I should have said something to them sooner. I honestly thought they'd get over it."

"It's fine," I say, though I can't count the number of times I wished Gem would say something over the past year. "I didn't think you even noticed."

"Of course I noticed, Han. I hate that they pulled all that crap, and I hate that I didn't call them out sooner. I should have said something the first time they changed the sleepover rules. But I promise, I'm going to keep a close eye on them. I don't want you to feel unwelcome at my house."

"I'm not sure that'll ever go away completely." I reach for

Gemma's hand and squeeze tight. "But I appreciate you looking out for me."

Gemma releases me and glances at her phone. "Okay, enough about my parents. Let's get you to your date!"

The drive to Gemma's house is filled end-to-end with advice for my date. She makes me promise to text her with updates the second it's over and wishes me luck as she slips out of the car. I catch her mom watching us from their front window, but I'm not going to let her put a damper on my day. Yet without Gemma's company, doubt creeps in and my limbs buzz with nervous energy as I make the journey to Morgan's place. My stupid palms get sweaty and slip on the steering wheel. Pre-date jitters turn my insides into a battleground. I feel like I might simultaneously throw up and pass out.

My phone's GPS guides me to a two-story ranch with gray-blue siding and bright-white trim. A SOLD sign still marks the yard. I pull into the driveway and sit with the engine running, trying to decide whether I should text Morgan that I'm here or knock on the door.

Before I can decide, a text comes through from Benton.

BH: No updates about the fire. The police asked if I had any leads, so I told them about Nolan. I hope that's okay.

I updated Detective Archer last night anyway, but before I can reply and reassure Benton that I'm fine, a second text comes through.

BH: Have fun on your date!

Microscopic butterflies flutter in my veins, and I send Benton a quick thank-you and a promise to meet tomorrow, as the front door swings open. Morgan sticks her head out and waves me inside. I cut the engine and unbuckle my seat belt. *Just breathe*, I remind myself, pushing away all thoughts of Hunters and detectives and car crashes. I won't let any of it ruin today.

Morgan is waiting inside the foyer when I reach the front door. A shy smile tugs at her lips. "I'm normally the person who yells at people for this, but I still need a couple minutes to get ready."

I follow her into the house. Boxes in various stages of unpacking line the walls. The dining room table holds what looks like their entire collection of pots, pans, and plates. "What's left? You look really cute." Her hair is pulled up in a ponytail, her red curls swinging against her shoulders. She wears denim shorts and a green sleeveless shirt that has a built-in belt around the waist. I wonder if that's what Gemma means by *structure*.

Morgan's cheeks flush, and she motions for me to follow her. "I haven't unpacked all my shoes yet. I have this great pair of hiking boots, but I can't find them. I just need another minute or two, promise. You can wait in here." She leads me through the house and up the stairs to her bedroom, depositing me in front of her desk while she disappears into her walk-in closet, which is crammed full of cardboard boxes.

Despite the state of her closet, Morgan's personality is already climbing over the walls. She's definitely neater than I am. Her bed is made—mine almost never is—complete with little throw pillows in blues and purples. She has a collage of pictures pinned above her desk, her surrounded by friends in matching outfits. *Costumes*, I realize. They must be her dance friends from

Duluth. I bet she misses them. I doubt messages and video calls make up for being forced to move right before senior year.

The focal point of the room is a pair of six-foot bookcases filled to bursting with novels. She's arranged them by color, and the rainbow effect seems fitting. I scan the titles and find a lot of my favorites. She even has books about fictional elementals, stories I've read and secretly loved even though the magic inside is nothing like the truth of my Clan.

I find more books on Morgan's desk. The one on top is a slim pink book with . . .

Wait. Are those girls kissing on the cover?

"Adler's books are great. Have you read any?" Morgan emerges from the closet with the elusive pair of brown hiking boots.

I shake my head and pick up the book. "Is this about lesbians?"

Morgan nods. "Well, one of the main characters figures out she's a lesbian, but her love interest is bisexual. The other main character is this totally hilarious, foul-mouthed rich boy. You could borrow it if you want."

"Is it any good?"

"So. Good." Morgan takes the book from my hands and flips through to a couple of earmarked pages. I stifle a cringe. *Who tabs book pages?* "It's so much fun. There's kissing and . . . other stuff."

Morgan's face flames bright red, and my cheeks burn in response, my brain happy to fill in said *other stuff* with ideas of my own. I push the thoughts away. This is so not second-date conversation.

"Anyway." She passes the book back to me. "You should check it out and let me know what you think."

I take the book from her, our fingers brushing, which sends

a little thrill down my spine. "I will." I trace the book's cover with my thumb. "Are you ready to go?"

"Yup. Sorry for making you wait." Morgan slips her phone into her back pocket, laces up her boots, and we head out for part one of my master plan.

⌗　☀　⌗

The drive to the first portion of our date doesn't take long, but by the time we find suitable parking and emerge from the car, the sun is past its peak in the sky.

"Where are we?" Morgan asks, shading her eyes from the glare. The sky is a perfect blue, dotted through with fluffy white clouds.

"The Salem Woods." I open the back door and pull out a wicker basket. "There are some great trails here, and I thought we could have a little lunch."

Morgan lights up, keeping pace with me as I head toward the entrance of the trail. "Please tell me you have dessert in there."

I nudge her with my shoulder as we slip past the edge of the woods. "Maybe," I tease, though in truth, I have something even better planned for after lunch. The trees swallow us up, and we make our way down the twisting path.

Walking together, with the sun warming my skin and the rich power of the earth gently nurturing my magic, the bit of awkwardness I felt on the way to Morgan's melts away. I shift the picnic basket to my left hand and let my right hand—the one closet to Morgan—swing free. Our fingers brush together as we walk. Once. Twice. Finally, she glances at me, a tinge of color in her cheeks, and threads our fingers together.

My heart beats just a little bit faster.

"So, are we heading anywhere in particular?" Morgan glances through the trees and traces small circles on my wrist with her thumb. "This place kind of reminds me of home, except we had more pine trees. I bet it looks amazing here when the leaves turn."

"It really does. We'll have to come back in the fall. It's almost like walking into a sunset with all the red and gold in the leaves." I've painted out here at least half a dozen times for that very reason. I adjust my grip on the basket, feeling the strain in my shoulder but determined to hide it. "There's a little clearing up ahead. I figure we can eat there."

We continue down the path until we come to a gnarled old tree that bears the scars of this spring's thunderstorms. I step off the worn trail and help Morgan pick her way through bushes and closely grown trees. Here, there's not enough room to walk side by side, so I have to lead the way, following the thread of water energy I feel up ahead. When we're close, I stop.

"Is this it?" Morgan glances around, and I can see the slight disappointment in the slump of her posture. There's nothing special about this place. Yet.

"Not quite, but I want you to stay here." I set our picnic supplies on a fallen tree and reach for her hands, gently resting them over her eyes. "No peeking until I come back."

Morgan shifts uncomfortably. "Please don't sneak up on me when you come back."

"I won't. I'll be right back." I grab the basket and slip through a knot of trees that opens up to a little clearing. The energy here is unlike anywhere else I've found in these woods. A small stream winds through the space, and there's something about the natural mix of earth, air, and water that settles deep in my bones. I set down the basket and perch at the edge of the stream, dipping my fingers into the cool water. With one hand in the water, one against the soft earth, and the wind in my hair, a calmness settles over me. All I need now is fire.

With Morgan waiting on the other side of the trees, I crack open the basket and lay out the blanket I stored on top. I pick a spot that's near enough to the stream to hear the gentle trickle of running water against the rocks but far enough away to be completely dry, and unpack our lunch. With a quick glance to make sure Morgan is still out of sight, I coax the earth into holding up the thin taper candle I brought. It looks like I simply pressed the base into the ground, but this way there's no risk of the candle tipping over. I strike a match and light the flame, and as the fourth and final element sparks to life, I step back to survey my work.

It's perfect.

I planned out every detail of this date with Gemma, and this was our compromise. Since I can't tell Morgan what I am, I can at least show her the place where I feel my magic all the way to my marrow. For a second, I worry that this was a bad idea. The Hunter knows who I am. He could have followed me out here, a place so secluded no one could hear me scream, but I shove the thought down. I promised myself a Hunter-free day. Besides, my air magic would have alerted me to another human lurking in the woods behind us. I would have sensed their breath.

When I return to Morgan, she's waiting patiently with her hands still covering her face. "I'm back," I whisper so I don't startle her. She smiles, and her excitement warms me like the sun. "Keep your eyes closed. I'm going to lead you to the spot."

Morgan reaches out one hand, using the other to shield her view. "Don't let me fall."

"Never," I promise, and lead her through the trees and into the clearing. When we're a few feet from the blanket, I stop. "Okay, this is it."

She opens her eyes, surveying the little picnic with the single candle flame swaying in the wind. "Hannah . . ." Something catches in her throat.

I can't read her reaction, and she doesn't say anything else. Panic hammers at my ribs. She hates it. Oh god, she hates it. Maybe this was a bad idea. I should—

Morgan reaches for my hand and draws me close, her touch stalling my worried thoughts. "This is amazing." She leans in and brushes the softest of kisses against my lips. "How did you find this place?"

And just like that, all my worries melt away. I take a spot on the blanket and pass Morgan one of the water bottles. "My grandmother lives on the other side of the woods, so I've spent a lot of time on these trails. I found this spot last year."

"Do you come here a lot?" Morgan reaches for the little triangle sandwiches I packed. She takes a bite and gives me an amused look. "Is this peanut butter and Fluff?"

A small flutter of embarrassment warms my face. "What can I say? I'm a baker, not a chef." I point to the other plate. "Those ones are Nutella though, if you prefer. And I packed fruit, too." I snag one of each kind of sandwich while Morgan pops a grape into her mouth. "I don't really do much out here during the winter, but otherwise I come as much as I can. It's my place to be alone."

At that, Morgan looks up from her sandwich. "Am I the first person you've brought here?"

I nod and grab one of the grapes. The skin is perfectly firm, and the inside explodes with flavor. "Most locals don't even walk the trails, let alone wander through the trees without them, and I don't think I've ever seen tourists out here. I wanted you to have a place that no one else knows about. I hoped it might make the town feel more like home." I wipe my fingers on my jeans, and when I glance back at Morgan, she's staring at me. "What?"

She smiles and shakes her head at me. "Do you realize how incredibly sweet that is?"

Before I can respond, Morgan leans in close, the tip of her nose brushing against mine. There's a smile on her lips, a bit of mischief in her eyes, and that's the last thing I see before she kisses me.

The first kiss is tentative, like we're trying to remember how to speak a forgotten language. Her lips are soft and warm on mine, the tenderness sending a small chill down my spine. But then her fingers tangle in the hair at the base of my neck, and there's this shift. This hunger. It builds low in my belly and rises into my chest as her kisses grow deeper and her tongue slips past my lips.

I reach out, needing something besides her lips and her hands to anchor me. My fingers brush against the soft cotton of her shirt, and she pulls me up to my knees. There's a flash of heat as my arms circle her waist, my fingers finding a strip of exposed skin. Morgan shivers beneath my touch, and I can't get enough of her. Her kisses and her warmth and the way she makes my entire body sing. The way she makes me feel so utterly *seen* in a way I never have before.

Wind whips around us, tugging at our clothes, our hair. It batters against us, but I don't care. I don't care about anything— not Veronica, not the Council, not even the Hunter. All I care about is the girl in my arms and the way she's pulling me closer and closer, like she's feeling the same desperate need that's thrumming hot through my veins.

Morgan trails her hands down my arms and reaches for the hem of my shirt, pressing her palms flat against the skin of my back. Heat blossoms behind me, so hot it almost feels like—

I pull away, breaking the kiss, and press down, down, down on all the feelings raging inside. Now that there's space between us, I can parse out the magic flowing freely in my veins. I shove the magic deep inside, locking it away. The wind calms, and the heat behind me dies. I risk a glance. The candle is already melted to a tiny nub.

"Is everything okay?" Morgan brushes a thumb along her bottom lip, her face flushed.

"It's so much more than okay." I smile even as I can barely catch my breath. I reach for her hand and weave our fingers together. My heart is pounding in my chest so loud I'm sure she must hear it. "That was . . ." I search for the right word, but I'm distracted, trying to get a firm hold on my magic. *I can't believe I let it get so out of control.*

"Yeah." Morgan sighs, laughing a little to herself. The corners of her lips crinkle as she bites back a smile. "That was." She clears her throat and sits back down on the blanket. "Right, so. Dessert?"

I settle on the blanket beside her and place a chaste kiss on her cheek, a silent thank-you for changing the subject. "That's part two of the date."

"Part two? How many parts are there?"

A mischievous grin tugs at my lips. "I guess we'll have to see."

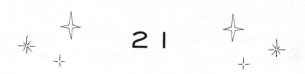

21

MORGAN AND I FINISH our lunch and lie on the blanket, swapping secrets and stories as we watch the clouds float by. Like me, Morgan's an only child, and we bond over the lack of siblings to blame when we broke something in the house. She tells me about the time she made the disastrous mistake of putting a metal bowl in the microwave when she was ten, and I reenact my dad's expression the first time I made my own cookies from scratch and mixed up the teaspoon and tablespoon measurements. Turns out, too much salt can absolutely kill a recipe.

Finally, we hike back to my borrowed car and head toward town.

"Now will you tell me your brilliant plan?" Morgan asks, resting her hand against mine on the gearshift.

I slow as the light turns yellow and stop as it goes red. "If you're up for it, I thought we could go back to my house and take over the kitchen. I have a new blondie recipe I want to try."

"Blondie?"

"It's kind of like a brownie, but more on the vanilla spectrum." My light turns green, and I inch forward so I can make a left once traffic passes.

"That sounds amazing."

"I haven't made this version yet, so no promises, but it should be good." I head down a residential street and sirens wail in the distance, growing louder. I glance in the rearview and catch sight of the flashing lights, so I pull over.

Fire trucks fly by us, their horns blaring. My heart plummets to my toes, and I know. I just *know* the Witch Hunter has stuck again. I hit the gas harder than I probably should, my tires squealing against the pavement.

"What are you doing?" Morgan asks, her voice high and panicked.

I don't answer. I'm too focused on the trucks ahead of us. I lose them around a corner, but I can still hear their sirens screaming. I follow them around the bend, the familiar route prickling at the back of my head. And then I see it.

Billowing gray smoke reaches up into the sky.

Someone's house is going up in flames.

A minute later, I taste the ash on my tongue, and I finally break my silence. "My house is this way," I whisper, and Morgan's hand slips from mine as I grip the steering wheel. *Please don't let it be my house.* But who else's could it be? The Hunter already knows who I am, and he's fought with fire before.

We're forced to stop at another light while the trucks race through. I lean forward, trying to determine how high the smoke reaches, to see if the firefighters are too late to save anything.

"It's green."

Morgan's voice jolts me out of my thoughts. I barrel through the intersection, trying—and failing—to keep the panic at bay. It crawls up my throat, closing off my airway.

Dad.

He wouldn't let the fire get this big. He must have gone for a walk. If he were home, the house would be safe. I turn down the next street. Only a couple blocks more to my place. I dig into my pocket and pull out my phone. "Call my dad." I punch in my four-digit code and pass the phone to Morgan.

"What do you want me to say?" Morgan opens my contacts and scrolls through. "There's nothing under *Dad*. What's his—"

"Walsh. Timothy Walsh." The sky glows orange from raging flames that flicker above the roofs and trees between us and home. I take the last turn too fast, tires screeching against the pavement.

"Hannah, watch out!" Morgan reaches for the wheel, and her touch jolts me back to reality.

I slam on the brakes, narrowly missing the car stopped in front of me. I throw the car in park and clamber out into the street, standing frozen on the side of the road. The smoke is thicker here, black as night, choking my lungs, covering us with ash.

"Is that . . . Is that your house?" Morgan asks, scrambling out of the car after me.

My voice won't work. I nod and watch the firefighters hurry for the hydrant. The flames roar, destroying everything: every memory, every photograph, every painting. Everything besides the clothes I'm wearing.

I reach into my pockets but come up empty. "My phone." I need to call Dad. He'll know what to do. He can fix this. "Where's my phone?"

"Here." Morgan passes it back. "He didn't answer."

But I barely hear her over the explosion of windows, the shattering glass, the shouts from firefighters in oxygen masks. I find Dad's number in my favorites and dial.

It rings and rings and rings.

"He's not answering." My throat is raw. Tears prickle at my eyes. I dial again and the phone rings on and on.

One of the men beside the fire trucks holds his radio to his ear. His face crumples. "Where the hell are the paramedics?" he shouts. "We've got a body inside."

No. No, no, no, no.

"Dad." I race forward, past the barricade, straight toward the line of firefighters. "Dad!"

Someone catches me around the waist, pulling me up short. My knees buckle, and I sag in their arms. I scream again, but the person behind me holds tight.

"Hannah, stop." Morgan's voice is in my ear, her breath upon my neck, but it feels cold compared to the fire raging in front of me. "There's nothing you can do."

"No." I struggle against her, but she's stronger than me. "I can stop the fire. I can put it out." I reach for Morgan's hands to pry them off me. "I can *save him* if you just *let me go.*"

A surge of adrenaline spikes through me. I scream and kick and fight like hell, but Morgan holds on. With a strength that doesn't seem possible from someone so slight, she keeps me trapped in her embrace, the only thing stopping me from running into an inferno.

"I know it's scary. I know it hurts." Morgan's voice cuts through the fresh sirens approaching behind us. "But you can't go in there."

"I have to! My dad—" I refuse to finish the sentence. He's not in there. He can't be. Morgan *still* won't let me go, but maybe I'm close enough. Maybe I can stop the fire from here. I reach out, searching for the flame's power.

But it's too strong. Too far away.

My legs stop working, and I collapse against Morgan. She holds me up, keeps me off the ground, keeps me from shattering into a hundred million pieces.

Sirens pull up behind us. More flashing lights. More noise. It's all a blur of red and orange and blue and white until I can no longer distinguish the police lights from the dancing flames.

A second set of hands grips my arms, but I can't make out the face through the haze. A deep voice worms through all the noise and shouts, cuts through all the panic.

"Hannah, listen to me. It's going to be okay." His fingers dig deeper, and the pain snaps me to the present. Detective Archer takes form before me. "I need you to focus. Tell me what's happening."

I stare at him and feel five years old. "My dad . . ." Tears close my throat, cutting off my words.

"We were on our way back from a hike when we saw the fire trucks." Morgan shifts until my face is tucked into her neck. "We think her dad might be inside."

Detective Archer places a hand on my back, but I flinch away from his touch. He was supposed to prevent this. He was supposed to keep us safe. The detective moves back into my line of sight. "Hannah, are you sure he's in there?"

"I don't know." My voice cracks, and I hold tight to Morgan like I might get sucked into the earth without something to tether me here.

The detective looks to Morgan. "Do not let her move from this spot."

"Yes, sir."

And then he's gone, pushing through the throng of firefighters, looking for someone who knows what's going on.

Morgan gasps. "Oh my god . . ."

"What?" I pull away, but Morgan tightens her grip.

"You don't want to see this," she says even as she loosens her hold enough so I can turn. She keeps one hand firmly around my wrist, stopping me from running into the burning house.

But none of that matters when I finally see.

A fireman rushes down the lawn with my father draped across his back. Paramedics hurry forward with a stretcher, others racing ahead with their medical bags. It feels like centuries before they have him strapped in. One of the paramedics, a short Black woman with a determined expression, climbs on top of the stretcher and starts chest compressions.

"No." The world tilts. I hit the ground. Everything goes dark.

It's a struggle to open my eyes. I try to sit up, but I can't move. It takes another few moments to realize I'm on a stretcher with a protective strap across my chest. There's an oxygen mask on my face and people crowded all around.

"Hannah? Can you hear me? How do you feel?" Detective Archer stands behind a pair of paramedics.

I yank the mask off my face. "Where's my dad? Is he all right?"

"He's on route to the hospital. The doctors will know more once they examine him."

"But was he alive? Did they get him breathing?"

"Miss, you need to keep the mask on." The paramedic eases it onto my face and pushes the stretcher until it's flush with the back of the ambulance. She shares a look with the man across from her, like they're ready to lift me inside.

I shoot a panicked look at Morgan.

"I'll take your car and meet you there," she promises.

Before they can stop me, I pull off the oxygen mask again. "Call Gemma. Tell her to call my mom."

I don't even see Morgan nod before I'm shoved into the back

of the ambulance and the doors slam shut. The vehicle jolts, rolling forward until there's nothing but sirens and flashing lights.

They won't let me see my dad.

I pace the waiting room, afraid to stop moving. If I sit, I'll have to admit that this is happening. The hospital released me as a patient two hours ago once they confirmed my vitals were fine. Morgan perches at the edge of a chair, my seat beside her empty, watching me pace.

Despite the NO CELL PHONES sign, I cling to mine like a lifeline. Mom called while I was waiting for the doctor to approve my discharge. She ended the field trip early, but the bus is stuck in traffic on the way back from Boston.

My heartbeat falters each time a doctor comes in, but they always call someone else's name. The stress and the wait have my stomach in knots. I need answers. Now.

"Hannah, sit. You'll make yourself dizzy." Morgan rubs at her face like she's the one who's lightheaded. "They'll be out as soon as they have an update."

"I know." I pause, coming to a full stop for the first time in hours. "You don't have to stay. I'll be okay."

Morgan stares at her hands before glancing up at me. "I want to be here for you."

I sink into the chair beside my date, reaching for her hand. She twines her fingers through mine, and I finally feel like I'm grounded to something real. Someone who's not going to let me float away. "What am I going to do?"

Morgan rubs her thumb along my wrist as she thinks. "Take it one step at a time, I suppose."

A humorless chuckle gets caught in my throat. "If I knew what any of those steps were, maybe I could do that."

"Well, one step is definitely contacting your mom, which you've done. Is there any other family you should call?"

I shake my head. "Neither of my parents have siblings." I should probably call my grandmother, but I can't. Not without bursting into tears and spilling our secrets in front of the entire waiting room, and I won't risk missing news about my dad by slipping outside to make the call.

Anger ripples through me, hot and bitter. The Council is supposed to protect us. The whole point of their existence is to keep us safe from Hunters.

They failed.

I'm not waiting for Detective Archer. I'm not waiting for the rest of the Council to decide the best course of action. I'm done with all of them.

I'm going to find this Hunter myself and make him pay for what he's done.

"Hannah, what's wrong?"

"Besides everything?" I snap, spewing my hurt all over her.

Morgan considers me, like she's searching for something and isn't sure she likes what she sees.

"Hannah!" The squeak of crutches follows Gemma's voice. She swings into the waiting room, eyes searching the rows of seats. "Hannah?"

I stand and start toward my best friend. "Over here."

Gemma maneuvers through the crowd and drops her crutches where we meet. She crushes me in a hug, and tears spill down my cheeks. I soak in her familiar presence. Finally, someone who understands. Someone who gets how bad this all really is.

"How is he?" she asks as she pulls away, wiping tears from my face with her thumbs.

"I don't know. The doctors haven't said anything. And my mom is stuck in traffic and my house is gone and I don't even have any clothes or anything." The story comes pouring out: Morgan and I following the fire trucks to my house, the firemen carrying Dad out of the blaze.

"It's okay, Hannah. We'll figure this out." She hugs me tight and whispers into my ear. "Do you think this was the you-know-what?"

She means the Hunter.

I nod.

Morgan steps up beside us. There's a questioning turn to the raise of her brow, but she doesn't ask what Gemma said. "Do you have somewhere to stay tonight?"

Gemma holds my arm for balance. "She'll stay with me."

"Miss Walsh?" A woman stands in the entryway to the ICU. "Miss Walsh?"

I hand Gemma off to Morgan and hurry over. "Is my dad okay? Is he awake?"

The woman, whose hospital badge says *Dr. Cristina Perez,* looks over my shoulder at the waiting room. "Do you have another parent here?"

"My mom is on her way." I squeeze my phone, willing it to ring. It doesn't. "Is he okay?"

Morgan and Gemma come up behind me. Dr. Perez glances between them.

"They're fine. Please, just tell me what's going on."

She nods, her expression neutral, which only worries me more. "Why don't you come with me."

The four of us weave through the busy halls of the hospital while Dr. Perez tries to prepare us for what we're about to see. "Mr. Walsh is still in critical condition. You can see him, but you should know he's on a ventilator. We don't know how extensive the lung damage is."

Before we even get there, I can see it. Dad unconscious on a bed, tubes and wires sticking out everywhere. "Why can't you wake him and find out?"

"There's a degree of swelling in his brain. We have him sedated, but we don't know yet what will happen when we reduce the drugs. For now, we're giving his brain time to recover before we try."

"Swelling? How did that happen?" My knees go weak, and I stumble. Morgan is there in an instant, catching me by the elbow and keeping me on my feet.

Dr. Perez glances at her clipboard. "It looks like he hit his head when he fell."

I think of the Hunter at Veronica's house. *Or someone knocked him out.* That would explain why the fire spread. How it overpowered him.

Explanations and timelines continue, but I don't hear them. I know I'm right. The Witch Hunter did this. He must have realized you can't kill Elementals with fire, at least not while we're awake.

"Your father will likely be unconscious for a few days. Maybe a few weeks. We'll continue to monitor the swelling, but he might need surgery to relieve the pressure." The doctor gestures to a closed door. "You can go in and see him if you like."

I stand there, staring at the door like I haven't the slightest clue how to open it. Dad made chocolate chip pancakes for me and Gemma this morning. I don't know how to reconcile that man with the one waiting for me in this room.

"Thank you, Doctor. We can take it from here." Gemma reaches for the door and opens it. "We're right behind you."

My heart lodges itself somewhere in my throat. I can't do this. I can't go in there. Even from the doorway, the room is too bright. Florescent lights glint off thin tubes that run from Dad's arm to the IV bags.

Morgan reaches for my hand and squeezes. The pressure of her touch grounds me. Blinking back tears, I take the first tentative step into the room.

The air weighs heavy with death. Thick and stagnant. A ringtone chimes. My pulse quickens, and I check my phone. Not mine.

"Shit. Sorry." Gemma pulls out her phone and presses it to her ear. "Mom? I'm at the hospital with Hannah. I'll talk to you later." She hangs up and puts the phone in her pocket.

"You should call her back. Make sure it's okay if I stay over tonight." I take another step forward but stop shy of the bed. *He looks so pale.* I wrap my arms around myself, trying—failing—to hold it all together.

"Are you sure?"

"It's okay, Gemma. I'll keep her company." Morgan holds the door open for Gem and then slams it shut behind her.

"What are you doing?" I turn and find Morgan leaning against the door, blocking the exit.

"Sorry. I didn't mean to close it that hard." She holds up her hands. "I just need to ask you something. In private. This is the first chance I've had since you said it."

"Said what?" Panic threads through my veins, and my magic stirs. I reach for the air, absorbing its strength, ready to use it in an instant if I need to.

"I'm not going to hurt you, Hannah. I just want to talk."

"So talk."

Morgan shakes her head, and there's this gleam of hope in her eyes that throws me off balance. "You said something at your house, something *familiar*. I've been spinning it around in my head since we got here, but I need to know if you meant it." She pauses and runs a hand through her hair. "You said you could stop the fire. How?"

I never should have said that. I press my magic down, releasing my hold on the air. "I don't know. It was the heat of the moment."

"I considered that, but you were so sure. And then I thought about the woods and the stream and the candle. You seemed so at home." Morgan steps forward, her hands still raised in surrender as if I'm the one holding *her* hostage. "Please tell me you meant what you said about the fire."

Wait. Is Morgan . . . I shake the thought away. No. There's no way. I would have sensed her magic the first time we met if she were an Elemental. "I didn't," I lie.

But I've never been very good at lying.

Morgan's eyes narrow. She lowers her hands and tilts her chin up, a challenge. She holds my gaze, the blue of her eyes shining in the artificial light. "Three Sisters blessed the world."

Impossible. My heart beats so loud I'm sure she can hear it. I step forward, meeting her dare. "And were banished for defying their Mother."

A slow smile spreads across her face. "You meant it. You could have stopped the fire."

I nod, even though there's still a hollow feeling in my chest that tells me I would have failed. That I wasn't strong enough for a fire that out of control, that hungry.

"You're an Elemental, aren't you?" Morgan says the words with such awe, such kinship, that I'm about ready to burst from the relief of it all. She can help me. With her and Gemma, there's no way the Witch Hunter will get away with this.

"I am." Despite my father's unconscious form behind me, I actually smile. It feels amazing to admit that to someone who truly knows what it means. "But you're not. I would have known."

A shadow crosses Morgan's face. "No, I'm not."

Her hesitation confuses me. "Are you a Caster?" Maybe she knows Detective Archer.

She shakes her head. "I'm a Blood Witch."

22

THE ONLY SOUND IN the room is the beeping of Dad's heart monitor.

I'm a Blood Witch.

I stare at the girl before me, whose kind eyes narrow in my silence. I step closer to my dad, shielding him as all the pieces click into place. The exacting control over her body when she dances. The impossible strength in her arms when she held me back from the blaze.

"You can't—" It's not possible. Lady Ariana said there weren't any Blood Witches in Salem. Mom said we got the scrying wrong, but we didn't. Morgan is here. She's an only child living with her parents. She's part of a large dance group. All the pieces are there. Everything fits. I bet there isn't even a Hunter in Salem. "Was it you?"

Morgan's eyebrows rise high. "Was what me?"

"This!" I gesture to Dad's still form, and the sight of him breaks something in me. "Someone has been stalking my coven all summer." I reach for my magic. The temperature in the room drops several degrees, and the air whips at our hair. "Was this because of you?"

Morgan crosses her arms. "Why? Because I'm a Blood Witch? The thing of nightmares?" She glares at me. "I'm not stalking you, Hannah. And there's not some Big Bad Blood Witch out to get you. My parents and I are the only ones in the state. That's precisely why we picked Massachusetts."

I ignore her certainty. Her logic. "Right, I'm the idiot for suspecting a Blood Witch. Because you're all softies at heart." I shudder. "I've seen the dangerous magic your kind weaves."

"My *kind*?" Morgan practically screeches the words. I hold tighter to my power, ready in case she attacks. "I thought you of all people would be more understanding. I guess you're not as accepting as I thought."

Her words cut deep, shame infecting the injured flesh. I release my hold on the air, letting the room settle between us.

"Not all Blood Witches are evil," Morgan continues before I can respond. "Even those with questionable morals are few and far between. Though, apparently, Elementals *are* just pyros with a superiority complex."

Tears sting my eyes, fear and shame and worry closing my throat. "But what about my dad?" I sit at the edge of his bed, the weight of everything buckling my knees.

Morgan's anger, her defensiveness, deflates. "I'm sorry, Hannah. I know this must be hard for you." She searches for my gaze, her blue eyes questioning. "But why did you suspect a Blood Witch at all? We have no quarrel with your coven. And we certainly aren't the type to play with fire."

I wipe the tears from my eyes and drop my gaze. "I met a Blood Witch once, a few months ago in Manhattan. She . . ." My words die in my throat, and I can't bring myself to look at Morgan. "She hurt me, and when all this started, I thought she had come here to kill me."

"How did she even know you were an Elemental?" Morgan sits beside me at the very edge of Dad's bed. "We don't usually reach out to other witches. You tend to hate us."

Though I want to deny her claim, it's true. Everything I've ever learned about Blood Witches has been a cautionary tale. Scary stories to keep Elemental children in line. Even the Council only keeps one or two Blood Witches in each rank at any given time. "Well, your goddess is the one who got the Three Sisters banished from Earth."

Morgan rolls her eyes at me. "Would you want to be constantly punished for something your creator did thousands of years ago?" She nudges me with her shoulder. "But really, why did that witch try to hurt you? Most of us aren't like that."

"It's kind of a long story. I was on this class trip and stumbled into a feud between her and these Caster Witches." Shame burns my cheeks. "They were trying to permanently bind the Blood Witch's magic. She thought I was part of their group."

Beside me, Morgan goes very still. "Were they successful?"

"No. She's fine. She got away." I pull out my phone, only to remember the pictures I'm looking for aren't in this new one. "When there was an animal sacrifice this summer, I thought she had come for revenge. Eventually, I figured out the sacrifice was this Reg I know, Evan, but I also found runes on the Witch Museum down the street from my work. I never found out where those came from."

"Oh, actually?" A blush creeps up Morgan's cheeks. "Those were mine. I normally wouldn't leave something like that out in the open, but my family left Duluth for a reason. Those runes were meant to provide protection, to keep my family hidden from what we left behind."

"But my parents didn't sense any magic in the blood."

"One of the first things we learn is how to mask our magic from others. Most Elementals and Casters don't like us. You suspect us of everything."

"Sorry," I say, but something sticks in the back of my head and holds on tight. "If you're supposed to hide your magic, why did you draw them somewhere so public? And how are you here at all? I thought the Council banned Blood Witches from Salem."

"My parents petitioned the Council for permission. We needed to be somewhere no one would look for us." Morgan shudders, and I wonder what she's running from. "As for the runes, the energy from all the Reg traffic helps amplify the power. Trust me, if I could get the same result from drawing runes at home, I would."

I lean into her shoulder, letting her steadiness hold me up while I reach for my dad's hand. "If everything I've learned about Blood Witches is wrong, what do you really do?"

Morgan rests her head on top of mine, her long hair brushing against my neck. "I'm sure a few of your fears are rooted in truth. Some of us can turn Regs into puppets. Control hearts and minds. But we generally keep our gifts turned inward, which makes us pretty physical as a Clan. A better control over our blood means a better control over our bodies." She pauses, and there's a smile in her voice when she continues. "I've been told our confidence makes us charming."

"Hey, I never said you were charming," I tease, the tension loosening in my chest.

"Says the girl who painted me an apology card *and* baked me cookies because you wanted a second date." Morgan laughs, but there's so much warmth there I don't even care that it's at my expense. "Some of our most prominent witches are healers. I bet no one ever told you that."

"Wait. You have healing magic, and you didn't think to say something?" I leap from the bed and gesture to the man struggling for breath—struggling for *life*—behind her. "Help him!"

"I can't." Morgan slips off the bed, her eyes full of regret. "I'm not fully trained."

"But you have some training," I insist.

She nods. "I do. But—"

"Please, Morgan. You have to try." I reach for her hands, threading my fingers through hers. "We can't let him die."

Morgan steals glances at my dad. "It might not work," she whispers, though her blue eyes sparkle as her magic stirs to life.

"Could you make it worse?"

She shakes her head. "I don't think so."

"Then what's the harm in trying?" I ask, not bothering to hide the tears that carve down my face. "I'm not asking for a miracle."

Morgan considers me for a long moment. She whispers something under her breath, but then she nods and approaches the bed. "It might not work," she says again, as if I didn't hear the first time.

I don't say anything. I don't want to scare her off from what she's about to do. Morgan slips the simple metal band from around her middle finger and pulls a thin pin from a groove along the ring's inner edge. "Are you sure about this?" she asks, and when I nod, she pricks my father's forearm.

A single bead of red rises to the surface. Morgan swipes her finger across the blood and wipes it along her palm. After a moment, the blood soaks through her skin like it was never there at all, and Morgan places her hands in the space around Dad's head.

Her hands tremble, and a crease forms along her brow. The room fills with static as my father's energy reacts to her magic. Morgan flinches, cursing under her breath.

"What's wrong?"

She doesn't turn, doesn't open her eyes. If anything, that crease in her brow furrows deeper. "Blood clot," she whispers through gritted teeth.

"Can you get it out? Or dissolve it? Or whatever it is doctors do?"

"I think so. Just . . . don't move."

I hold my breath and cross my fingers that no doctors or nurses or *best friends* come to the door. I've watched enough medical shows to know a blood clot is not a good thing.

Several tense seconds later, Morgan pulls her hands away and stumbles back. I reach out to catch her, but she rights herself before we touch.

"Are you okay? Will he wake up now?"

Morgan stumbles for the chair and collapses into it. "I don't know. He's still in really bad shape, but I've done all I know how to do." She glances up at me, breathing hard. "Now do you believe we're not all evil?"

"I really am sorry about that." I tuck a bit of hair behind my ear. "You were right, I never should have suspected a Blood Witch, especially when there's a Witch Hunter in town."

At that, Morgan's eyes grow wide. "There's a Hunter? Here?" A quiver runs through her voice, a thread of fear that verges on panic. "Not again."

"Again?"

Morgan nods. "Maybe you were right. Maybe this is all my fault."

"What are you talking about?"

"My ex, Riley, the guy back in Minnesota . . ." Morgan rubs her hands across her impossibly pale face. "He's a Hunter. He must have followed me here."

"You dated a Hunter?" I push my shock aside, focusing on what this news means for my coven. We finally know who's behind all this. We finally have the upper hand. "Why is he after you?"

Morgan looks at me like the answer is obvious. "Why else? Because I'm a Blood Witch. They hate us the most."

Behind me, someone gasps.

Gemma stands in the doorway, leaning on her crutches.

"What. The hell. Is a Blood Witch?"

23

"WELL?" GEMMA SWINGS INTO the room and closes the door behind her. She glances at my father's still form and lowers her voice to a fierce whisper. "Someone better start talking."

Morgan sneaks a look at me. "Is Gemma . . ."

I shake my head. "No, she's a—"

"So help me, Han, if you use that word again." Gemma collapses into an empty chair across from Morgan and sets her crutches on the floor. "I take it Morgan knows about what you are?"

"She figured it out, Gem. I swear I didn't tell her."

"Wait." Morgan holds up her hands. "You told Gemma? That's *forbidden*."

"Uh, hello? I'm right here." Gemma glares at us. "Stop dancing around the words. Just say it. Hannah's an Elemental."

Morgan eyes widen, and she looks like she might pass out.

Gemma lets out a smug, wordless sound. "Now, will someone please tell me what the hell a Blood Witch is? Because it sounds terrifying."

Morgan grimaces. "Why does everyone think we're so creepy?"

I shrug. "Blood grosses people out."

"*Hannah*," Gem warns.

"Right. Sorry." I can't believe I'm doing this. Again. "There are actually three Clans of witches. In addition to the Elementals and Casters I already told you about, there are also Blood Witches." I look to Morgan, and she nods for me to continue. "Morgan's one of them."

"Great," Gemma mumbles. "Another witch. So glad I'm your token Muggle friend."

"Gemma."

"It's fine. Forget it." She turns to Morgan. "So, what can you do?"

Morgan fidgets with her hands. "It's so weird telling this to a Reg. How does she even know about you?"

Gemma makes a face, but I focus on Morgan's question. "It happened when the Hunter ran us off the road. I had to use my magic to get us out of the sinking car."

"Oh, right. Of course." Morgan looks to Gem and fusses with the ring on her finger, the one with the hidden pin. "Basically, my magic gives me better control over my body. Faster healing. Increased endurance and strength. That kind of stuff."

"Oh. That's not nearly as gross as I assumed." But then it's like something gels in her head. "Did you say *healing*?"

Morgan casts me a worried look, but she nods.

"That's perfect!" Gemma points to her cast-covered leg. "You can fix this. And help Hannah's dad." She adds that second part almost like she forgot he was in the room with us.

"I tried to help him, but I wasn't able to do much." Morgan twines her fingers together and won't look at either of us. "Healing others is a lot harder than our natural self-recovery."

"Oh." Gem shifts in her seat, her gaze lingering on my dad. There's a worry in her eyes that stabs at my heart. I have to look away when she turns her focus on me. "What about the third group, the Caster Witches? What do they do again?"

"They're more like your typical stereotype of a witch. Casters make potions and cast spells. That sort of thing." I smirk at Morgan. "They tend to be very buddy-buddy with Wiccans and other pagans."

Gemma's eyes grow wide. "Wait, so is Wiccan magic real, too?"

"Yeah. I mean, it's not anywhere near like what the Clans can do, but it's real." I think of Evan, of what happened to his father after he attempted magic he didn't fully understand. I really hope Lauren has him on a better path.

"Wow." Gemma taps her fingers on the arms of the chair. "That is so cool."

Morgan fidgets in her seat and pulls out her phone. "I can't believe Riley found us. I have to warn my parents."

"I need to update mine, too." I reach for my phone to text my mom. "Is it okay if I tell them? About you being . . ."

"A Blood Witch?" Morgan finishes for me, and heat flames my cheeks. I need to stop treating her Clan like it's a curse. She nods. "Of course."

"Hannah." Dad's voice is weak, but it cuts through the room, silencing Morgan. I turn as his eyes flutter open. "Hannah, is that you?"

"I'm here. I'm right here." I rush to his bed and reach for his hand, careful not to pull out the IV lines attached there. "It's going to be okay." I glance at Morgan and hope she can see the gratitude in my eyes.

"Where's your mother?"

"She's coming, Dad. She'll be here soon."

His eyes go wide. "The Hunter. He . . ." Dad's lips keep moving, but no sound comes out. His hand goes limp. His eyes roll back in his head. The alarms go off, screaming, piercing, shattering the calm of the room as Dad begins to shake.

Doctors flood in, pushing us out, dragging us away. The door slams in my face.

"Dad!" I bang on the window, but Morgan pulls me back. "Let me go! We have to get in there."

"Let the doctors work. They'll help him."

Gemma follows us down the hall. "Do you want me to call your mom again?"

Before I tell her that yes, yes I do want my mom, the elevator opens. Mom steps out, her phone pressed to her ear. "I don't care what he says. I want to speak with him. Tonight." She looks up and catches sight of us. Her phone drops from her hand and clatters against the floor. "What happened?"

"Dad, he . . . he . . ." I dissolve into tears, and Mom crushes me in a hug, smothering me in her familiar scent of chalk and honey.

"Mrs. Walsh?" An unfamiliar voice speaks behind me.

Mom shifts but doesn't let go. "Yes?"

"We spoke on the phone a few minutes ago. We thought your husband was doing well, but we've hit some unforeseen complications." The doctor, a tall white woman with curly black hair pulled into a bun, clears her throat. "We're taking him into surgery."

"What happened?" Mom's grip around me loosens and falls away. She sways on her feet, but I reach for her hand. We anchor each other. Two lost ships in a storm. "Where is he?"

The doctor closes the file she's holding. "We're taking him to the OR now. I can show you to our private waiting room."

Mom nods and picks up her phone. She glances to Gemma

and Morgan. "I appreciate you girls staying with Hannah, but I think we need some family time now." Mom gives me a look that says our family is about to include those bound by magic, not just by blood.

"I'll call as soon as I know anything," I promise.

Gemma crushes the air out of my lungs when she hugs me. "Call me if you need a place to sleep tonight."

Morgan offers a small smile. "If you need anything, anything at all—"

"I know how to find you."

With that, my best friend and my . . . and Morgan leave. Mom and I follow the doctor to the private waiting room, and when we're alone, I tell her about Morgan. She's shocked at first, jumping to some of the same conclusions I did, but when I explain that her ex is a Hunter, Mom texts a frantic update to Lady Ariana. After that, neither of us speaks for a long time. There's nothing more to say. Mom doesn't need to tell me the same fears that are running through my head are also in hers. Each worry is meticulously etched across her face.

So, we wait.

And hope the doctors are good at their jobs.

-�︱-　　⁎　　-�︱-

Mom and I flinch whenever someone passes the doorway to our private waiting room, our personal circle of misery. The hospital staff walk by without so much as a glance inside, without the barest acknowledgment of the fear that breeds in our hearts like a festering wound.

As the hours tick past, I come up with a plan. Once Dad is out of surgery, Morgan's parents can heal him fully, and then this Hunter is *mine*. Well, ours, anyway.

The room around me is filled with Elementals, with family bonded by magic and tragedy and fear. A family both born and chosen. My people. My community. My everything.

The Hunter picked the wrong coven—the wrong *family*—to mess with.

By the time my grandmother arrives, everyone is already here. Ellen Watson sits beside Rachel and Sarah Gillow while their parents speak in hushed tones. Mr. and Mrs. Blaise sit to my right, pushing food and drinks on me every few minutes. Veronica and her brother are here with their parents, but I don't have the emotional energy to even acknowledge her.

Lady Ariana stands at the center of the little room, and I've never seen her look more tired. Dark circles sit below her eyes, making her face look gaunt and almost hollow. Beneath her cracking composure is the same fear in my veins, fear for the loved one still in surgery.

"Is he coming?" Mom stands, her knees popping as they straighten for the first time in hours.

"Agent Archer is parking the car. He'll be up shortly." She looks past Mom and settles her unusually soft gaze on me. "I'm sorry, Hannah. You were right about our coven being in danger. I should have believed you from the moment I saw the sacrifice in the woods."

Her warmth is uncomfortable, especially since she was right. The sacrifice *was* a Reg dabbling in dangerous magic, just like she said, but I nod anyway. Even that small motion closes my throat and threatens tears. Lady Ariana shouldn't fracture like this. She's supposed to be the one who gives us strength.

"Has the agent—" Mom pauses when footsteps echo in the hall. She waits for the pair of nurses to pass before continuing. "Has he finished the tracking spell?"

"Almost. They're crafting two spells—it seems his assistant isn't entirely convinced this Riley fellow is in Salem—but still it shouldn't be more than a day." Lady Ariana smooths a thin hand across her white hair, but she can't disguise the way her fingers shake. "He will explain everything when he arrives, after he speaks with the team that took down the last Hunter."

This time, I do find my voice. "How many Hunters are there?"

"Nationally?" Lady Ariana shakes her head. "The Council isn't entirely sure."

I use the chair's arms to shove myself to my feet. "And what about locally? How many Hunters are in Salem? In Massachusetts?" When Lady Ariana doesn't respond, the room spins. *What have we gotten ourselves into?*

"Relax, Hannah." Mom grips my arm, her breath coming out white before her, and I finally notice the thrum of magic beneath my skin. My worry has latched on to the air, sucking out all the heat.

"Relax? How am I supposed to relax?" But even as I say the words, the air warms. I glance over at Lady Ariana, at the power in her stance, and know she's reclaimed ownership of the elements.

Footsteps cut through the silence, the click of dress shoes against tile floor. We stare at the doorway, waiting for the latest doctor to move out of earshot.

But the tall man doesn't pass our door. Instead, Detective Archer walks in, his little notebook in hand. "Miss Walsh." He nods in my direction.

"You." I storm over to Detective Archer, hands clenched into fists. Magic rising in my chest. "You were supposed to protect us. How could you let this happen?"

"Hannah!" Mom's horrified voice slows my rage. But only for a second.

"No, Mom. I'm sorry, but no. This man," I say, pointing at the detective, "wasted time following me across Salem instead of doing his job, and now Dad's . . . He's . . ." I can't even finish the thought.

"Hannah." This time, it's Lady Ariana who speaks my name, and it holds a power Mom's voice doesn't. The air around me grows thick. Heavy. It weighs on my limbs until I can't move.

The detective has the decency to put away his stupid notebook. "I'm sorry I wasn't faster, Hannah, and I'm so sorry about your home and your father, but I *will* stop this Hunter. My assistant is working on the tracking spells as we speak. It's only a matter of time."

"We're out of time, Detective. How many of us have to lose our homes before you stop this? If this isn't Riley, what other suspects *do* you have?"

I pause, and when he doesn't immediately respond, my anger flares. "Here, I have plenty. I've already given you Nolan Abbott—grade-A asshole and the right build to be Veronica's attacker. And then there's Savannah Clarke, the girl you first questioned me about. She threatened me at the Cauldron this week. Have you looked into either of them yet, or were you too busy sucking face with my boss to do your job?"

"*Hannah*," Mom snaps.

Detective Archer holds up a hand. "It's okay, Marie. Your daughter has every right to be upset."

No shit.

"I know I haven't earned it, but I need you to trust me." He steps forward, closing the space between us, bending forward until our eyes are level. "I did look into Nolan. So far, everything points to him being a Reg. He'll get community service for breaking your window, and if he's involved with the Hunters, I'll handle him. I promise."

A woman clears her throat before I can respond. "Excuse me? I'm looking for the Walsh family."

The detective steps aside, and I catch my first glimpse of the doctor in our doorway. She's the one from the waiting room, Dr. Perez. She looks disheveled now. Exhausted. Younger than I remember.

Mom takes a tentative step forward. "How is he?"

Dr. Perez grips the file in front of her like a shield. "We did everything we could."

We did everything... The room quivers around me. Detective Archer grabs my arm, and I realize I'm the one who's shaking. "No." I squeeze my eyes shut. This isn't happening. It's not real. "*No*. He's in recovery. He's fine."

"I'm so sorry." Dr. Perez approaches my mother and presses a small metal band into the palm of her hand. "I thought you might want this."

Mom uncurls her fingers and crumples when she sees what's inside, a sob catching in her throat. I catch a flash of gold before she clutches it to her chest, and my universe shatters when I realize what it is.

Dad's wedding ring.

My knees hit the ground. My lungs won't inflate. I can't breathe.

There's movement around me. Voices. Then shoes walking away. The flutter of a white jacket. Hands on my back. My shoulders. My arms. Tugging. Pulling. Pressing. I suffocate inside someone's hug.

And the world ceases to exist.

24

I WAKE IN A bed that isn't mine. My chest is tight, my eyes itchy and dry, but I have no memory of how I got here. The ground shifts beneath me as I turn. *An air mattress.* On the bed beside me I catch a glimpse of blonde hair and the edge of a pink cast.

Gemma.

And then it all comes rushing back.

My chest burns and my eyes fill and I'm doubled over and I can't breathe.

Dad's gone.

"Hannah?" Gemma's bed creaks and the air mattress dips with her weight. "Are you okay?"

I shake my head and grip her hand. "No." The word carves up my throat and scrapes over my tongue.

Gemma wraps her arms around me and holds me while I break into a million pieces. She shivers as my magic steals all warmth from the room, but I can't feel the cold. I can't see anything beyond the endless loop of my mother's broken expression.

Puffs of white air tell me Gemma's speaking. Saying she's sorry and that it'll all be okay. But I don't hear the words. The doctor's voice drowns out everything else. *We did everything we could.*

Everything we could.

Everything.

None of it seems real. Yet it's the *only* thing that's real.

I don't know how much time passes there on the air mattress—days, weeks, years—but eventually, I let Gemma drag me downstairs to the dining room for breakfast. Her parents try to talk to me, but I can't even look at them. I want my mom. My grandma. But they're both with Detective Archer, making sure they stop the Hunter, making sure I'm not next.

Gemma's parents leave for work, and I force myself to keep moving. I shower, the water masking my tears, but then I'm left standing in Gem's room with a towel and no clothes. Because my house is gone, too. I have nothing. I am nothing.

Mrs. Goodwin washed last night's outfit, but I don't want to wear it. The blood may be invisible, but it's there. Dripping off every thread.

Dad's gone.

I can't do this. I can't wear the same clothes I wore when he left us. "Gemma." My voice comes out rough and crackly from disuse. "I can't."

"Okay," she says, as if anything will ever be okay again. "I'll find something else. We'll get you dressed." She digs through her closet and comes up with a handful of items I've forgotten here over the past couple years.

I settle into an old pair of my jeans and the *I'm so gay I can't even think straight* T-shirt Veronica got me for Christmas, the one Gemma saved the day we purged my room down to a single box of keepsakes. The same keepsakes I burned last week.

Not that it matters. Everything is gone now.

Gem deposits me on the couch and brings me a mug of hot cocoa. I'm only halfway through the cup when Morgan comes over. She and Gemma speak in hushed tones and then settle on either side of me. They steal glances at me like I'm about to fall apart, burst at the seams, and maybe they're not wrong. Maybe I am about to lose it.

Something buzzes in my pocket. I pull out my phone, but it won't stop shaking. There's text after text after text of *I'm so sorry* and *I heard about your dad* and *I'm thinking of you.*

"Please take this." I shove the phone away, and Gemma grabs it up. "I can't . . ."

"It's fine. I got it. I'll let you know if anything important comes through." She sets the phone on her other side, safely out of reach. Out of sight.

"I know there's nothing we can say to make this better." Morgan reaches for my hand and squeezes tight. "But if there's anything you need to talk about or anything we can do, we're here for you. We've got your back."

I nod, but there's nothing they can do to give me what I want. They can't bring back my dad. No magic is that strong.

The room falls silent for a long time. I stare at the floor, where the carpet's stained a little red. Wine. Blood. It makes little difference. Then slowly, ever so slowly, the gears begin to turn inside my head. They *tick, tick, tick* until an idea burns away the fog. "Anything?"

Morgan nods. "Of course."

"Anything," Gemma agrees.

I exhale a shaky breath. "I want to find the Hunter."

I want to kill him.

"Hannah." Morgan pulls her hand away. I'd forgotten it was there. "Hunters are dangerous. And unbelievably hard to trace. We should let the Council handle this."

"They had their chance. They failed." Energy builds inside me until my knees are bouncing and I can't sit a second longer. I stand and pace the living room, air swirling around me. Morgan stares, something strange flickering across her face. I turn to Gemma. She wants to be part of this. She can be swayed. "Please, Gem. I need this. I need to do something."

Gemma looks between me and Morgan, uncertainty flickering in her eyes.

"Gemma, please." My voice breaks, and I don't even have to fake it.

"Fine." My best friend sighs. "I'm in. But if we're doing this, we're going to do it right."

"Of course." Whatever it takes to get her to agree. I'm going to stop this Hunter. Make him wish he never set foot in Salem. "Morgan?"

"You're sure about this?" Morgan waits for my answer, and I only nod. My blood is boiling, my magic itching under my skin. "Well, I'm certainly not letting you do it alone. Count me in."

Gemma looks between us. "So where do we start? Hannah said the Hunters were supposed to be wiped out. How are they back?"

I see the masked Hunter in my head. Hear the stories Lady Ariana told. My magic burns like acid, desperate for a way out. The house trembles as the earth beneath us shakes.

"Maybe you should sit down." Morgan reaches for me, but I back away. I can't stop moving. If I stop, I'll break. I'll shatter like glass.

Eventually, Morgan sighs and looks at Gem. "I'm not entirely sure. We thought the Council took out the last group of Hunters back in—what? The sixties? They must have gone underground. I don't know what brought them back out of hiding, but something obviously has."

Gemma shifts and grabs a pillow, shoving it under her broken leg. "So, what? They're out there tracking down witches? How many people have they killed?" Her words pierce my armor, and I suck in a breath. "Sorry, Han."

I nod, but tears prickle at my eyes. I push down, down, down on the feeling. Bury it deep. My arms shake. The pictures on the walls rattle.

"Hannah, you have to stop." Morgan's up a second later, blocking my path. She places her hands on my face, leans her forehead to mine. "You have to breathe."

"I can't."

"Then let me help you." She slips off her ring and reaches for the small pin. "Can I?" There's a pulse of fear at her suggestion, but I trust her. When I nod, she pricks my finger and gently wipes the blood away.

A numbing sensation washes through me, and I manage my first deep breath since the fire, tears slipping down my face.

"We don't have to do this," she whispers, her power humming through my veins. "We don't have to talk about him."

I don't know which *him* she's referring to, but my heart rate slows. A shuddering breath fills my lungs. The house stops shaking.

Somehow, I find my voice. "I need this. We have to stop him." *I have to stop him.* I let Morgan bring me back to the couch, and the cushions swallow me up. Once my friends help me find the Hunter, I'll take him down myself. I won't put anyone else in his crosshairs.

"How do we identify the Hunter?" Gemma asks.

"That's the tricky part. It's basically impossible to tell." Morgan rubs the back of her neck with one hand. "Hannah already knows this, but I accidentally dated one."

"What?" Gemma asks, her voice pitched high with shock.

Morgan nods. "Hunters are hard to find but not impossible. The biggest giveaway is how they insinuate themselves into the witch's life. They have to make sure their target is a witch before they . . . do what they do."

Before they kill. That's what she won't say. I hate this. Hate the Hunters. Hate the questions that fill my brain to bursting. *How close did Morgan come to dying? How did she manage to escape when my dad couldn't? Why him and not her?*

"Wait, so your ex tried to kill you?" Gemma asks.

"Yeah. I had a rough junior year." She clasps her hands together and won't look at either of us. "Riley was the sweetest guy at first. When his parents went out of town one weekend, we decided to cook dinner together instead of going out. I slipped and sliced my finger."

She holds up her thumb, but it looks perfect. Unblemished. "I tried to play it off, but he noticed the cut. And then noticed how quickly it disappeared. If he were a normal Reg, it might have been fine. But Hunters spend their entire lives training to spot witches. He knew what I was the second he saw my healed thumb. It was . . . not good."

"Damn, that really sucks," Gemma says. "Do you think Riley followed you to Salem?"

"That's what I thought, but Detective Archer called my parents last night. Riley isn't here." Morgan pulls her knees to her chest. "My family has the worst luck, picking two towns with Hunters in them."

A bitterness coats my tongue. Her dad isn't the one lying in a morgue. Mine is. But before I can say anything, before I can utter something I'll regret, a different voice worms its way inside my head.

Help!

Veronica.

Hannah, please. Hurry!

Panic destroys whatever was left of the calm Morgan magicked over me. This time, the advanced air magic shouts loud in my head, Veronica's message coming in crystal clear. *He's here!*

I'm off the couch a second later, searching my pockets for my phone. I spot it by Gemma and lunge for it, dialing her number by memory. It rings and rings and then picks up. Static greets me on the other end. Followed by a crash and something shattering.

"Veronica! What's happening? Where are you?" Worry slithers up my throat. *Not again. Not again.*

A door slams. "He's back, Han. The Hunter. He's back."

"Where are you?" My power surges. The ground rumbles. "Veronica!"

Veronica shouts. In the distance, there's another scream, high and terrified. "I'm home. He's got a—"

Gunfire rings out.

And the line goes dead.

25

"I HAVE TO GO."

"What happened?" Gemma asks at the same time Morgan says, "I'm going with you."

"Absolutely not." I can't lose anyone else. I rush out of the living room and throw on my shoes. "Call the police and ask for Detective Archer. Tell him the Hunter's at Veronica's house. Gemma, call my mom. I'm going after him."

"You're *what*?" Morgan chases after me and blocks my path to the door. "You can't go after a Hunter alone. It's not safe!"

"Get out of my way." Power ripples across my skin. "Now."

Morgan holds her ground. "Take me with you. I can help."

"Move." I grab hold of the air's energy. The wind picks up, pulling at Morgan's hair. "I won't ask again."

"Hannah . . ."

She doesn't get a chance to finish. I tug on the air's current, pushing Morgan away from the door and shoving her into the living room. I'm through the door a second later, slamming it closed behind me. Outside, the earth hums beneath my feet. I turn and urge the bushes to grow around the door handle, blocking them inside.

And then I'm gone. My heart lurches as I jump inside Dad's car, but I force the emotions away and slam the key into the ignition. I race to Veronica's house, trying to send air messages as I go.

Veronica doesn't respond, and worries scream through my head on an endless loop.

Don't be dead. Don't be dead. Please, don't be dead.

As Veronica's house comes into view, I'm surprised to find it smoke-free. The house looks empty. Untouched. I don't hear any sirens in the distance, but I'm sure Morgan has them on their way.

Guilt tries to rise up, tries to drown me in panic, but I push it down. I push everything down until there's only vengeance. Only power.

I park and leap from my car. Lady Ariana must have pulled the protection detail from Veronica's house now that her binding tattoo has worn off. I don't see anyone I know parked on the street.

Worry flames the embers of my magic, and it hurts too much to keep it locked beneath my skin. So I let it out, let my power tug at the air and shake the earth as I race up the steps. All my worst fears have already come to pass. Why should I care about the rules?

The front door is unlocked, and I slip inside. Every sense is on high alert, yet there's nothing but echoes in the house. Echoes of power. Echoes of fear. The air reacts around me, dancing with my hair, swirling around my skin. If the Hunter is here, I'm ready.

I check the first floor. Each room is vacant but clearly disturbed. Chairs knocked onto the ground. Picture frames shattered, glass sparkling on the carpet. Dirty footprints that lead upstairs.

Air swirls tighter, curling into my hands, ready to attack the Hunter if he leaps out of one of the bedrooms. My feet lead me to Veronica's room, pulled by the gravity of all the time I've spent inside, of all the memories.

There's a bullet hole in her doorframe. The door itself is smashed inward, hanging on broken hinges.

I force my magic away when I see what's inside.

"Savannah." I rush into the room, sidestepping a pool of blood that I refuse to look at. She's tied to Veronica's desk chair, a gag in her mouth. "Are you okay?"

Her reply is muffled, and tears stream down her face. I reach for the gag first, untying one of Veronica's scarves. She gasps when her mouth is clear. "He took her. He took Veronica."

"Was she alive?" I reach for the knots tying Savannah to the chair. "Who did this to you?"

"I don't know." Savannah winces when her broken arm, still in its cast, is freed. "He shot her. In the arm I think. She was still conscious after, but then he hit her with the butt of the gun. I didn't see his face."

Sirens wail in the distance. "It's going to be okay, Savannah. The police are on their way." I kneel before her and work at the ropes holding her legs. "Do you remember anything else? Did you hear a voice? See hair color? Anything?"

She shakes her head. "He was wearing all black. A mask and gloves and everything."

"There must be something. Even if it's small." *Come on, come on. Before the police get here.* I grip her arms, squeezing tight. "Anything else? Please, try to remember."

Savannah shakes her head, tears streaming down her cheeks. "You have to save her. We're supposed to go to college together in the fall. And I . . ."

"You what?" I snap, losing patience when she trails off.

"I'm in love with her." A sob catches in her throat. "I've been in love with her since we were freshmen. You have to get her back. Please."

"Then help me. There has to be something else." I kneel in front of her. "Give me something, Savannah. Veronica's life depends on it."

That, at least, gets Savannah to nod. To close her eyes. While she thinks, I pace the room, stealing glances out the window. Police cars race down the street toward us. We're running out of time.

"Wait. There is something."

Finally. "What?"

"He must be in college. He had a fraternity tattoo." Savannah traces one finger across the inside of her right wrist. "When he picked up Veronica, his sleeve lifted enough to show it."

"What was it? What did it look like?" I sneak a look out the window. The first car screeches to a halt across the street. "Can you describe it?"

Savannah nods. "It was a triangle. It looked like a delta."

My heart stops cold. "What?"

"Delta, the Greek letter."

It can't be. "Are you sure?" A memory surfaces, and it turns my stomach. *It's delta. The symbol for change. It's the only thing in life you can really count on.*

Savannah glares at me, looking more like her usual self. Or, at least, the only side of her I ever had a chance to know. With her feelings for Veronica, I probably only saw the harshest parts of her personality, not the real girl underneath. "Of course I'm sure. My mom was a Delta Sigma Theta. I'd recognize that symbol anywhere."

I'm out the door a second later.

"Where are you going?" she calls, but I'm already halfway down the stairs. "Hannah!"

I pause at the sliding glass door, boarded up from the last time I was here. "He's not in a fraternity. It was Benton Hall."

"Benton? Wait! Where are you going?"

"I'm going to save her."

26

BENTON'S THE WITCH HUNTER.

I speed through town, a single certainty pulsing through my veins.

Benton Hall killed my father.

Through the haze, I hear my phone ringing on and on. I don't bother checking the screen to see who it is. I won't let anyone talk me out of this.

It's time for Benton to burn.

Somewhere in the back on my mind, all the pieces fit together. Benton befriending me in art class, joking and laughing and creating all year. Then it's summer and he's asking me out, keeping me close.

He's the one who attacked Veronica. He's the one who ran me off the road and broke Gemma's leg. The one who destroyed my home. Tried to destroy Nolan's—

I slam my foot on the brake as I reach the turn and fly around the corner.

Benton's the one who set the fire at Nolan's house. He must have gotten trapped on the second floor when Veronica added her power to the flames. I can't believe I played detective with him while he plotted to kill my family. I should have left him to die at Nolan's house. If I had, none of this would have happened.

My dad would still be alive.

As the Hall mansion comes into view, my hands clench around the steering wheel. There will be nothing left when I'm done. I throw the car in park and lean across the seat, digging through Dad's glove box for the matches he kept there. I clutch them tight in my fist and hurry out of the car. The earth trembles the moment my foot touches grass, the air whipping around me. Every element reaches for my power. I stow the matches in my pocket, keeping the fire close but unlit.

I won't let the house burn until I know for sure Veronica isn't inside.

As I approach, the mansion seems to grow taller, more threatening, but its size won't keep me out. It won't scare me away. I bound up the marble steps and rest my hands across the mahogany wood of the front door. My magic itches, presses, wants me to burn my way through the entrance, but instead of the matches in my pocket, I reach for a different element.

The wooden door trembles beneath my fingers, then *CRACKS*. It pulls away from its hinges and falls forward into the foyer. I'm greeting by vaulted ceilings and silence.

"Benton!" My voice echoes back at me, over and over. No one responds.

Air whips through the house, searching for signs of life. Nothing. No one. A frustrated scream tears from my lips. Every window shatters, shooting glass onto the lawn. I hope it ruins his pool.

The stairs catch my eye, those damn six-foot oil paintings mocking me. Generations of Witch Hunters line the steps. How many of us have they killed over the years? How are we just finding out about them now? At the top of the stairs, Benton's senior portrait completes the line.

I tap my pocket, the matches there a temptation. Once I find Veronica and make sure she's safe, I'm going to burn this whole place to the ground, starting with Benton's portrait.

Hannah . . .

Mom's voice is at my ear, inside my head.

Hannah, where are you?

Gemma must have called. Told her I went after Veronica.

Dammit, Hannah, answer—

I tug on the air, and it swirls around me, blocking out whatever message Mom has sent. I am *not* giving up, not when I'm so close. I'll figure out where Benton took Veronica, and then we'll see how *he* handles his life burning down around him.

Once I'm upstairs, it doesn't take long to find Benton's room. I hate it immediately. A king-sized bed sits centered against the far wall, and there's still room for a huge desk, sofa, TV, and gaming corner, with plenty more room to move around. The far wall is a testament to his privileged life, full of trophies and medals like the ones he feigned embarrassment over the last time I was here.

I knock the whole thing down with a burst of air—delighting in the sound of snapping metal as the trophies break—and search the rest of the room for clues, anything that will tell me where he took Veronica. Where he plans to kill her. I swallow hard at the thought, overturning his bed and spilling his shelves onto the floor.

My magic flares as my frustration grows. Picture frames rattle against the walls until they fall, shattered glass shining like diamonds on the carpet.

There are two doors in the bedroom, both closed. I check the first, a bathroom. The Halls definitely use a maid service because there's no way any teenager keeps their bathroom that immaculate. The glass door of the shower shines like crystal.

The urge to throw something against the glass, to shatter it everywhere, rises up in my chest. I hate that Benton has all this when he's the reason my home was destroyed. When he's the reason my father is gone and I have *nothing* of his to hold. Not a single keepsake. Everything he ever touched is ash.

Magic swirls in my chest, begging me to light a match. To release the element that really knows how to rage.

"Hannah? What are you doing here?"

Magic and adrenaline flood my system. My hands tremble. Air swirls through the bathroom, tugging at my clothes, and I reach for the matches in my pocket.

The *click-click-click* of Benton cocking a gun sends chills down my spine. He must have returned after my initial check of the house. "I really wish you wouldn't." He sounds almost sad. "Why couldn't you leave it alone?"

I turn to face the Hunter, and he's closer than I expected, the gun just a few inches from my face. "What, like you left my family alone?" I flex my hands, drawing a pocket of denser air into my palm.

Benton steps closer, the gun pressing flush against my forehead. "I can shoot faster than you can conjure."

I let the pocket of air drop away. "Where's Veronica? What did you do to her?"

"She's alive, for now." His hand shakes, but from cold or fear, I can't tell. "I really wish you hadn't come. I didn't want to kill you."

"You had no problem killing my father."

"Hannah—"

My phone rings, loud and obnoxious, and we both flinch. The gun drops. Just an inch.

But it's enough.

I shove into Benton with all my weight. We fall to the floor, the phone and gun skidding in opposite directions. The house shakes beneath us, trembling as I reach for every element I can touch. Pipes burst in the bathroom. Wind separates us, pushing me near my ringing phone. I answer.

"It's Benton. He's trying to—" A scream cuts off my words as Benton grabs the back of my head and pulls me upright, away from the phone. "You don't have to do this, Benton. You don't have to kill us." I try to shout, but the words come out breathy and weak as he wraps a hand around my throat.

"Yes. I do."

He grips the barrel of his gun, lifts it above my head, and swings.

27

EVERY INCH OF ME hurts when I wake. It starts with my head—Benton must have hit me—but the ache spreads all the way down to my toes. Like I've been thrown down a flight of stairs.

Maybe I have been.

My eyelids struggle open, and the light sends a fresh wave of pain through my head. When my eyes adjust to the brightness, I realize I'm surrounded by rich black leather, cramped and shoved into the tiny backseat of a two-door sports car.

With Veronica.

I try to call her name, but I can't. Duct tape covers my mouth, the discomfort masked by all the other pain in my body. But though I can't form the words, my voice hums in my throat.

Benton glances in the rearview mirror, and there's a glint to his eyes that I've never seen before. "You weren't supposed to wake up."

The tape over my mouth muffles the *fuck you, asshole*, but even as I glare at Benton, panic rises, threatening to drown out all my training.

Where is he taking us?

What is he going to do?

Why didn't he just shoot us?

At least my hands are bound in front of me. I rip off the tape, cursing at the pain. My eyes sting, but even as I taste blood on my lips, I try to focus. "Veronica? Veronica, wake up." I reach out and feel for her breath. It's there. Faint, but there.

I inhale deep, trying to draw courage from the air, but it doesn't help. Nothing helps.

"She's not going to wake up."

"Excuse me if I don't trust the guy trying to kill us." I lean forward and search under the seats, looking for something— anything—that might be helpful. If I can untie my hands, I can at least get an air message to my mom.

Benton flashes me a look I can't read. "Trust? That's rich, coming from the girl who broke into my house." His fingers tighten around the steering wheel. "Do you have any idea how much a door like that costs?"

"Screw you." I reach for my magic and I find . . . nothing. The swirl of power in my chest is there, I can *feel* it, but I can't access it. Can't try my grandmother's advice to steal the breath from Benton's lungs until he passes out cold.

Benton must see the tense concentration, the panic, the worry, because he smiles. "It feels amazing, doesn't it? To be completely human for once."

"What did you do?" My head swims as he takes another sharp turn, and I slide across the leather seat, closer to Veronica. He probably gave me a concussion with the blow from the gun, but that's not enough to block my magic. "What did you *do* to me?"

"It's an old family recipe, actually. We're so close to getting it right." Benton sighs, and there's this hitch in his voice. "I tried so hard to keep you out of this, Hannah. I wanted to save you, but you wouldn't leave it alone."

His words send a chill down my spine. The effect is sobering, but it doesn't clear away the fog slowing my reactions. "What are you talking about?"

Benton glances in the rearview again, his eyes shimmering. "The drug's effects aren't permanent yet, but soon we'll be able to save you. Instead of killing you, we can make you human."

"We *are* human. We've always *been* human." I try to sound reassuring, but I can't hide the bitter rage swirling inside. "We've never done anything to you."

Veronica is still unconscious beside me, oblivious to the danger we're in. I reach out and stroke the hair from her face, and my fingers glance across cool metal. I pull the bobby pin from her hair and hide it between my hands, my heart thudding loud in my ears. I don't think I can angle it right to cut away the tape at my wrists, but if I could free my ankles, I'd have a chance to escape.

"Your kind is a danger to society. We can't take that risk."

I ignore Benton. Clearly, the other Hunters have him convinced he's a hero, and I'm not going to waste precious seconds trying to undo whatever brainwashing they've done. Instead, I pull my knees into my chest, wincing as the movement pushes a wave of nausea through me.

Focus. I swipe the sharp end of the bobby pin across the tape, but it's too dull. There's no way it'll cut through fast enough. I shift the pin and angle it so the edge pokes through the layers of duct tape. I retract the metal and puncture the tape again and again and again, forming a jagged line of holes in my binding. I flinch each time the tape *pops* as the pin pokes through, but Benton doesn't seem to notice.

Shit. I suck in a breath when the next stab misses and goes through an existing hole, stabbing my leg. I wince as it breaks the skin, drawing Benton's attention. "How did you figure out what we are?" I ask, desperate to distract him from what I'm doing.

He taps his thumbs against the steering wheel and signals for his next turn. "We received word of a family of witches moving east, so we've been on high alert for signs of magic. I noticed Veronica first." He glances in his mirror, like he can see her slumped against the window. "At the party in the woods. I thought it was weird how quickly the fire went out, so I set a trap for her at Nolan's. I set a small fire outside the bedroom door to see what she'd do."

I can see it. Veronica opening the door to flames, dampening them without a second thought. Restarting them after she and Savannah were clear so Savannah wouldn't notice what she'd done. "I should have let you die there."

Benton winces. "That's how I found out you were a witch, too. But you were different from the others. You used your curse to help me. I wanted to return the favor. I wanted to wait, to save you. We just needed a little more time to perfect the cure." He glowers at me. "But then after you attacked me at Veronica's house, I knew you had to be stopped."

"Excuse me for not letting you kill my ex." The bobby pin tumbles from my grip, but there are enough holes in the tape now. I shove my fingers through and get ready to tug. "And we aren't *sick*. There's nothing to cure."

Benton shakes his head and pulls off the road. As the wheels spin against gravel, I tug with all my strength. The tape gives way with a drawn-out *riiiiip*.

I lean back and bring my knees to my chest, pushing Veronica out of the way with my bound hands.

"What are you—"

But Benton doesn't finish his question. I kick my leg through the space between the front seats, catching him on the side of his head. I rear back to kick again, but he's faster than I am. He blocks my attack and slams the car into park. I try again, my back pressed against the seat, but Benton swings open his door.

The front seat folds forward, and Benton reaches inside, dragging Veronica out. They disappear from my line of sight, and I can only assume he's laying her on the ground.

The Hunter leans into the car to pull me out next, and I let him. I'm not going to make my final stand in the backseat of a car, flailing like a cornered cat. But once my feet hit solid ground, I bolt. I run as fast as my legs will carry me, heading back toward the road, hoping someone will drive by and spot me. Spot the murderer chasing after me.

But I'm not fast enough.

Benton tackles me from behind. I hit the dirt. Taste blood.

And everything goes black.

-|-   *   -|-

If I wasn't concussed before, I am now. I roll over on my side and throw up, my insides spilling all over the ground. My mind is mushy, my vision full of shadows. Beside me, Veronica groans.

She's still alive. *We're* still alive.

A series of coughs wracks my body, and I heave. I'm dizzy and disoriented. Unsteady. I dig my fingers into the rich earth, reaching for its energy, trying to tap into its strength, its calm. Nothing. I'm still cut off from my magic. The realization clenches my insides, but I have nothing left to expel.

How long until the drugs wear off?

How long can we survive without our magic?

I collapse onto my back. Beside me, Veronica's eyelids flutter as she finally starts to stir. Her brows shoot up when her gaze finds mine. "Hannah? What's happening? Where are we?"

"I don't know," I whisper back, my voice hoarse.

The hollow, dull clang of wood smashing against wood draws my attention. I turn to the sound, but my head swims. Despite the nausea, I force myself up until I'm sitting.

Benton throws another piece of wood onto a large pile. It's at least five feet across and nearly up to his waist.

We need to get out of here.

I try to stand, but my legs aren't working. Fear slows the blood in my veins when I glance down. There will be no escaping. Not without our magic. Benton has bound our legs together, from ankle to knee. We're as good as dead.

"Veronica." I keep my voice low so Benton won't hear. "Veronica, can you feel the elements? Any of them?" The earth's power sits untapped beneath me. So close yet untouchable.

She closes her eyes and furrows her brow. She falls silent and still, and I wonder if she's passed out again. But then her eyes flutter open, filled with tears. "No." Her whole body quivers, her voice breaking as tears carve down her bloody face. "Hannah, I'm scared. I don't want to die."

"We'll find a way out of this. We'll be fine." I push down the terror. If only we had our magic, we could call for help. We could warn the coven.

I glance over at Benton, and when I realize what he's doing, my heart stops.

Benton raises a pole into the sky, at the center of his pile of wood and kindling.

He's going to burn us at the stake.

The Witch Hunter stands in front of his finished pyre, hands on hips, head tilted to one side. Like he's making sure everything is even. Balanced. After a beat, he turns and faces the witches he spent the summer hunting.

Veronica turns, following my gaze. "Benton?" Confusion rides high in her voice. "What are you doing?"

I scoot back an inch, putting myself between my ex and our would-be killer. "He's a Witch Hunter, Veronica. He's the one who shot you."

"He *shot* me?" Veronica looks down at her arm like she's finally understanding where the pain is coming from. "Why?" Veronica asks, breaking into sobs as Benton slinks toward us. "Why are you doing this?"

"Your kind shouldn't exist." Benton squeezes his eyes shut, like he can't bear to look at us. "You especially, Veronica. You almost killed me that night at Nolan's house, all because you're poisoned with a power no human should have."

"We're just as human as you are," I snap. "Maybe more, since we've never *killed* anyone." I don't mention how strongly I still want to kill him, how much I want him to suffer for what he's done. Instead, I search for power in the air, in the earth beneath me—*anything*—but they're still outside my reach.

Something I can't name flashes across Benton's face, but whatever it was, he shakes it away until his face is blank. Emotionless. "How many of you are there? A dozen? Two dozen? I know your sickness is hereditary, so your parents are like you. Veronica's little brother, too."

Behind me, Veronica thrashes against her bindings. "Don't you *dare* go near him. Or I'll—"

"You'll what? Use your magic to 'make me pay'?" Benton paces back and forth between us and the pyre. Tracking his movement makes my head swim. "Deny it all you want, but when push comes to shove, *your kind* are the monsters. You're the things we humans fear in the dark."

"How is this any different?" I ask, struggling against the tape on my hands. "You pretended to be my friend and then you *murdered* my dad!"

"That wasn't me." Color creeps into Benton's face, and he won't meet my gaze. "I took too long to do my job. The Order was asking questions, so my parents had to take matters into their own hands."

"What?" I can't stop the tears now, and they blur Benton out of my sight. Somehow, the revelation finds new ways to hurt me. I can see it. His parents, full-fledged adult Hunters, stealing into my house and ambushing my dad.

Behind me, Veronica shudders an inhale. "You don't have to do this," she says, her voice high and pleading. "You can let us go."

The Witch Hunter considers us, his eyes glimmering. "If I don't kill you, the Order *will*. And then they'll kill me for being too weak to do my job." He lifts his shirt, revealing a patchwork of angry bruises all along his torso. "I thought you were going to catch me, Hannah, when you noticed the bruise along my jaw. I almost let the truth slip when you asked."

I remember that day at work, how he defended me against Nolan. I hate how grateful I felt in that moment. If only I knew then what I know now, I could have stopped him. I could have saved Dad.

"When my parents found out you'd been at our house, they gave me an ultimatum. If I ever wanted to make it as a Hunter, I needed to kill my first witch within the week. I tried to do my job on the bridge, but I didn't see Gemma until the car was already going over the edge." He drops his shirt, covering the bruises. "We aren't supposed to hurt humans. The Order doesn't tolerate mistakes."

"We could protect you," Veronica says, and I try to stop her. I want Benton *dead*, not protected by the Clans, but I can't get my voice to work. She tries again. "If you let us go, we could protect you. I swear—"

"No one can stop the Order," Benton snaps. "And even if you *could*, it doesn't change what you are. Your abilities are an abomination." Benton bends and leans his face close to mine. "I wanted to save you. I tried to kill Veronica first to buy you more time. I could have cured your whole family if you hadn't interrupted."

"Fuck you." I spit in his face and kick up with my bound legs. My shoes catch Benton in his already injured stomach, and it takes him a moment to find his breath. I scoot back, but I only make it an inch or two before he recovers.

He picks me up by my shirt, tearing the collar, and drags me away from Veronica. I struggle with every ounce of strength I have left, digging my heels into the ground, making it as hard as possible to pull me to the pyre.

The Hunter doesn't care. He throws me over his shoulder and carries me the rest of the way. I try to kick him, but the angle is all wrong, and I can hardly keep my eyes open.

Splinters stab at my shins, my calves, my arms as Benton throws me against the woodpile. He grabs the tape and ties me to the stake.

"Please, Benton," I beg, tears streaming down my face. "Don't do this."

He ignores me. When he's finished, he drags Veronica over. She puts up even less of a fight. Only her voice rails against him, all the strength gone from her body.

When Veronica is taped to the stake behind me, our backs flush, Benton jumps down from the pyre. He steps back to examine his handiwork and picks up a red plastic can I didn't notice before. He uncaps the top. The smell hits me a moment before the liquid covers the wood beneath my feet and splashes against my legs.

Gasoline.

"Benton, please. Don't do this." Veronica's words come out choked, slurred by her tears. "You can't kill us like this. You can't. You have the gun. Just end it."

But the Hunter shakes his head. "We will no longer hide our work behind accidents." Benton sloshes the gasoline onto our legs, and I can see it. Hunters orchestrating car crashes and house fires all across the country. Taking out Clan witches without raising suspicion for fifty years. "Your deaths will be a message."

When Benton moves out of sight, soaking the rest of the wood with gasoline, Veronica's hand finds mine. "I'm sorry," she says. "For everything." She grips my hand so hard it hurts. "And I'm sorry that you saw me with Savannah. I wasn't trying to hurt you. We just sorta . . . happened."

I try to tell her it's okay, that I want her and Savannah to make it work, that I'm falling for Morgan, but I can't get the words past my lips. Everything hurts. I can barely breathe through the tears and sharp smell of gasoline. I manage to squeeze her hand, but even that's a struggle.

"Hannah . . ." She tries again. "I don't want to die like this."

Dad's voice is in my ears, reminding me I'm not a hero. That

I should have left Benton in the house for someone else to save. But then Veronica's hand tightens in mine. "We're not going to die. Not like this," I tell her, tugging at my tape, reaching for the elements. Pushing against whatever Benton has done to me. "It's not over. Not yet."

"That's where you're wrong." Benton drops the empty can and pulls a blowtorch from the messenger bag on the ground. He lights it and finally meets my gaze. "It's very much over."

Then Benton Hall steps forward and sets the world on fire.

28

I'M GOING TO DIE.

Fire licks at my feet, looking for a way in, but I don't burn. Not yet. I'm not sure how this drug works, but it must not erase our magic completely. We can't control it, but it's still there, buried somewhere inside. Not that there's much comfort in that.

The smoke is thick and toxic, choking off my lungs. Flames lick along the path of gasoline and consume the wood beneath my feet. The smoke grows denser and more toxic with every breath. Panic clears my cloudy mind, but I can't find clean air, can't call it to me.

Behind me, Veronica coughs and chokes. Her grip on my hand goes slack. Loosens. Drops.

"Veronica!" I can barely hear myself over the roaring fire licking at my legs. My skin may not burn, but the tape that binds me melts and my jeans catch fire. The fabric crumbles to ash around my legs. "Veronica, hold on." My voice dies in a fit of coughing. Shadows crowd out my vision as my brain is starved of air.

Benton stands before us, but his expression is hidden in shadow. I try to yell at him, to curse him, to beg him to stop, but there isn't enough breath in my lungs to form the words. Soon, he's barely visible through the smoke and the red-orange flames blotting out my vision. But I don't want Benton to be the last thing I see before I die. He can't be.

I close my eyes and imagine the future I'll never see.

Mom is there, inside my head, grieving but never alone—surrounded always by the rest of the coven. Lady Ariana moves the families out of Salem, keeping everyone safe. Gemma goes with them, an honorary Elemental, under our protection for the rest of her life. Even though I know it's impossible, I allow myself the dream.

Veronica shows up next. I reach for her hand, but I can't feel anything besides the heat pressing, pressing, pressing against my skin, waiting for an opening, a way around the Elemental protection no drug can wipe away. Only death.

Shadows drag me down, and the person inside my head next is Morgan.

Her laugh. Her red hair shining in the sunlight. The way the corners of her lips crinkle when she's trying not to smile. The moment she realized I was an Elemental and used her Blood Magic to help my dad.

Dad . . .

I hope he's waiting for me on the other side. Hope he's there with a laugh and a shrug and an embrace that crushes away the pain. We can watch over Mom. Make sure she's all right. Make sure . . .

An explosion rocks the pyre beneath me. There's a ringing in my ears. Light flashes, glowing red on the other side of my closed eyelids, and then I'm drowning. The fire below me hissing and screaming its own death.

Shouts cut over the noise, and then I'm ice. Shivering and cold. Hands grip me. Wind whips in my face, and I can *feel* the ground rising up to meet me. But the collision never comes.

And then the hands are back. On my face. My neck. My

wrists. The pressure hurts. I want it to stop. I just want to sleep and let the afterworld take me. I want my dad.

Pressure slams into my chest. I cry out and gulp in a huge rush of clean air.

I cough, the movement shaking my whole body. Somewhere in the back of my rattled, oxygen-deprived head I realize the tape is gone. My limbs are free. My skin survived unburned.

More voices join the one beside my ear, but I can't hang on to their words, can't separate the jumble of vowels and consonants and sounds beyond the high-pitched wail of distant sirens.

Until, suddenly, I can.

"Open your eyes," a woman's voice commands. Her hands on my shoulders. Another gust of air rushes into my lungs. "Hannah. Open your eyes."

She sounds so insistent, like she's not used to being ignored. But I'm so tired. So bone-weary and exhausted. Why won't she leave me alone? I want to sleep until death comes to find me.

The ground rumbles like it's displeased with me. The shaking jumbles my mushy brain, and I hear myself groan. "Hurts . . . Stop . . ." My tongue is heavy and thick, but the words come out.

The voice above me sighs, the only clue she's relieved. "The police will be here soon. You must deny any knowledge of the boy's motives."

The boy's what? And then I place the cold, concise voice above me. "Grandma?" I force my eyelids open, but even that hurts. Smoke stings my eyes, but I turn my head, searching. "Veronica? Is she—"

"She's fine. You both are." Lady Ariana, my grandmother, looks at me with more warmth than I thought she was capable of feeling, let alone showing. "You stubborn, foolish girl." I must be imagining things, because I think she sounded proud.

Veronica's shape comes into view. She's lying on the ground a few feet away, her shoes burned and falling apart. But the steady rise and fall of her chest, combined with Lady Ariana's assurances, lets me hope she's really okay.

"How did you find us?" I glance up at my grandmother. She snaps her fingers, creating a fire all her own, and tosses it toward Benton's pyre, reigniting the blaze. Speaking of Benton. "Where is he?"

"Agent Archer is handling the *Hunter*." She practically spits the word and gestures to my other side. "He got your message and tracked the boy."

I turn and find Detective Archer leaning over Benton. My coworker, Cal, stands behind him with a vial of green liquid in his hands, whispering something I can't hear. I must have hit my head harder than I thought. "What's Cal doing here?"

"He's the agent's assistant. He's putting the finishing touches on a binding spell." A murderous expression flashes through my grandmother's eyes as she stares at Benton's still form. "The Hunter won't be able to share his knowledge of the Clans, no matter how hard he tries."

Archer pours the glowing green liquid down Benton's throat. The Hunter coughs, sputtering awake. He tries to break out of Archer's grip, but Archer flips Benton onto his stomach and secures the handcuffs as a horde of police officers swarms through the trees.

"Over here!" he calls. "Read his rights and take this scum back to the precinct."

Officers descend upon Benton, and he almost seems relieved as he's dragged away.

Detective Archer rushes to my side, Cal on his heels. "I need medics! We've got two down. Smoke inhalation. Possible burns."

The medics race toward us, two flat boards between them. Someone shoves an oxygen mask on my face, and it's the most glorious thing in the world.

Detective Archer kneels beside me and brushes something off my face. "Don't worry, Hannah," he says. "We got him. You're safe." Beside him, Cal offers an encouraging smile.

And then they're gone, the paramedics shooing them away. I flinch when they stick a needle in my arm and maneuver me onto the stretcher.

This time, as my mind fades to unconsciousness, I am not afraid.

29

I DRIFT IN AND out of consciousness. Each time I wake, I'm somewhere new. The ambulance. The emergency room. Someplace with white walls and florescent lights. With mask-covered faces and concerned eyes.

The next time I wake, I'm alone.

Machines beep all around me, a steady rhythm that's probably my heart. Which doesn't seem right. Shouldn't you be able to tell it's broken just from listening?

The machine keeps on beeping, ignoring my concerns. I glance down at the bed beneath me. It's comfortable enough, I guess, but it isn't mine. It squeaks when I move. The sheets are scratchy, irritating against my tender skin.

I want to go home.

Tears spring to my eyes when I remember I *can't* go home. My home is gone. Burned to ash. If Benton had his way, I'd be ash now, too. How long has it been? Why am I still here?

"Honey? Are you awake?" A warm voice washes over me. Beside my bed, a figure stands and her worried face comes into focus.

"Mom?" My voice cracks, and I collapse into tears. I try to apologize, to explain why I had to go, but everything is a mush of half-formed words and wracking sobs that close my throat.

Mom listens to every strangled apology. She strokes my hair

out of my face, brushes away tears, holds my hand. When I'm finished, a single tear escapes the confines of her lashes. "I'm so, so glad you're okay." She squeezes my hand tight in hers, careful to avoid the IV needles that push fluids into my veins. "But please, don't *ever* do that again."

I nod, but the movement sends my head swimming. I wish Dad were here. He'd stand behind Mom, his hand on her shoulder, nodding his agreement. Yet there'd be this glimmer in his eye, telling me that he was proud of my rescue efforts, despite the risks. But I don't say that to Mom. I don't know how much more of this she can take. Don't know if I could say the words even if I tried.

The fight with Benton may be over, but I sure as hell didn't win.

—|— —☀— —|—

The next few hours pass in a blur of doctors and nurses and white coats. People check my vitals, shine lights in my eyes, and mess with the IV fluids. I spot Gemma and Morgan outside my door, but Mom shoos them away so I can rest.

But I don't want rest.

I want answers.

No one will tell me what's going on. Mom won't entertain any questions about Benton or the other Hunters in his cell. My grandmother visits, briefly, to remind me I'm only allowed to speak with Agent Archer about what happened. Veronica's parents pop in on their way back to Veronica's room to thank me for saving their daughter.

No one mentions my dad. No one mentions the boy in jail. At least, not where I can hear them.

Dad's colleagues are somewhere in the hospital. Police officers. Lawyers. The secretary he's had since I was a baby. Mom won't let them near me, but she passes on their well wishes.

At least the doctors speak directly to me instead of going through my mom. They tell me I'm lucky, that my lungs look great—all things considered.

That's what they say. *All things considered.* They tell me it's a miracle I didn't suffer tremendous burns. That I'm lucky. Blessed even. I need a new T-shirt: *Someone tried to kill me, and all I got was this stupid concussion.* But the real injuries won't show up on their scans.

I think they know that.

A knock at the door has Mom putting down her magazine. She raises a brow when Detective Archer walks in, carrying a small bag in one hand. "I thought we agreed: no interviews until tomorrow. She deserves a good night's sleep before reliving this nightmare."

Detective Archer stops beside my bed. "I'm sorry, Marie. I tried to put it off, but the chief insists. Your husband was an important man. The DA is pushing for a quick trial."

At the mention of my dad, Mom loses the little color she had left in her cheeks. She nods and settles back into her chair.

"I actually need a private word with Hannah, if that's all right." The detective casts a glance my way as he says my name, but he doesn't meet my eye. "Please."

Mom presses her lips into a thin line, but she nods. "Of course, Detective." She glances at me before she goes. "Can I grab you anything from the cafeteria?"

I shake my head. Food reminds me of Dad, which reminds me he's gone, which sends me spiraling into despair, and I don't have time for that right now. When the door closes behind Mom, I stare at the detective. I haven't forgotten his failures. He may have saved my life, but that doesn't mean I trust him.

Detective Archer clears his throat and takes a seat in Mom's chair. "How much have you heard?" he asks, which seems like an odd place to start.

"Not much."

Archer runs his hands through his hair. "Mr. Hall has been processed and questioned. We'll know more tomorrow, but the DA is confident she can get the judge to deny bail. He's going to be in jail a very long time."

A long time isn't *forever*, but I'll deal with that later. "His parents?"

"They aren't in Salem. Records show they flew to Florida two days ago, right after the fire. We believe they're hunting down a family of Blood Witches near Bradenton. We'll stop them." Detective Archer finally meets my gaze. "I'm really sorry I didn't take them out sooner."

"You should be." My throat closes, and I force a cough to dislodge the emotion there. "What's that?"

Detective Archer lifts the bag like he forgot it was there. Color brightens his cheeks. "Lauren asked me to bring this for you. She tried to visit, but your mom sent her away. Cal sends his well wishes, too." He hands me the bag.

"When were you planning to tell me about Cal? How long has he worked for you?" I remember Cal acting grossed out when I suggested he might find the detective attractive. His reaction makes so much more sense now.

"Mr. Morrissey joined the Council when he turned eighteen. We were paired up when I moved to Salem last month." Archer leans his forearms on his knees. "Cal's a big part of how we made it to you fast enough. Without his help, I wouldn't have finished the tracking spell in time."

"Can you thank him for me? I don't think I'll be at work for a while." When Archer nods, I shift in my hospital bed and turn my attention back to the gift Lauren sent. My hands shake as I peel away the tape. Inside, nestled among light blue tissue paper, is a small stone on a silver necklace. And a note. "Did you read this?" *Is it safe? Can I read this without losing myself? Does she say his name?*

"Take your time. I can wait."

Lauren's flowing cursive greets me inside the card. My eyes fill with tears before I even read past my name. I blink them back, shove the feelings down as hard as I can, and read:

> *Hannah,*
>
> *I'm so very sorry to hear about your loss. I know this isn't much, but I hope this necklace brings you some small comfort. This black tourmaline stone is from my personal collection, and it has always provided strength when I needed it most. I hope it can do the same for you. If there's anything you need, anything at all, do not hesitate to ask.*
>
> *Blessed be,*
> *Lauren*

My heart lurches in my chest until it's hard to breathe. Dad always kept a piece of black tourmaline on his nightstand for protection. It was lost with the rest of our belongings. I grip the necklace tight in one hand.

"Are you okay?"

I glance at the detective. I'd almost forgotten he was here. "Yeah." I brush the tears away. Though my magic is still missing, I find a small bit of strength from Lauren's gift. "There's something you should know. About the Order."

Detective Archer nods for me to continue.

"The Hunters . . . Their plans are evolving."

"How do you mean?"

"They're developing a drug. Something to strip the Clans of their powers." I shiver and hold the stone to my heart. "Permanently."

The detective curses. "Did he say how close they were? How soon?"

"I don't know. Benton said our deaths were supposed to be a message. That the Hunters aren't going to hide anymore." I shut my eyes and reach for the air around me, but there's nothing. "Whatever this drug is, it's still holding strong."

Detective Archer scribbles something in his notebook. "I'll get a sample of blood from when you first came in. We'll test it and see what we're up against."

"Detective?"

"Yeah?"

"This is bad, isn't it?"

The detective sighs. "Yeah, Hannah. It's bad." He stands and shoves his hands in his pockets. "But this isn't the first time the Hunters have tried to wipe us out. We won't go down without a fight."

30

I DON'T WANT TO be here.

The little ranch-style house looms before me. Its white siding and yellow trim is so cheery it makes me want to puke. *It's only temporary.* At least, that's what I keep telling myself, but it doesn't make this any easier.

It's not home.

"Come on, Hannah. I promise it's not as bad as it looks." Mom leads me toward the front door and swings it wide. She disappears inside, leaving the door open behind her.

Mom and I had been staying in a hotel since I got out of the hospital, but the Council finally did something right and found us a rental. I take a deep breath, the air providing strength. It's been five days since I almost burned to death. Five days, and my powers are only just starting to come back. Bit by bit.

"Hannah, come on." Mom pokes her head out the door. "I've got a surprise for you."

"I'm coming." I trudge down the crooked sidewalk and up the porch steps. Mom's been doing her best to act cheery for me, but I can see under the mask. I wish I knew how to make it better for her. For both of us. "What's the big surprise?"

Mom points down the hall. "In your new room. Second door on the left."

Your new room. I shove down the urge to remind her that

I don't *want* a new room. That I want my old room and my old clothes and my old life. She's trying. I have to try, too.

The hideous beige carpet compresses under my steps. I reach for the door and flinch as the hinges creak open.

"Surprise!" Gemma flies into view, hopping on one foot while balancing her cast in the air. "Good to see you're up and moving. About time, slacker."

Gemma's cheer grates at my soul, but I force a smile and allow her to crush me in a hug so hard it cracks my back. "What are you doing here?" I try to inject some warmth into my words, but I'm not sure I succeed.

"Oh, you know, getting things set up a bit." Gemma whistles and Morgan steps out of the closet carrying Gemma's crutches. "Thought we'd make this place feel a little more like home."

"What are you—"

And then I see what they've done.

My closet is full, packed with all the clothes I used to love. There's the T-shirt with the Rubik's Cube and my UMass hoodie. All my favorite jeans and yoga pants. New versions of nearly everything I lost. "How did you do this?"

"It was mostly Gem. She overheard your mom talking to the detective about needing new clothes. Gemma suggested she let us handle the shopping." Morgan passes Gem the crutches. "We didn't mean to ambush you."

"The ambush was the *point*." Gemma rolls her eyes and hops back over to the closet. "Look, I even got all those shirts with the ridiculous puns on them. I made Morgan pretend they were for her."

Morgan blushes. "I didn't mind. I find them hilarious."

"Which is why *you're* the girlfriend and *I'm* the best friend."

Gemma freezes and shoots me a look. Her overly excited facade cracks, and I see the nerves she's trying to hide. The uncertainty. She knew, in the way best friends do, how to handle my breakup, but we're in uncharted territory now. "I mean . . . Hey! Look over there." Gemma points to the back corner of the room.

I play along and turn to where she's pointing, but there's nothing. When I look back, the door is closing behind her. "You'll thank me later!" she calls, her voice muffled.

Even though I should probably be offended at her lack of tact, the normalcy of her meddling soothes me. At least *something* hasn't changed.

"I never told her we were official or anything," Morgan says.

"I know." A soft smile pulls at my lips, and I grip tight to the necklace Lauren gave me. "That's Gem for you."

Morgan nods. Silence settles between us, neither sure how to close the divide. Then Morgan reaches into my new closet and pulls out a white plastic bag. "I got you something else. The clothes and everything came from the Council, but this is from me."

I let her pass me the bag. My hands tremble as I peer inside and find a sketchbook and a set of graphite pencils.

"It's not much, but I thought you might want a creative outlet. When you're ready." Morgan fidgets, like she's unsure what to do with her hands. "I wish there was more I could do."

"Thank you. This is . . . It's great." Her concern punctures through the hard facade I've been building brick by brick. I set the bag on the bare bed. The tears spill over, my chest contracting around my broken heart until it's hard to breathe.

"I'm sorry," she says, resting a hand on my back. "About everything."

Morgan's there when I turn, and I crumple into her embrace. We stay like that for a long time.

Until, finally, something inside starts to stitch itself back together.

Dad's funeral ended an hour ago, but I can't move.

The service—despite my request for something small—was packed. Thanks to Dad's boss, the district attorney, his death has been all over the news. I haven't been able to look at the internet since the fire. It's littered with Benton's face. Occasionally, they show Dad's formal ADA headshot. I hate that picture, though. It's nothing like the goofy man I know.

That I *knew*.

Instead of the small service I wanted, the graveyard was full of uniforms. The entire police force came. Every single witch from our coven was there, some flying in from as far away as Arizona. Gemma and her parents came, too, of course. Dad's friends from law school. Mom's friends from work. Lauren and Detective Archer. A lot of people cared about my dad.

But I still wish I could have been alone with him. One last time.

Which is why I'm here. Sitting on his freshly covered grave. It's raining—of *course* it's raining—but it's only the combined strength of the rain and the earth beneath me that keeps me from falling apart completely.

Dad . . . I reach my hands into the earth and look for any sign of my father's presence. But there's nothing there. No spark of life. No hint of magic. I don't understand this reality. I don't understand how life can just soldier on without him. None of this makes sense.

I reach into the fresh earth, searching for life, and *pull*. Slowly, ever so slowly, a flower curls up from the dirt and unfurls its petals. I'm breathing hard from the effort. It shouldn't be this difficult, but the lingering effects of Benton's drugs make every bit of magic ache. At least the flower is there. Alive. Proof that I'm still an Elemental.

But the feeling of victory doesn't last.

Every second that's filled with anything other than grief leaves me unbearably guilty. Every smile an affront to Dad's memory. Laughter an abomination. I know he wouldn't want this for me, but I don't know how else to be. Can't imagine a time when this won't hurt so much.

And then there's Benton.

He's proof that the Hunters are back. That they're more determined than ever to wipe us out. I still don't understand how the universe chose to spare me yet take my dad, but I'm going to find out. I'll wring the answers out of Benton, by force if I have to. This time, I'll have magic on my side.

Lightning streaks across the sky, bright and angry. I should get out of here, meet Mom back at our temporary home before she worries. I stand, brushing the dirt off my jeans.

I love you, Dad. Thunder rumbles in the distance. *The Hunters won't hurt anyone else. I promise.*

Detective Archer was right. There's a war brewing.

And I intend to win.

ACKNOWLEDGMENTS

Writing is a solitary pursuit, but publishing is a team sport. Thanks first to my agent and champion, Kathleen Rushall, who gave this book a second chance at life and connected me with Julie Rosenberg, editor extraordinaire. Without these two fabulous humans, this book wouldn't be in your hands. A big thank-you to the teams at Penguin and Razorbill (Ben, Corina, Alex, Kim, Krista, and many others!) for bringing Hannah and her friends to life. And a special thank-you to Libby VanderPloeg, whose wonderful illustrations so beautifully capture our quartet of leading ladies.

The journey to publication has brought many wonderful writer friends into my life. A big thank-you to Shannon, Kerrie, Kara, Kurt, Patty, Maurice, and Akeen at my local writing group, who suffered through many of my early writing attempts. Love to the DV squad for their support and friendship over the years—and a special shout-out to Karen and Jenn for our Twitter book club turned publishing coven. To my fellow mentors in the Author Mentor Match program, your advice and support is invaluable. I can't imagine navigating this industry without you.

To Rory, Gabe, and Ava, thank you for your advice and feedback during the editorial process. To my dear friend and wonderful critique partner, David: you've been there from the very beginning. I couldn't have done this without you.

I'm lucky to have a family full of supportive and down-to-earth people: Mom, Chris, Cameron, Taylor, and Tristan. Kim, Rod, and Pat. My awesome grandparents, aunts, uncles, and cousins. My friend and colleague Jaimee, who let me talk through countless story problems over the years. And a special thank-you to everyone who read my early, cringe-worthy writing attempts. I'm sorry for putting you through that.

Finally, to my wife, Megan: this story would not exist without you. I cannot thank you enough for all the love and support. You believed in this dream from the very beginning, and for that I am eternally grateful. Thank you for your patience during deadlines, plot problems, and first draft woes, and thank you for finding humor in the little things—I dedicate all my funniest typos to you.